Getting Worked Up

Sapphire Falls, book two

Erin Nicholas

ISBN: 978-0-9915579-6-7

Editor: Heidi Moore
Cover artist: Laron Glover
Copy edits: Fedora Chen
Digital formatting: Author E.M.S.

DEDICATION

To "my team"…my husband, kids, mom & dad, sister, friends and family who believe in me, let me flake off on chores, who understand when I scribble in my notebooks at ballgames, play rehearsals and during movies, and who know I *can* cook but that I *choose* not to (ha!) — I couldn't do it without you!

And to every reader who has ever emailed me, written a glowing review, messaged me on Facebook or told a friend about my books… I couldn't do it without you either!

CHAPTER ONE

"Naked in his bed when he gets home, wearing the engagement ring on a chain around my neck."

Phoebe Sherwood wrote the words as she spoke and then folded the piece of paper and put it in the beer mug Hailey Conner held out for her.

She bent her head to write again. "On one knee on his porch with the engagement ring—and pizza—when he opens the door."

She folded option two and put it in the beer mug.

On the third piece of paper, she wrote, *Public proposal in the town square during the festival.*

After Phoebe added the scrap of paper to the mug, Hailey put her hand over the opening and shook the tiny squares before pulling her hand back and grinning.

"Okay, pick one."

Phoebe glanced at the other women at the table.

Lauren Davis rolled her eyes. "How come none of those papers say 'just man up and tell him'?"

"It has to be a grand gesture at this point," Hailey said. "Phoebe's been in love with him for three years. She should have told him how she feels about him at least two years ago. Now he's in love with someone else, so she has to make a real impression."

It was a little amazing to Phoebe that Hailey, of all people, understood this.

"And he's a little slow," Hailey went on, "so this has to leave no question about what she wants."

Phoebe frowned. "Hey. He's not slow."

Hailey laughed. "Then how do you explain that he's the only person in Sapphire Falls who doesn't know you're in love with him?"

"I..." Phoebe looked around the table. Lauren saluted

her with her margarita glass but didn't deny what Hailey had said. "Adrianne?" Phoebe asked her best friend.

Adrianne shrugged. "Mason didn't know."

Even Phoebe had to laugh at that. Mason was Adrianne's husband. And he definitely wasn't slow. In fact, he was a genius. Literally. He had an IQ of one hundred and thirty six to prove it. But he didn't pay attention to much beyond his world-renowned agricultural discoveries and his wife.

"That doesn't make me feel better," Phoebe said. She sighed and drank from her own margarita glass. When the tequila and lime were gone, she set the glass down with a thump and took a deep breath. "Okay, let's do this."

She reached for the beer mug with the three options for how she was going to let Matt know how she felt about him.

"You sure about this?" Adrianne asked just as Phoebe touched one of the papers.

Phoebe sighed. "I have to be. I'm running out of time."

"What do you mean?" Lauren had just motioned to the waitress for a refill on her margarita.

"He's going to propose to her."

The three women at the table with her all froze and stared at her, completely silent for several seconds. Which in itself was an amazing thing.

"Matt's going to propose to Nadia?" Hailey asked.

"How do you know?" Lauren asked when Phoebe nodded miserably.

"He told me."

Matt told her everything. Especially big things like proposing to the woman he'd met only six months before.

Phoebe dropped her forehead onto her arms on the tabletop. Matt was proposing. The guy who was happily, purposefully single. The guy who had been her best friend her whole life. The guy who she'd loved for three years. The guy she'd *not* thrown herself at—repeatedly—because he wasn't ready to be serious about anyone.

The waitress approached. "Need a refill?" she asked.

"I think you better bring a pitcher," Lauren said.

"He told you?" Adrianne finally asked.

Phoebe lifted her head. "Yeah. Last night. He called me to come over and showed me the ring." She took a shuddering breath. "It's gorgeous."

"What did you say?" Hailey asked.

"What could I say? I told him it was gorgeous."

Lauren gave a frustrated huff. "How about 'I'm in love with you. Don't marry her'?"

"Because I…" This was going to sound so stupid. "Because he won't believe me without a huge gesture. I need the ring, at least. Naked or public square would help." She sighed and frowned at the beer mug. "In fact, let's take the front porch on one knee thing out. I think I definitely need naked or the public square. Maybe I can figure out a way to combine them without getting arrested."

Adrianne snorted, Hailey dug the second option out of the mug with a grin and Lauren asked, "What do you mean he wouldn't believe you?"

"We've been friends forever and…" She swallowed. "We've talked about it before."

Lauren set her glass down and sat up straighter. "You've talked about being in love with him before?"

Phoebe shrugged. "Kind of."

Hailey took the new pitcher of margaritas and filled Phoebe's glass. "Talk."

She sighed. "Okay, fine, when we were sophomores, I was crazy about Greg Harper. Matt and I were drinking strawberry wine at the river and talking one night and I told him I was in love. He turned to me with panic in his eyes and said, 'But you're supposed to marry me'."

The girls all froze with their glasses partway to their lips.

"What?"

"Are you kidding me?"

"*Matt* said you were supposed to marry *him*?"

She nodded, knowing how ridiculous it sounded. "At the time, I really was in love with Greg and I'd never looked at Matt like that. He'd been my best friend forever. So I told him that I thought he was just worried about losing me as a friend and that he wouldn't be the main guy in my life anymore. We agreed that was all it was."

She took a deep breath, regretting for the four billionth time that she hadn't just eloped with Matt that night. "He said that he'd always assumed we'd end up together when we were ready to be really serious. And I told him that maybe that would happen, but it wasn't something that we should talk about when we were tipsy. So we agreed that if one of us was truly serious about it someday, we'd make a big public gesture that took planning and foresight so the other would know we really meant it."

She took a big drink of tequila and lime.

"That was when I did start looking at him as more than my buddy, and it grew from there. But I've known that he wasn't ready to be serious. I mean, a relationship between us would be a lot more than messing around or dating. There would be no breaking up without turning both our worlds upside down, so it would have to be *the* relationship. The last one. The big one. So I've been waiting. Then Nadia came to town with Mason and Lauren and met Matt. And now…he's proposing to her."

Hailey shook her head. "Wow."

Lauren added, "Damn."

Adrianne grinned. Phoebe frowned at her and then noticed that Adrianne was looking at someone, or something, over Phoebe's shoulder.

She turned and saw Mason. Phoebe started to roll her eyes. The two of them were amazing together. And sickening. Especially when Phoebe so wanted what they had together and was on the verge of watching it all slip away.

But then Mason shifted to his right and she caught sight of the guy with him.

Holy hot new guy, Batman. She swung to face Adrianne. "*Who* is that with Mason?"

It wasn't that she was looking for a replacement for Matt or anything. But this was Sapphire Falls. Hot new guys didn't happen often. It was kind of like seeing the Northern Lights. You might like the regular night sky just fine, but that didn't mean you wouldn't rush outside to look at the rare, colorful streaks of light if they appeared.

His dark hair was nearly black, as was the stubble on his jaw, and the eyes beneath the thick eyebrows were just as dark. He was muscled but trim, like he went to the gym and specifically sculpted his arms and chest versus the thick, brawny muscles of the farm boys she was used to. His skin was tanned, but she'd bet he didn't have too many scars or calluses on those big hands holding his beer. His teeth were white—probably from whitening treatments and a lack of chewing tobacco—also unlike a lot of the guys here. If the obvious use of hair products wasn't a giveaway, his clothes definitely said *outsider*. Denim was the town fabric in Sapphire Falls. Along with cotton in the form of T-shirts or plaid work shirts and leather in the form of work boots. This guy wore khakis and a button-down dress shirt that should have been paired with a jacket and tie. They were both missing and he had the top button unfastened and the sleeves rolled up. Still, he looked too good to be hanging out at the Come Again.

Adrianne gave her a big smile. "I got you a present."

Phoebe's eyes widened. Hey, she was the first one to admit that it had been a while since she'd had a guy she'd wanted to do more than two-step with, but Adrianne was giving her *him*?

He wore dress shoes and probably socks that matched. Phoebe liked guys who were a little more laidback about their appearance and drank beer straight from the bottle or can. She preferred T-shirts to ties and while his end-of-the-day stubble was up her alley, she liked hair that was messed up from the wind and skin tanned from working outside.

She watched him take a drink of beer from his *glass* and then laugh at something Mason said. His laugh made the beer-out-of-a-real-glass thing a little less offensive. His eyes crinkled at the corners like he smiled a lot. He turned and leaned against the bar then. He moved with confidence, and if anyone could win her over to the khaki side it was him. His long legs and tight ass looked just fine in the tan fabric.

"That's really nice of you," Phoebe commented. If she hadn't been preparing to propose to her best friend, she might even be willing to see if he could country two-step in those khakis.

"You're giving her Joe?" Lauren asked.

"Joe?" Phoebe repeated. "You know him?"

Lauren lifted a shoulder. "Yeah. He works for us."

"Specifically, he works with me," Adrianne added. "He's the one who went to DC with me last month."

That was *Joe*? The new wonder boy that Adrianne had hired to help her with the government relations she headed for Mason and Lauren's company?

Innovative Agricultural Solutions—IAS for short—had started out in a lab in Chicago with Mason and Lauren alone, but it had grown quickly, and once Mason had fallen in love with Adrianne, he'd moved the actual planting and growing to Sapphire Falls. Their need for land had been a big boost to several local farmers, and the employees they'd brought with them who needed homes, groceries and gas and other things had helped the local economy.

The public relations and marketing people, along with accounting, government affairs and the other departments that didn't need to put their hands in the dirt, were still based in Chicago.

Lauren spent most of her time in Chicago overseeing business operations and acting as a kind of human-resources supervisor, while Mason oversaw all the scientists and projects, preferring to play in the dirt and sunshine beside his people. Since she'd met Mason, Adrianne handled their PR and all of their government relations—of which there were many. She was the perfect buffer between her genius nerdy husband and the government, media and everyone else who needed things broken down into lay terms and sometimes repeated more than once. As the company grew and their overseas projects became bigger and more successful, it became clear that Adrianne needed some help if she was ever going to have a chance to leave DC and spend time with her husband on their farm in Sapphire Falls.

Enter Joe Spencer.

Adrianne had gushed to Phoebe about how charming and smart and passionate Joe was. And how polished and sophisticated he was. And how impressed the vice president—yes, of the United freakin' States—was with him. Phoebe had never thought to ask what Joe looked like.

"I'm not giving him to you like *that*," Adrianne said. "But he can help with the Nadia and Matt situation."

"I thought he was here to get an in-person look at our operations," Lauren said.

"Sure. That too," Adrianne told her. "I mean, that's what Mason and I thought. But then…" she leaned in, her forearms on the tabletop, her eyes twinkling, "…he showed up on our doorstep last night at midnight."

"What?" Lauren asked, glancing at where Mason and Joe had taken seats at a corner table. "Why?"

"It's actually really romantic," Adrianne said. "He showed up, looking like hell. He had just gotten a text from Nadia telling him that *she* is planning on proposing to *Matt*. He tried calling her but she didn't answer, so he booked a flight, then rented a car and showed up. *"*

Phoebe's stomach dropped. "*What?*" she demanded. Adrianne nodded, still grinning, and this was no grinning matter.

"Nadia and Joe are long-time friends. They've known each other since they were kids, like you and Matt. Turns out, he's in love with her."

Phoebe slapped her hand down on the tabletop. "Are you *kidding* me? Brainiac Barbie has *two* hot men in love with her?"

Hailey giggled. "You call Nadia Brainiac Barbie?"

"Well, ever since Lauren gave her that makeover, she's not just the cute, geeky scientist; she's got that sexy-librarian thing going on."

"I am good," Lauren said.

"But you had to make Nadia over, didn't you? You really couldn't let her keep wearing the lab coats and the buns?" Phoebe asked. "You've never offered to give me a makeover."

"Well, for one," Lauren said, "I'm really best with nerds." That much they had to agree on. Lauren had met Mason in college and had known him for three days before giving him the big makeover that had turned the nerdy genius into one of the sexiest guys to ever come out of Sapphire Falls.

"For another," Lauren went on, "you don't need a makeover."

Phoebe cocked an eyebrow. "Well, thanks."

"Seriously. Nadia needed the makeover because she was clueless with eyeliner and she was shy. She needed some confidence and a curling iron. You on the other hand…" Lauren was seated next to Phoebe so she could sweep her gaze from Phoebe's head to her toes. "What would I possibly makeover on you?"

Phoebe couldn't help but grin. It wasn't just that Lauren had impeccable taste and always looked amazing herself, she was also a lesbian—well, bi-sexual, technically—so she looked at other women and their appearance a little differently than most.

"I'd totally be all over you if you gave me even the tiniest lesbian vibe," Lauren told her.

Phoebe laughed. "And if I ever had any curiosity in that…area…I'd come to you," she assured the other woman.

"Hey, what about me?" Hailey asked Lauren. "You've never even mentioned the thought of hitting on me."

"Honey, you *so* don't give off the right vibe," Lauren told her.

"And I do?" Phoebe asked.

"I'm not talking about the lesbian vibe," Lauren said. "I mean the I'm-sweet-and-accommodating-and-will-do-whatever-you-say vibe. That's what I'm looking for from here on out." She gave Hailey a once over. "And you, girl, do *not* have it."

No one could argue with that. Sweet and accommodating were not Hailey Conner's style.

"I'm not the will-do-whatever-you-say type either," Phoebe protested. She was, however, fairly sweet and often accommodating.

"That's one reason I haven't tried harder to get you naked," Lauren said.

"What's another reason?" Adrianne asked, wide-eyed.

"She likes men."

"Ah."

"*So*," Phoebe said to Adrianne, trying to get back on track—these women were incredibly intriguing…and very distracting. "Let's talk about this Joe's-in-love-with-Nadia thing."

Adrianne shook her head and picked up her story. "Okay, last month when we were in DC, Joe mentioned that he'd like to come to Sapphire Falls. He thought that getting an in-person look at the operation here would help him when he was in discussions in DC. I couldn't argue."

"He didn't mention Nadia then?" Lauren asked.

"I knew they were friends. She was his main reference for the job," Adrianne said. "But I didn't know how far back they went, and I didn't know he was in love with her."

"So he came to stop her from proposing," Hailey said. "But Nadia isn't here. She's gone for two weeks right?"

"She's in Haiti for the next two weeks overseeing the new crop for us. But he didn't know that," Adrianne said. "When he found out last night, he was pissed. We talked him into staying with us for the next few days to see the operations, get to know the town and make a plan." She pinned Phoebe with a direct look. "Which is where you come in."

"Yes, this gift thing."

"Joe is the answer to your problem, and he needs your help."

"He is? He does?" Phoebe asked, but her wheels immediately started turning. She looked over at Mason and Joe. They were drinking and chatting. They watched the dancers on the dance floor and the band, Mason kept an eye on Adrianne and...Phoebe sat up straighter as she realized that Joe was checking her out.

"What did you tell him about me?" she asked Adrianne.

"Nothing. I didn't even tell Mason why I thought tonight was a good night for them to have a beer together. But it's perfect."

Hailey leaned in, one of her I'm-not-convinced-I-care-but-I'm-willing-to-hear-more frowns in place. As mayor of Sapphire Falls she wore that expression a lot when confronted in the grocery store or post office by citizens with concerns. "Go on. I'm intrigued."

Phoebe was frickin' intrigued too. Any plan that didn't involve her getting naked in the public square to convince Matt how she felt sounded great to her.

"Isn't it obvious?" Adrianne asked.

"Yes," Phoebe answered. It was to her.

Lauren yawned.

"Spell it out," Hailey said.

"He tells Nadia how he feels, sweeps her off her feet, she breaks up with Matt and he's all mine," Phoebe said.

"Sounds easy," Hailey said. "But if she's in love with Matt—"

"Look at him," Phoebe said, gesturing toward Joe's table. "Come on."

Hailey laughed. "I thought *you* thought Matt was the epitome of all men."

"He is," she agreed. "But—" she glanced at Joe again, "—*that's* gonna be hard to say no to if he's coming at you with romance and sex, you know?"

Hailey nodded. Adrianne nodded. Even Lauren nodded.

"Plus, Nadia's known Joe her whole life. She's known Matt for six months. That's totally to Joe's advantage, just like me knowing Matt so well. It's pretty hard to ignore someone who's been there with you through so much for so long." At least, she hoped that was true. She and Matt had a lot of history. That had to count for something. Of course, she didn't really know anything about Joe and Nadia's relationship. Still, he'd known her for a long time. Unless he was a moron, he knew stuff about her that would matter when it came right down to it.

Lord, she hoped he wasn't a moron.

"Oh, and there's something even better," Adrianne said excitedly.

"Awesome, what ya got?" Phoebe asked.

"Apparently, Nadia's had a crush on Joe for years."

Okay. Now they were talking. "I can *totally* work with that," Phoebe said enthusiastically. "Him, looking like he looks, a history with her and a past crush? Oh, yeah, this will be a piece of cake."

"So you'll have him sitting here waiting for her when she gets home?" Lauren said. "You really think she's just going to dump Matt like that?"

"Well, see, here's the brilliance," Phoebe told her, the entire plan coming to her like magic.

Because Nadia was Matt's girlfriend and Matt was Phoebe's best friend, Phoebe had heard Nadia gushing about her new life in Sapphire Falls plenty of times. She loved it here. Phoebe suspected that eighty-percent of Nadia's feelings for Matt actually stemmed from her feelings for his hometown, friends and family. "Nadia is in love with Sapphire Falls. She's crazy about our little town. Matt embodies everything she loves about it, and with him she's smack dab in the center of everything from the town festival to the baseball team's championship win to the park rebuilding project. She's nuts about all that stuff. She likes the simple life, the sense of belonging, the laidback good times. And Matt's the king of all of that."

Matt was involved in every aspect of life in Sapphire Falls—volunteer fireman, Little League coach, president of the alumni association.

"Good point," Hailey admitted. She knew perfectly well that there were only three people in Sapphire Falls who could take the job of mayor away from her if they wanted it. Matt was one of them. Phoebe and Adrianne were the other two.

It wasn't that Phoebe thought Nadia was aware that her affection for her new home and lifestyle had spilled over to the guy who embodied that home and lifestyle.

But Matt deserved better. He needed a woman who knew and loved all his layers, not just the Crown-Prince-of-Sapphire-Falls layer. Phoebe had known him since they were four. She knew every endearing and annoying thing about him. That was real love—knowing every way the other person would irritate the crap out of you but wanting to be with him anyway. Phoebe could absolutely say she knew every way Matt was less than perfect. No way could Nadia feel the same way about him. She'd known Matt for six months. Anyone could look good for six months.

"So what does that mean for Joe?" Lauren asked. "He's not from here and he's definitely not a Sapphire Falls golden boy. That guy grew up in the city. He has dinner with politicians. He's a charmer, but not in the good-ol-boy way Matt and the guys here are. He's charming in the slick and sophisticated I-can-sell-ocean-front-property-in-Iowa way."

Phoebe grinned. "But he's going to hang out with *me*. And I've got two weeks until Nadia gets back from Haiti. I'll turn him into a Sapphire Falls favorite son with a week to spare. If we combine everything she loves about Matt into *that* package, and add the cherry on top—the fact that she's wanted him in the past—Brainiac Barbie won't have a chance."

Hailey raised an eyebrow in an expression that was rare indeed—she looked impressed.

Figuring that meant she was as ahead as she was going to get at this table, Phoebe finished her margarita and shoved her chair back. "Okay, I'm going to go introduce myself to my new best friend," she said with a smile.

It wasn't going to be a hardship spending some time looking at Joe Spencer over the next few days, that was for sure. She just hoped his charm and polish could be adapted to small-town Nebraska.

If anyone could help him with that, it was her.

"Hey, Ad, help me out by getting your husband busy with something else, 'kay?" Phoebe said.

Adrianne grinned. "No problem."

"I'm going to go kiss my wife," Mason said, pushing back from the table as he drained his glass.

Joe thought maybe this was the perfect time to make his escape from the small-town bar where he knew no one and where he'd gotten a funny look from the bartender when he'd asked for a glass with his beer.

"Thanks for the drink, Mason." He started to rise as well.

"Hi, Joe. I'm Phoebe."

Joe looked from his boss into the brightest blue eyes he'd ever seen. That they happened to be on the knockout redhead he'd seen sitting with Adrianne and Lauren seemed like icing on the cake.

"Hi, Phoebe." He couldn't help the grin he felt stretching his mouth.

"Joe," she said, pulling out the chair next to him and taking a seat, "you're gonna want to buy me a drink."

He might be in town for another woman, but there was no way he could look himself in the mirror in the morning if he said no to that. "My pleasure."

"A beer. No glass." She looked pointedly at the glass in front of Joe.

Right. He signaled the waitress, raised Mason's empty bottle and then held up two fingers. When in Rome and all.

Then he studied the woman beside him. He'd noticed her right away. She was the kind of woman who got noticed wherever she went. Which meant the type he'd bought drinks for all the time—in his past life. The life he'd had before he'd awakened in a hotel room in Phoenix— though he hadn't known he was in Phoenix when he first woke up—alone, naked and unable to remember the previous twenty-four hours. Other than the multiple shots of Patron and the gorgeous blond who'd occupied the bar stool beside him at the casino in Vegas earlier in the night. She'd worn a shimmery gold dress. Very shiny. Like Phoebe. Which meant Phoebe was the type of woman he should stay far away from.

He was here for Nadia. Quiet, reserved, conservative Nadia. Nadia, who didn't even wear jewelry most of the time, not to mention shiny, shimmery clothes. He was going to marry her and settle down in this tiny, boring, casino-less town and he'd get over his penchant for gambling, drinking and flashy women. He was safe here. So he could talk to and admire this gorgeous thing without worry.

He sat back in his chair. Phoebe's hair, a deep red color that glowed with strands of gold under the bar lights, was a mass of curls held back from her face by a bright green silk scarf. The scarf was tied behind her head and trailed down the back of her neck over the tank top in the same sparkly green. She wore white denim capri pants and tiny white sandals.

Of course, he couldn't see her shoes while sitting at the table.

Joe frowned. He hadn't realized he'd cataloged so many details—including her tiny feet—from across the room.

When he met her gaze, the bright color of her scarf complemented the glitter of mischief in her eyes and her bright smile.

Bright. Bold. Tempting.

Definitely a woman he should steer clear of.

"Hey, Phoebe," the waitress said as she set their beers down. "Sandra had a baby girl. This morning. Twenty-seven hours of labor."

Phoebe bounced out of her chair and grabbed the waitress. "Oh my God, that's awesome. I knew it! Right? I told you it was a girl."

The waitress squeezed her back, grinning. "You did. And she took your name suggestion too."

"Shut up," Phoebe exclaimed. "She named her Macie? No way."

The waitress nodded. "She loved it. She's going to send you a gift."

"No," Phoebe said firmly. "No, no, no. I'll send it back. You tell her that."

The waitress laughed. "I know. I already told her. I

guess we'll see if she listens."

"Well, if I get a package from Sandra, I'll send it back along with something that costs twice as much."

"Okay, okay." Still grinning, the waitress moved off.

Phoebe reclaimed her chair, but as soon as her butt hit the seat she pivoted and yelled after the waitress, "Unless it's my birthday or Christmas. Then she can totally send me something!"

"I'll tell her."

Phoebe turned back to smile at Joe. "I am about to be one of your favorite people *ever*."

Joe narrowed his eyes. "Is that right?"

"I understand that you're here because you're head over heels for Brianiac Barbie."

Joe frowned. "Who?"

"Nadia. Sorry, *Dr.* Nadia."

"Um, okay. Yes, I'm in town to see Nadia."

Phoebe leaned in. "Oh, honey, you're gonna have to do better than just *see* her."

"Is that right?" Something about this woman rubbed him the wrong way, but he couldn't put his finger on it. Maybe it was that he could *not* keep his gaze off the earrings swinging in her ears. They were big gold hoops. Just gold, just circles. There was nothing strange or weird about them. But they were big. And shiny.

Like Phoebe herself.

He liked big, shiny things.

No, that wasn't entirely true. He was *attracted* to big, shiny things.

Like neon signs and sequined bustiers and Porsches.

"It is right. But don't worry," Phoebe said. "I'll make sure you're doin' everything right."

Her smile was big and shiny too.

"Actually, I think I'm fi—"

"Phoebe Sherwood, you've got to be fuckin' kiddin' me," another loud voice interrupted. The owner of the voice was, shockingly, dressed in flannel.

Phoebe blinked up at him. "Oh, hi, Travis."

"Cassie said you're puttin' your fruity girl drinks on my tab?"

Phoebe shrugged. "You owe me fifty bucks, and you're not payin' up. Figure this is one way to get it out of you."

Travis didn't look upset. He looked amused as he crossed his arms and stared down at her. "I do not owe you fifty bucks."

"You do. You said that if I sank that putt you'd give me fifty bucks. I'll admit it was an *amazing* shot," she said, "but I made it and you owe me."

"You don't have any proof," Travis protested. "You had Janie distract me. For all I know, you picked it up and dropped it in the hole."

Phoebe sprang to her feet, her expression a cross between menacing and hurt.

Joe sat back in case any fists started flying. He also patted his wallet. He'd put his money on the fiery redhead.

"You were too drunk to remember half that game, so I knew it would come to this. I had Drew record that shot with the camera on my phone while you were busy making out with Janie." She pulled her cell phone from her pocket, ran her thumb over the screen a few times and then thrust it in Travis's face. "There. See?"

Travis frowned as he watched the video. Then he shook his head. "I don't remember anything about that shot except you bragging you could make it and me betting the money."

"Well, now you have proof. And don't think I'm not going to spend every dime of that fifty bucks in here. Tonight. In fact..." Phoebe swung her chair around until the seat faced out from the table. Then she climbed up on it and said loudly, "Excuse me!"

The people in the immediate vicinity quieted but it took some shushing to get the whole room to stop talking. But it happened. Joe was impressed.

Travis looked a little pale.

"Travis is buying a round for the house!"

A loud cheer went up, Travis cursed and smacked Phoebe on the butt, but he headed for the bar to pay up.

"How tough was the putt?" Joe asked as Phoebe reclaimed her seat at the table.

"Oh, impossible." She took a drink of beer.

"But you sank it."

"Nah, I did that video later. He was too out of it to know the difference."

Joe raised an eyebrow. Sneaky and shiny…not a good combination in a woman in his experience. "Why the grudge against Travis? He an ex or something?"

She grinned. "A friend. I gave fifty bucks in his name to the Girl Scout troop in town for their park clean-up project. The bet or the bar tab was the only way to get the money back from him."

"Why not just donate it in your name?"

"'Cause it's way more fun for every little girl in town to run up to say hi to him everywhere he goes. He has no idea why they all even know who he is. It's hilarious."

Joe smiled simply because her smile was so big.

"So anyway," she said. "I want you to know that I'm fully committed to getting you and Nadia together. But I need to know a few things first."

Joe frowned. "You're going to help me get together with Nadia?" Okay, that was a new one. He wasn't sure he'd ever had a drink with a woman he was attracted to only to find her trying to set him up with another woman. Unless of course it was intended to be a threesome. That had happened. A few times.

"Yes."

"Why?" Maybe there was a threesome thing happening…

"Because I don't want her to be with Matt."

Joe just looked at her for a moment before understanding dawned. Ah, no threesome then. Which was fine, considering Phoebe was exactly the kind of woman— and threesomes were exactly the kind of thing—he was trying to avoid. "Got it. Matt's the ex."

"Matt's the hasn't-been-yet," Phoebe told him, "and if we don't break Matt and Nadia up before the last night of the festival, he's gonna take her on that big ol' Ferris wheel and propose."

Joe sat forward. No. That was *not* going to happen. He was here to ensure that did *not* happen. "Don't worry. I'm on it. There's only one proposal Nadia's going to hear."

Phoebe looked at him and nodded. "I really appreciate the enthusiasm. That's important. But you can't just charge in there and propose the moment she steps off the plane in Omaha."

Not only could he, but that was precisely the plan. "Yes, I can."

"No." Phoebe reached out and put her hand on his arm, her expression serious. "Joe, you can't do that. You'll just fluster her and piss Matt off."

He ignored her hand on his arm—kind of. She wore multiple rings and bracelets that clinked at her wrists. All were shiny and…okay, not that big, but still…he ignored them. Mostly.

"I don't give a shit about Matt."

She nodded. "Yeah, exactly. But you should."

"Matt and his feelings are not my problem."

"But see, they kind of are."

No. Nadia had known Matt for six months. Six *months*. Joe had known her his entire life. At least all the parts he could remember. That was supposed to count for something. And dammit, she'd *promised* him. "Nadia and I have history."

"Which is definitely in your favor. But you can't build your entire campaign on that."

"My campaign?"

"Your campaign to win her heart," Phoebe said, putting one hand dramatically over her chest.

"I don't need a campaign," Joe said with a scowl. "I need to talk to her. That's it. Just once."

"Will this talking involve a diamond ring?" Phoebe asked.

"Yes."

"Then no."

"No?" This woman was something. He was gritting his teeth even as he was tempted to lean closer and see if the waft of green apples he'd sensed had come from her.

"I can't let you do that."

"Because you have to protect poor Matt's feelings?" Joe asked.

"Because you'll crash and burn, and then where will we be?"

Before he could respond to that he heard, "Phoebe!"

A woman was yelling to her from several feet away. Joe sighed. He was trying to have a drink and a conversation—okay, an argument—with Miss Fucking America here.

"You are in so much trouble, bitch."

Well, maybe not Miss America…

"Hey, Amanda." Phoebe gave the woman a little wave.

"You've been keepin' those hot cowboys all to yourself all this time?" Amanda said.

That got his attention. Joe sat up straighter and looked at Phoebe. "Cowboys? Plural?"

She grinned. "Sometimes."

"And they have rope and they know how to use it." Amanda laughed and blew Phoebe a kiss. "You're my favorite, girlie."

Joe was still watching Phoebe. Her grin grew.

"You're welcome." Phoebe laughed and turned back to Joe.

"You have multiple cowboys that you share with your girlfriends?" He took a long draw of his beer. Sapphire Falls had just gotten a whole lot more interesting.

Phoebe gave him a wink with those playful blue eyes. "Yeah, *I* had to pay for them, but I let my friends borrow them for free."

"Ah, happy to hear that I could make a little cash on the side if needed."

She laughed out loud then. "Oh, Joe, honey, don't think you could pull the cowboy thing off. Or the ropes."

He lifted an eyebrow. Little did she know. He might prefer silk to rope, but in his experience, once he pulled the silk ties out, the woman didn't care what he was wearing.

He resisted telling her that, but he really did want to see if he could make Phoebe Sherwood blush. Though if she was used to a bunch of cowboys, it might take him some effort. He could do it, but it would take more creativity on his part.

"You don't think I have what it takes to fit in here in Sapphire Falls, huh?" he asked.

"Exactly," she said, with enthusiasm. "That's what I'm saying. You need to fit in here to win Nadia back, and I can help you."

"Don't tell me Nadia's met your cowboy friends." He wasn't alarmed by that so much as stunned. Nadia was *not* a tie-me-up kind of woman.

At least, he didn't think she was.

Phoebe laughed. "Not yet. Hailey had them before Amanda."

"You just pass them around?" Not that he thought the guys would mind.

"They're books, Joe," she said, grinning.

"They're…books?" He wasn't following.

"The hot sexy cowboys using ropes? They're in books. Romances. Really sexy romances."

Ah. That made more sense. "That you share with your

friends."

"Right."

"Right." Joe took a long drink of beer. "Are they gay romances?"

Phoebe's eyebrows went up with that. "No. I mean, there's more than one guy sometimes, but they're with a woman. She's the center of the attention."

Joe nodded. "You ever loan those to guys?"

She tipped her head, looking at him with interest. "Huh. No, not yet. But now that you mention it, that's a great idea."

"Yeah?"

"We have lots of rope around Sapphire Falls that's not being used to its full potential."

Joe couldn't help it. He grinned. This woman was loud and bright and bold and gave off a vibe that attracted him and at the same time caused him to be wary. But she made him smile.

"Now back to our plan," she said.

He figured they had about two minutes before someone else needed her for something.

"Phoebe, I have a plan. Thanks, but I don't need your help."

"You have it all covered? Everything's good. You're confident, good to go, no worries?"

"Right."

"You do realize that you're competing against Matt Phillips."

Joe frowned. "So?"

"So, Matt's like a celebrity here. No, more like Prince William is in England."

"Royalty, huh?" Joe asked. Good grief. So the woman was in love with Matt, but royalty was a bit much.

"Well—" she lifted a shoulder, "—yeah. He's got a lot of power around here, everyone's interested in what he does and he's got the charm and the brains and the looks and—"

"I got it," Joe broke in. "He's King Matt. Great. Whatever."

"Yeah, and he's about to propose to the woman *you* want."

"But she doesn't know how I feel."

"You're just going to tell her how you feel and she'll fall into your arms?"

"Something like that."

Phoebe shook her head. "It's not enough."

"It's kind of hard to get a big ego around you, huh?"

She chuckled. "Sorry. It's not you, it's…him."

This was annoying. Part of him liked Phoebe. She seemed like a lot of fun and he definitely liked looking at her. But he didn't need coaching or mentoring or whatever in how to win Nadia over. She'd been in love with him since they were seventeen. And she'd promised to marry him. Okay, they'd been eighteen. And tipsy at her sister's wedding. But Nadia was responsible and intelligent. All he had to do was remind her—as if she could have forgotten—and they'd be right back on track.

"Thanks, Phoebe. I understand your heart's in the right place, but I'm fine."

"Hmm." She studied him for a moment. Then she tipped her beer back and finished it off before shrugging and pushing to her feet. "Okay, Big Joe. Can't say I didn't offer. You hang out here, observe, chat, do it your way. Go for it. But if you change your mind, let me know. I'm easy to find."

He didn't doubt that for a second.

In spite of himself, he watched Phoebe wind her way between the tables on her way to the bar. Her hips swayed as she went, and he couldn't help but smile. She really was something.

CHAPTER TWO

An hour later, Joe was no longer smiling.

And Phoebe Sherwood was still something.

She hadn't sat down for more than five minutes and even then it had been to perch on the edge of a barstool.

He'd been sitting at his table, nursing another beer for the past sixty minutes, unable to take his gaze off of her for more than a few seconds. The place was packed and loud, there were even two other redheads here, but he couldn't stop watching Phoebe.

She seemed to…sparkle.

And he felt like a dumbass for even thinking that.

But it was true. She sparkled all over the damned place. On the dance floor with guy after guy, at the bar with her friends doing shots of God knew what, hugging people as they came and went, chatting, making everyone around her smile.

Miss America for sure.

At the moment, she was smiling up at a tall guy who was leaning close, apparently telling her a story for her ears only. She twirled a curl around her finger as she listened to him and then tipped her head back and laughed. Not a chuckle, not a giggle, but a laugh. Joe swore he could hear it from where he sat. Or he could feel it. Or something stupid like that.

He tightened his grip on his beer bottle and gritted his teeth.

The guy's smile was amused as he watched Phoebe, but there was some heat in his gaze as well. He studied the creamy expanse of her throat, looked into those blue eyes, put a big hand on her left hip and leaned close again— much closer this time—to whisper in her ear.

She laughed again and pushed him back playfully, rolling her eyes.

The guy tipped his head and said something else.

She grinned but shook her head.

Joe sat up straighter. Was the guy propositioning her? Whatever he was saying, she was answering no. Which meant the guy should be walking in the other direction instead of...pulling her out onto the dance floor.

Joe sat back.

She was going willingly. As she'd gone with all four of the other guys who'd done that same thing. Not to mention the two guys *she'd* pulled out there.

Joe shuddered. He couldn't believe he'd sat here tolerating country music for this long already. There was no way in hell he was stepping on the dance floor. Unless, of course, it was to take a swing at the guy who was now swinging Phoebe around. Literally. Her feet were off the floor, they were twirling and she was laughing like she'd never had so much fun in her life.

Why that annoyed the shit out of Joe, he really couldn't say.

Then things got worse.

"Matt!"

Several voices called out the greeting, and Joe groaned. His Royal Highness was here.

Joe watched as the other man made his way through the room to the bar. He was welcomed by everyone he passed and it took him a few minutes to make it across the sixty-foot expanse. Joe glanced at Phoebe. She was still dancing and hadn't noticed Matt's arrival. But they clearly hung out with the same people. Matt took his place amongst the group Phoebe had been with most of the past hour. Obviously, she would notice him eventually.

Joe settled back in his chair and lifted his beer. This would be interesting.

Two girls, who looked to be in their early twenties, took seats at the table to Joe's right. For the most part, his back was to them, but they sat in the chairs closest to him and he could hear every word they said.

"Matt going to be one of the guys at the dunk tank," the young brunette said.

The blond giggled. "Oh, I know. I'm saving up my money."

"He really is gorgeous, huh?"

"Definitely. Did you hear that whatever he raises at the tank he's going to match out of his own pocket?"

"He's so sweet," the brunette gushed.

"And the best math teacher ever," the blond added.

Joe rolled his eyes. So they were here to list Matt's attributes. Terrific. Just what he needed.

"Oh, definitely," the other girl agreed. "And my brother is so excited to be playing football for him. This could be their *third* state championship."

Wow, what more reason could a woman have for falling madly in love with the guy? Joe thought sarcastically.

"And he's funny."

"He is. But smart funny. He doesn't tell stupid jokes."

"Right."

Okay, Matt was good looking, sweet, generous, smart and funny. Great. Got it.

Joe pushed to his feet. He should get the hell out of here. He didn't know anyone, didn't like the beer and had heard more about Matt Phillips in five minutes than he'd ever really wanted to. Even if it was set up, he could feel the tension in his neck. This was the guy he was competing with. Nadia thought she was in love with Matt, and Matt was the most popular guy in Sapphire Falls.

Joe started for the door but couldn't help but glance over at where Phoebe was being swept into a new man's arms for another dance.

It was that damned sparkling thing, he was sure, but it took him longer to look away than it should have.

Phoebe was also in love with Matt.

He quickly changed directions and headed for the bar

where Matt was picking up the second shot someone had bought for him. He found a space three people down from Matt and ordered a scotch—anything had to be better than more of the bottled beer they offered.

Discussion continued around him and it took Joe exactly eight minutes to realize that no, he didn't fit in here. The conversation included mentions of things like hydrologic models and crop residue management and the new tight-end recruit at the University of Nebraska and the sand volleyball tournament at the upcoming town festival.

Joe didn't know a damned thing about any of it.

If Nadia was in love with Matt, she couldn't have picked a guy more different from Joe if she'd put them both up on a white board and listed all their qualities.

Which, knowing Nadia, she might have done.

She'd clearly picked his opposite.

Nadia had made no secret of the fact that she hadn't approved of his lifestyle for a long time, especially the past year. She worried about him, but she'd also grown frustrated with him. So, her analytical scientific mind might have very well sought out a man as different from Joe as she could get.

Now he really should go.

He finished his drink and turned from the bar. His gaze landed on the table where he'd first seen Phoebe sitting with Adrianne, Lauren and another woman. Lauren was now alone.

He headed straight for her.

Lauren had been around Sapphire Falls long enough now that she had to know more about the people and activities here than he did, and she was a no-nonsense person he could trust not to bullshit him.

"Hey, Lauren." He pulled out the chair next to her and sat.

"Hey, Joe. Welcome to Sapphire Falls."

He smiled. "Thanks."

She just looked at him for a moment. "Feel like you fell down the rabbit hole?" she finally asked.

"Absolutely."

"It's a pretty different world."

"You know Matt?"

Lauren smiled. "I like a man who can get to the point. Yes, I do know Matt."

"Is he everything Phoebe says he is?"

"If she says that he's the guy everyone wants for everything, then yes."

Joe groaned and leaned back in the chair, crossing one ankle over the other. "And is Nadia as gaga over the town as she seems?" He and Nadia had been exchanging emails on a regular basis ever since she'd left Chicago to go to Haiti with IAS last year. He knew that she'd fallen in love with the country and the people and the work she was doing. Then she'd come to Sapphire Falls and the enthusiasm had ramped up times a hundred.

Lauren nodded. "Yes. She is."

"Phoebe seems to think that the way to her heart is to become involved and accepted here."

"Makes sense to me," Lauren said with a shrug.

"Seriously?"

"What's the worst that could happen? You get to know some nice people, maybe have some fun, and it can't make Nadia *less* impressed, right?"

Joe sighed. Lauren was the second smartest person he'd ever met. Her best friend and business partner was the first. He should listen to her.

"Tell me more about Matt."

"He's a really nice guy. Really nice. If you're into that kind of thing."

"Hmm."

"You're nice too, Joe," Lauren said with a chuckle.

"No, I'm charming. That's different." She laughed and he said, "Really. Charming you can fake. Nice you can't.

At least not for long."

"Well, Nadia's crazy about him, so maybe you need to learn some nice."

"That's what I'm thinking." He wondered how exactly to do that. "What else is she crazy about?"

"She's downright giddy about this town festival," Lauren said. "It's funny to watch. I've known her as this serious scientist girl in the lab for a year. Then she's here for three days and suddenly she's into river parties and sand volleyball and country dancing."

Joe grimaced and glanced at the dance floor. "Country dancing?"

"Oh, yeah," Lauren said with a big grin. "She *loves* to dance."

"Shit," he muttered.

Lauren laughed.

That was hard to imagine. Nadia was quiet, conservative, introverted, more interested in data than dancing. Or at least, he'd thought so.

If not, maybe Nadia was more his type than he'd thought. Which was a little problem considering he was looking for a quiet, introverted girl. Who didn't dance.

But even as he thought it, he knew this wasn't truly a problem. He got it. Nadia had grown up in a rotten family—more rotten than even his own. She'd found a warm, welcoming group of people here who cared about her and who she could relax with. That would, no doubt, make her more prone to things like dancing and sand volleyball—though he would have to see that to really believe it.

He was happy for her. He didn't want to take her away from this. In fact, he wanted it too. He wanted to know what it was like to spend time with people who didn't think only of themselves and the moment they were in, who understood consequences and who had morals.

Yep, that would be really nice.

He knew what he had to do to get Nadia back and to get started on this life.

He just didn't want to do it.

"Fine." He looked at Lauren. "You're the smartest woman I know."

"I know that."

"You have ten seconds to figure out any other way for me to get Nadia back besides spending the next two weeks with Phoebe Sherwood."

Lauren looked toward the dance floor, then back up at Joe. "I can't think of a single reason why that's a bad thing, actually."

He raised an eyebrow. "Not even one?"

"Nope."

"Half of one?"

She laughed. "Nope."

"Really? 'Cause I can think of a couple."

Lauren crossed her arms. "Is that right? Give me an example."

"She's…" He looked to where Phoebe was spinning— literally—around the dance floor.

Just then she let out a loud, "Yee haw!"

He turned back to Lauren. "She's very…sparkly."

Lauren's eyebrows shot up. "She's *sparkly*?"

He gestured to Phoebe. "She *is*. She's loud and bright and there's no way to ignore her."

"Yes, she is loud and bright and I don't think you should ignore her." Lauren was smirking at him.

"But she's…" Yeah, he couldn't tell Lauren that Phoebe was *exactly* his type. His past type. The type of woman that he used to be drawn to.

But wow, did it feel like he was attracted to her *now*. No, he corrected, it felt like he was attracted to her *type*. Bad habits were hard to break.

"She's what?" Lauren asked.

He looked at Phoebe again. "Sparkly," he muttered. He

didn't meet Lauren's eyes when he said, "See you later," and headed for Phoebe.

"See ya'" she called after him.

The song was just ending and Joe was there when Phoebe spun to the edge of the dance floor. "Okay, let's go."

She was breathing hard and her cheeks were flushed from dancing. He liked that look on her.

He was almost on top of her toes when she grinned up at him. "You sure?"

"Yeah, I'm sure." He knew he sounded less than enthusiastic.

"You're all mine?" she asked.

He kind of liked the sound of that—which meant he should say no way.

"You bet," he told her instead. "Whatever that means."

"I'll show you exactly what that means." She took his hand and pulled him toward the door.

∽∾

This was going to be fun.

Phoebe wasn't sure why she thought so or if she was right, but she had a feeling about Joe. She didn't know much about him except that the only people in Sapphire Falls that he knew were three scientist types from the city—Mason, Lauren and Nadia. Okay, he knew Adrianne too, but she also wasn't a Sapphire Falls native. Adrianne had been in high-powered sales and marketing in Chicago before coming to Sapphire Falls. Between the four of them, Phoebe had a pretty good idea what things about Sapphire Falls would be a culture shock and what wouldn't.

It was important to get the culture shock out of the way for Joe so that he didn't show it to Nadia. She wanted a hometown boy. Joe was going to get a crash course in living in Sapphire Falls—the good, the bad and the homemade booze.

"Where are we going?"

Joe was following, his hand still in hers, as they stepped out onto the porch that ran the length of the Come Again.

"We're on a tight timeline and I'm afraid you have a lot to learn. So I'm going to show you the spot in Sapphire Falls that is most important to your plan."

"I have a plan?"

She grinned. He was kind of cute. And she really liked the feel of his hand in hers. She had expected soft and smooth skin, the hands of a guy who worked in an office and didn't know much about using tools and getting dirty. But his hand was rough, not I-work-on-a-farm-and-gloves-are-for-wusses rough, but also not baby-butt smooth either. His hand was big and firm and warm. All very good adjectives as far as she was concerned.

"You will have a plan," she promised. She headed around the east corner of the bar toward the darkened building that butted up against the Come Again.

He followed her all the way up the steps and to the door of the obviously closed-for-the-night building before he asked, "Are we supposed to be here?"

"Sure."

"I think they're closed."

"You're right." Phoebe fished in her front pocket for the key and inserted it into the lock.

"You own this place?"

She laughed. "Hell, no. This is my aunt's place." Phoebe pushed the door open and gestured for Joe to step inside.

He shook his head. "You first."

"Are you scared of the dark?" She went in ahead of him and reached to the left to hit the lights.

"I'm scared of women I don't know taking me into dark places without telling me why." Joe came through the door, stopped and looked around.

Phoebe laughed. "Oh, Joe, if I was going to kill you and hack you up into little pieces, I'd take you way out into the country. I know lots of places I could hide your body where they'd never find you." She crossed the room to the glass shelves that held her Aunt Mary's infamous brew. "That is, assuming anyone realized you were gone. You're new here, and frankly, Mason's easily distracted."

Joe didn't exactly laugh at that.

Phoebe did.

"Adrianne knows I'm here."

"True. But Ad and I are tight. She'd have my back."

"Uh huh. Where is this very important place that you think I need to see tonight?"

She grabbed a bottle from the third shelf and turned back to him. "Joe, do you trust me?"

"Not really."

That was only fair. "Then you have to at least give me the chance to prove that you can."

He narrowed his eyes. "Fine. But maybe you should give me a general idea of what to expect."

She looked down at the bottle in her hand. "Are you much of a drinker?"

He snorted and she looked at him in surprise.

"Um, yeah. I can hold my own."

"Well, that will make this initiation a little easier on your system. But you're still gonna feel like crap in the morning."

He actually smiled at that. "Initiation, huh?"

"And this is just the beginning." She headed for the door, grabbing his hand on her way past.

He followed for a few steps before he said, "By the way, I *am* scared of the term initiation."

"Yeah, you probably should be," Phoebe agreed, trying not to smile.

They were down the steps of the liquor store and halfway across the parking lot when he asked, "So you don't have to pay for liquor in Sapphire Falls?"

"I'll have Mary put it on my tab."

"A girl with a tab at a liquor store. Be still my heart."

Yep, he was definitely cute. "Everyone who knows Mary personally gets a tab. And she knows pretty much everyone. She won't take credit cards or checks so we all settle up once a month. As long as it's before her bills are due, she's happy and it's easier."

Joe looked back at the tiny liquor store. "Anyone ever stiff her?"

"Not more than once. Being cut off from all the alcohol for thirty-seven miles is worse than any other threat she could come up with."

"She controls *all* the alcohol?"

"She and Tex own the bar, the liquor store and the gas station—all the places where you can buy liquor."

"The restaurant doesn't serve alcohol?"

"Sure. They get their stuff from Mary and Tex. And if Mary says not to serve someone, they don't get served."

Joe shook his head. "No one gets upset about the liquor monopoly?"

Phoebe shrugged. "They're nice people, pretty laidback and don't overcharge. There's not really any problem."

"Small towns are weird."

Phoebe grinned and stopped by her truck.

"Is Tex from Texas?" Joe asked.

"Nope."

"Of course not."

Phoebe pulled the driver's side door open. "Get in."

"This is yours?"

"Yep."

Joe frowned at the truck. "This red F150 pickup is yours?"

"Yes. What's wrong?" she asked.

"It's…*big*. And bright. And…" he sighed, "…shiny."

Well, he wasn't wrong. But speaking of things that

were weird… She frowned. "Have you hit your head?"

"That would be a much better explanation," Joe said as he headed around the front of the truck and to the passenger-side door.

Whatever that meant. As he climbed into the truck and slammed the door, Phoebe decided she didn't want to know.

It only took seven minutes to get from the Come Again to the gravel road that led to Phoebe's place. She loved living out in the country. The road, the house, the fields were as familiar as the backyard of the house she'd grown up in. The farm had been her grandparents' and she'd spent as much time there as she had in her childhood home in town. When they'd left it to her, she'd been touched and thrilled.

They were far enough out of town now that Joe wouldn't be able to find his way back without her.

"So what's the deal with you not telling Nadia how you felt before all this blew up?"

Joe looked over. "Beating around the bush isn't really your thing, huh?"

"Not really, no."

"I could ask you the same about you and Matt."

"The thing with Matt is easy," Phoebe said. "We've been friends forever, so we couldn't really date casually, you know? It had to be all or nothing. So I settled for nothing until he, we, were ready to do it all."

Joe nodded. "We have that in common. I knew Nadia was in love with me, but I knew I couldn't just mess around with her and I wasn't ready to settle down."

"And then she came here and met Matt and now you're suddenly ready?" Phoebe asked, frowning at the road in front of them.

"Yeah. Small-town life, here I come. I mean, I'll still be traveling a lot for IAS. I'll have regular meetings in Chicago and DC, but I'm thinking a town in the middle of nowhere with very little excitement will be a great home base."

She probably would have been more offended by the very-little-excitement comment if she wasn't busy being annoyed by his willingness to move to Sapphire Falls before he'd spent even twenty-four hours in town. Why did it bug her that Joe was willing to move here and change his life to be with Nadia? She was *glad* he was here. He was going to help her get what she wanted too. The fact that no one had ever made a grand gesture for *her* had nothing to do with this. Just because she had definite doubts about Matt's willingness to do something like that didn't matter—she wanted to be here in Sapphire Falls like he did. So it was a moot point.

She tried to make herself stop scowling. "What if Nadia wants you here full time?"

Joe sighed. "Then I'll…have to find a job in Sapphire Falls." There was a definite lack of enthusiasm in his tone.

She snorted. The positions currently open in Sapphire Falls included a morning cook at the café, a checker at the grocery store, a helper at the daycare and a farmhand for Larry Devin. And that was only until Larry's shoulder healed up and he could get back to work himself.

"You're ready to live in a small unexciting farming town? Really?"

"I need to be ready."

That didn't sound especially confident. "But you're not? Or you don't want to be?"

"I am." He pulled himself up straighter in the seat. "I'm ready. I want to be."

"Sounds like you're trying to talk yourself into something." That made her scowl return full force.

"I've just never done this before. I wanted some time to ease into it."

"Done this?"

"Been serious and—" he coughed into his fist and then

sheepishly said, "—monogamous."

Ah. "Longest relationship?" Phoebe asked. She couldn't help it. She was interested in Joe Spencer. Not *interested*, but interested in learning about him. She knew it was simply a product of him being almost the only male her age in the county that she hadn't known since diapers, but still, she found him intriguing.

"Two months," he said. "And I banged her best friend about halfway through."

Phoebe glanced over quickly. "Did you just say *banged*?"

He looked chagrined. "Sorry."

Phoebe couldn't help it. She laughed. "Wow."

"I know. I'm an asshole. Trust me, I know I'm not a nice guy. But I'm trying to change."

"No, it wasn't the banging-her-best-friend thing— though yes, that's an asshole thing to do—but it was the way you said it. It's refreshing. The guys here don't talk like that."

Joe looked skeptical. "All guys talk like that."

She shook her head. "Not around me. I'm like…their little sister. They don't say stuff like that when I'm around."

Joe snorted. "Those guys you were dancing with a little bit ago were *not* thinking of you as their little sister, Phoebe."

She sighed. Yes, they were. As much as she'd like to think they weren't. "What was the best friend like?" she asked, morbidly curious. "Did she seduce you? Or was it a drunken fling?"

Joe shrugged. "I don't know. No, she didn't really seduce me. It just happened. I mean, I'd always thought she was hot and I was probably feeling claustrophobic after two months of sex with the same woman."

Phoebe scowled at the road again. She knew guys around here that had felt that way about their girlfriends—

tied down, too serious too soon, bored, restless. And they'd always come to her with their sob stories and their guilt, wanting advice about how to break it off. But never had any of them made a move on her. Not even once.

"What's wrong?" Joe asked.

Phoebe glanced over. "Do you know that I'm the best friend of nearly every woman in this town…and several of the guys?"

"Aren't you supposed to just have one best friend? As in, the *best* of all your friends?" Joe asked, totally missing the point.

"*I* have one best girlfriend. Adrianne. And one best guy friend, Matt. But lots of women here consider me their best friend because I'm a great listener, I'm always willing to help them out and I happen to have excellent taste in shoes and clothes, interior design and party planning. I've bailed lots of people out lots of times."

Joe nodded. "That's nice. You're the go-to girl."

"Yeah, unless you want to have an affair apparently," she muttered, frowning at the road as she turned into her lane.

"You want to have an affair?" Joe asked.

"No. But I know lots of the guys in town probably do. That's a guy thing, right?"

Joe shifted on his seat. "I don't know about that…"

"You have to admit that at least one guy in this town has wanted to have an affair in the past ten years."

"Okay," Joe conceded. "Probably."

"And the chances of that guy dating or being married to one of the women who think I'm the best thing since Snickers was made into an ice cream bar are huge. Everyone here thinks I'm great."

"Okay," Joe said.

"And yet not one guy, not *one*, in the past ten years has tried to seduce me."

Joe grabbed onto the dash as they turned off of her lane

and headed across the field that would take them to the river. She typically took this slower. It wasn't a road. It was literally a large pasture, but tonight it felt good to hit the bumps and dips at high speed.

"I find that very hard to believe," Joe said, gripping the dash and the handle over the top of the window on his side.

"Well, it's true. Not one guy has tried to bang his girlfriend or wife's best friend—*me*."

"I'm...sorry?" Joe said.

"Me too." She jerked the wheel to take the truck through the narrow space in the fence that would lead to the river.

"You're telling me that you *want* your friends' boyfriends and husbands hitting on you?" Joe asked.

"Yes. I mean, no. Not for their sakes of course."

"Maybe they're all really great guys who would never cheat," Joe said. "Everyone knows people from the country are nicer."

"Yeah, well, it would have been nice to have to turn someone down once. Or twice," Phoebe said. She didn't mean it, of course. It would have been awkward and she would have been pissed at anyone for even thinking about cheating on one of her friends.

Still, she didn't quite believe that none of the guys in Sapphire Falls had ever had lustful thoughts about a woman other than his significant other. She did, however, believe that *she* was never the target of those lustful thoughts.

Phoebe backed the truck up to the edge of the bluff that overlooked the creek and took a deep breath before turning the engine off. She needed to let go of the tension. It was stupid. It didn't matter. She would be with Matt, and all that mattered were *his* lustful feelings.

She breathed again, looking through the windshield. This was her favorite spot. She wasn't sure why she'd brought Joe here instead of the usual party spot for the gang. She supposed it was that part of her mission was to get him to fall in love with Sapphire Falls, and this was, in her opinion, one of those spots that would either made him roll his eyes and yawn or stare in wonder.

Phoebe got out and went to stand at the edge. With the moon bright overhead, the water reflected like a silver ribbon twelve feet below the bluff. There weren't a lot of varying levels in Sapphire Falls, but this was one place where the landscape was more than flat, rolling fields. People who weren't from here regarded the fact that they could see for miles in all directions boring. But Phoebe appreciated the beauty of the plains as much as she did the bluffs, and she counted herself fortunate to have a little of both in her backyard.

The trees and bushes were bunches of dark shadows across the tiny ravine. The top of the bluff was flat with a sharp drop off to the water that could be dangerous if you didn't know it was there. The fall wouldn't kill you, but you'd be limping, that was for sure. Most of the bluff was farmable but for the twenty feet or so that butted up against the cliff that had been carved by the water over the years. Farther down the bluff, two hundred yards or so, where the land slowly eased down to the water on a gentle slope, was where the gang carried their coolers and other party supplies to the creek. But this higher spot was where Phoebe came to think.

She held her breath as Joe got out of the truck and came to join her at the tailgate.

For several seconds, neither said anything. Finally, he said, "Wow. This is…gorgeous."

Phoebe let her breath out, recognizing that it was ridiculous that she care or be glad that Joe found the spot beautiful.

"Different from your own backyard?" she asked lightly.

He laughed. The soft, husky sound seemed to wrap around her, and she sighed.

"I'd say. My backyard was concrete."

"You grew up in the city?"

"Penthouse suite."

Really different. "So no dog, no tree house, no fishing at the creek?"

He chuckled again. "I always thought tree houses were just in stories."

She felt herself smile. "In my experience, a childhood isn't complete without a tree house."

She couldn't see him clearly, but she could feel his smile drop. "Well, that might explain a few things."

Oh, she wanted to know more. Lots more. She wanted to ask him what he meant, what his childhood had been like, did he really think he could be happy in a place so different from what he was used to?

But she didn't say any of that. Her goal was to show him why Nadia loved Sapphire Falls, and she could do that without knowing his life story.

Nadia's affection for the town was one reason Phoebe liked her in spite of her homing in on Phoebe's future husband. In fact, since meeting Nadia, she'd found herself looking at her hometown with new appreciation. Nadia's enthusiasm for the lifestyle and the things that Phoebe had taken for granted her whole life had made Phoebe, and many others, smile more than once.

"Okay, so to fit in here you have to attend our social gatherings. Nadia loves hanging out with the gang. She goes on and on about how much fun we have with the simplest things. So I'm going to give you a crash course in hanging out in Sapphire Falls."

She let the tailgate down and boosted herself up to sit on the back, dangling her feet.

Joe joined her, sitting close enough that his arm brushed hers and she could feel the warmth from his body.

"I'm ready."

Looking to the other side of the creek, she thought about the get-togethers in Sapphire Falls with fondness.

She knew that parties in Chicago had to be as different from what they did here as it got. "Every good social event in Sapphire Falls has four main ingredients—the great outdoors, booze, tall tales and music."

"The great outdoors?" He looked around. "Like this?"

She could hear the amusement in his voice. "Yep, like this."

"What about when it's a hundred and five degrees out?"

"We dress skimpy, take lots of trips into the water and drink really cold beer."

He turned to look at her. Their eyes had adjusted and the moon was bright enough that she could see his expression. His gaze traveled over her. "I can't really find anything wrong with that."

She smiled. Damn. Joe Spencer was not her type, but there was something about knowing he was picturing her in skimpy clothes and wet from the creek that made her squirmy.

"And of course, there's always skinny dipping."

"I was hoping you'd say that."

"You skinny dip in Chicago?"

"Nope. I always thought that was another of those just-in-stories things. But I'm very happy to hear I was wrong."

Phoebe chuckled and reached for the bottle she'd brought from Mary's. "Stick around. You're gonna learn all kinds of new things."

"Not sure if I should be happy or worried about that."

She twisted the top of the bottle off and tipped it back for a drink. Then she handed it to Joe. "Booze."

He took the bottle and examined the label. Not that it would tell him much. It simply said "Strawberry." Mary made the labels on her home computer. The people who bought the bottles only needed to know if they were picking out strawberry, peach or grape, so the labels did what they were supposed to do. No one was too concerned about what was in it other than that.

46

"Okay, I'm officially worried." But he tipped the bottle back anyway.

Phoebe watched the swallow, the widening of eyes, the blown-out breath at the end and finally the cringe.

That was exactly what all newcomers did when they first tasted Mary's stuff.

"Booze," she said again. "You gotta get over the wincing thing. We consider that an insult around here."

"Got it." His voice was a little tight. He coughed and looked at the bottle again. "Do I want to know how she makes it?"

"Probably not."

"Okay."

Phoebe was strangely pleased that he took that in stride.

"That's a party staple," she said, pointing at the bottle. "There's beer and stuff too, but there's always a couple of bottles of this. Tradition is that it comes out later in the night and we pass the bottle, everyone drinking from it. We consider that a true taste of home. It's not sold anywhere else and it's made right here from fruit grown here, so you have to be willing and able to drink it without insulting our hometown and our ways with grimacing, coughing or flat-out refusing."

Joe wrinkled his nose. "Kind of like refusing to eat my grandmother's ostakaka at Christmas."

"Osta what?"

"It's a Swedish custard. And kind of an acquired taste."

She laughed. At least Joe had something to help him relate here. "If you didn't eat it and pretend to like it you were in trouble, right?"

"Right."

"Then, yes, it's like this."

He looked at the bottle skeptically and then took another swig. This time, he swallowed faster and without a frown. He did shudder a little at the end.

"Keep practicing," she said with a smile. "Now to the

tall tales."

"Lay it on me."

"You take a story—any story about anything, frankly—but it has to be true."

"Aren't tall tales made up?" Joe asked.

"Wait for it," she said with a smile. "You take this true story, whatever it is. I mean it can be going to the grocery store, visiting your aunt at the nursing home—"

"Losing half your college money at the craps table and then making it back times five at blackjack."

She blinked at him. "Uh, kind of. I mean yeah. You take the true story and then you make it more interesting. But only a touch. See, the technique is in embellishing without people knowing you're embellishing. If they call you on it, you have to confess—and drink. If you get away with it, you're good until the next time they come around to you."

"So I'd have to add some show girls and three big bouncers to my story," Joe said. He tipped the bottle back again.

She frowned. "I was thinking the losing half your college money and then the times five part was the embellishment."

"Nope, that was the true part."

Okay. Well then. "You don't think show girls and bouncers are overkill on the embellishing?"

"Got it. Show girls *or* bouncers, not both."

She really wanted to hear some of Joe's stories. Really. "You had some wild times, huh?"

He gave a humorless laugh. "Yeah. But I didn't know they were wild. They were par for the course in my family."

Oh, yeah, she couldn't wait for the first bonfire to hear more of this stuff.

"Craps and blackjack and show girls and bouncers are normal everyday stuff for me. Like you going to the grocery store and the nursing home." He drank again.

"What'd you grow up in a casino or something?"

"Exactly."

She stared at him. "You *grew up* in a casino?"

"Yep. My family has owned casinos for four generations. On the plus side, I learned how to count and do math at a very young age. On the negative, I saw my first pair of naked breasts at age nine, knew that I liked scotch better than whiskey by age fourteen and was a whiz at poker by fifteen." He paused. "Not that I thought any of those things were negative at the time." He seemed to be thinking. "I might have a hard time with embellishing."

She shook her head. "Joe Spencer, you are, hands down, one of the most intriguing people I've met in a long, long time." Which wasn't saying much, since she didn't get out of Sapphire Falls much, but still.

He gave her a half smile. "Stick around. You might learn some things from me too."

She laughed. "I'm sure. But this could be tricky," she told him. "I mean, you have an advantage because you're new, so we don't know you well enough to know if you're lying, and we don't know enough about your life to know what really happens and what doesn't. The disadvantage is even your true stories will sound over the top. You'll have to really get used to that booze. I have a feeling you're going to be drinking a lot."

He didn't say anything to that. But he drank again.

"Okay," she said, willing to change the subject that seemed to make him somber. "Next is music."

"This I *know* I'm worried about."

"Can you name three country bands? Past or present?" She leaned back and hit the play button on her old portable CD player she kept in the truck. She had fancier, newer equipment at home, but partying at the river meant the risk of sand and beer in the electronics.

He didn't even hesitate. "Nope."

"Then, yeah, you might need to worry." The Zac Brown Band started singing from the boombox and she saw Joe cringe.

"Oh, no, you will *not* disparage Zac Brown." She pointed a finger at his nose. "Or Garth Brooks. Or Johnny Cash. Or Miranda Lambert. Or…anything I play."

He held up the bottle of booze. "I think I know why you all drink so much of this stuff." He took another swallow.

Phoebe watched him. Not even a shudder that time. "You better take it easy, city boy. That's strong stuff. Ninety-percent alcohol."

"Good." He started to tip the bottle back again.

Phoebe grabbed for the bottle. He held it out of her reach and she leaned into him, her hand on his thigh to keep from tipping over.

The muscles under her hand were hard and hot.

They stared at each other for a moment.

She blinked up at him, feeling befuddled. She hated that. She wasn't used to guys being anything other than predictable and…manageable frankly. There was nothing about Joe that made her think she could manage him. Unless he let her. He'd gone along with everything to this point, but she sensed that if he dug his heels in, she'd have a hard time getting him to do anything she wanted.

She wasn't used to that at all.

"I can handle this," he said, his voice gruff.

He could handle what? Kissing her? Because that was all she could suddenly think about.

"You can?" she asked softly, knowing she wouldn't push him away.

Joe's gaze dropped to her mouth. She watched his throat work as he swallowed before speaking.

"No. I changed my mind. I cannot handle this."

He scooted six inches away and her hand slid from his leg. Then he drank again of Mary's strawberry booze.

Phoebe frowned. He obviously wasn't referring to not

being able to handle the alcohol. "You can't handle what?"

He lowered the bottle and wiped his arm across his mouth. "You."

Hey. That wasn't very nice. He didn't want to kiss her? He didn't want her leaning on his leg? Fine. Geez. All he had to say was…nothing. She definitely didn't want to hear that out loud. Or maybe he meant hanging out with her and learning about Sapphire Falls. She knew she could be overbearing and yeah, okay, she knew she'd been bossy with Joe so far, but she was trying to *help* him.

If he just wanted to be friends, fine. She was more than used to that. If he didn't want to be friends…well, tough shit. They had to hang out if he was going to impress Nadia. And he *was* going to impress Nadia. That was the ultimate goal. How Joe felt about Phoebe or how she felt about him didn't matter a damned bit in the end.

Phoebe grabbed the bottle before he knew what she was doing and took a long drink herself. She could always count on Mary to make things feel better.

"We don't have to like each other, but you're stuck with me, Joe," she said after the strawberry fire had burned its way to her stomach. "You need me."

Joe turned to her, his gaze intent on hers. "You want Matt, right?"

She frowned back. "Yes. I thought we'd established that."

"Just confirming. That's very important." His attention dropped to her mouth again. "Very important," he repeated firmly.

"Okay." Wow. Of course it was. But Joe was so intense about it that she felt irked without really understanding why. "Geez."

"I mean it, Phoebe. You have to be focused on Matt. You have to know that he's the one who can give you what you want. Right?"

She frowned. "What's the matter with you? Yes, of

course Matt's the one I want. He's the one I've wanted for three years."

"Why do you want him?"

This was weird. But okay, fine, it wasn't like she couldn't answer this question. "He's sweet and kind, he takes care of people and he's content with this simple life here with the people we love."

Joe was studying her. Then he shook his head. "That's not enough." He sighed. "Dammit."

Phoebe felt her eyes go wide. He seemed annoyed. And why he should care how she felt about Matt was a mystery. "What is your problem?"

"Sweet and kind and *content*?" he said. "Really? You think that's enough to keep you crazy about him forever?" He took the bottle away from her and drank. "Content? Seriously, who uses that as an adjective to describe the person they're hot for?"

She crossed her arms, biting back her initial retorts. "Maybe you don't understand being content."

"What?"

"You don't strike me as the type of guy to be content. You're always trying for more, aren't you? Always driven? Always thinking about how things could be bigger and better?"

She didn't know how she could possibly know that about him. She'd only known him for a couple of hours, and it wasn't like they'd shared deep, dark secrets. But she could feel it about him—the drive, the focus, the ambition.

He narrowed his eyes as he looked at her. "Yeah, I'm driven. Yes, I want to do more and be better. That's a *good* thing."

She shrugged. "Fine. That's you. But there's nothing wrong with already having the life you want and being *content* to enjoy it."

He didn't say anything for a few seconds, just sat watching her. "We're talking about Matt," he finally said.

"What about you?"

"What about me?" She shifted on the tailgate.

"Are you content? Here? With Matt?"

"Yes, of course." She was. Why was he questioning that? He didn't know her, didn't know Matt, didn't understand their life here. She and Matt made sense. She and Matt would be...her parents.

Her mother was content and often talked about what a blessing that was. To not want for anything. To not feel like there could be more. To look at the people in your life and accept them for who they were. To look at the things you had and be grateful. To look at the place you lived and know that it was your corner of the world, for better or worse.

Phoebe had never dreamed big. At least, not bigger than Sapphire Falls. And she didn't feel bad about that. This was her corner of the world and she was...yes, content here.

"Just because you don't understand it, doesn't mean it isn't true," Phoebe told Joe. She grabbed the bottle from him. There was only about a fifth of the booze left. Oops.

"I *want* it to be true, Phoebe," Joe said earnestly. "You have to get what you want from Matt. Not me."

She paused in mid-drink and swung to face him, so quickly she got a little dizzy. "From you? What would I want to get from you?"

"Doesn't matter," he said. "I'd give you anything. I'd do completely stupid, reckless, possibly life-altering things to give you whatever you wanted."

She stared at him, knowing her mouth was hanging open. "What in the *hell* are you talking about?"

Had he hit his head? Was he so drunk he didn't know who she was? Was she having some bizarre dream?

"The men in my family are idiots about crazy women."

"Excuse me?"

"I'm just telling you the truth." Joe gave a big sigh and suddenly lay back in the truck bed, staring at the night sky.

Hesitantly, Phoebe lay back beside him. Should she take him to the hospital?

"We're drawn to crazy women. Women who are confident and sexy and who instantly tie us up in knots. We love that rush, the heat, the never-felt-this-way-before feeling. And we get in way over our heads, way too fast. We're having the time of our life and the idea that it might go away makes us nuts—literally." Joe scrubbed a hand over his face.

Phoebe didn't even dare breathe. This was quite a rant and, in spite of her better judgment, she wanted to hear the rest of it.

Joe kept going, thankfully.

"So when the girl starts talking about leaving or moving on or whatever, we'll do anything to get her to stay. We'll put up our family business in a poker game or threaten her ex-Marine-boyfriend in a bar or agree to pull some strings at the IRS to get her back taxes forgiven." He sighed again. "We're morons."

What did this have to do with *her*? Phoebe bit her tongue and didn't ask, but it was killing her. And then there were the poker games and ex-boyfriends and the IRS. This had the makings of a very interesting story. Sure, it was possible it had nothing to do with her and he was simply drunkenly rambling. But there was some tie there with him wanting to be sure that what she wanted, she wanted from Matt.

Without warning, Joe rolled toward her, propping himself up on his elbow.

"So you can't turn these big blue eyes on me, okay?"

She stared up at him, having a hard time swallowing. Wow, the guy was intense.

"Um…"

"'Cuz, I already felt it with you." He lifted a hand and traced his index finger over her eyebrow and down the side of her face to the corner of her mouth. "I already got that feeling of wanting to get in over my head. That's not good."

His finger traced her bottom lip and Phoebe was pretty sure she stopped breathing. Holy crap...

"So no asking me for anything. Just turn it all on Matt. And I'll concentrate on Nadia."

Right. Nadia. And Matt.

But it would be a lot easier to focus on Matt if Joe stopped touching her.

She was going to have to think about all of this later. Or maybe not. Maybe not thinking about it was the safest thing. This was too crazy to even begin to dissect. And what would be the point? He was here about Nadia and Phoebe wanted Matt. That was easy. Nothing to wonder about and analyze there.

"Nad—" She had to clear her throat and was glad when Joe moved his finger from her lips. "Nadia is content here too, Joe. She loves it here. She wants to stay."

He nodded. "I know. That's good. She doesn't make me want to act crazy. I can be sane and normal here. I can have a white picket fence and spend Saturday nights at home and maybe even go to church or something. I want to be with her because, unlike the other men in my family, *I* understand that there are more important things than sex."

Okay. "We do have sex here in Sapphire Falls."

Where that came from she really couldn't say. But she did enjoy the curl to his mouth and the way his eyes seemed to heat.

"I'm glad to hear it. You should be having lots of truck-shaking sex, Phoebe Sherwood."

Well, she didn't know about the truck-shaking part...

"I should?" Now why had she said that? That was stupid. He was drunk and here to win another woman over, and Phoebe herself was trying to win someone else over. It did *not* matter what Joe thought about sex.

His mouth stretched into a full smile with that, and she

had to take a deep breath.

"Of course. You're made for blow-your-mind sex."

CHAPTER THREE

Phoebe didn't know what to say to that. Was that a compliment? It felt like one. Even though she wasn't really sure what he was talking about.

"Because of my breasts?"

She knew a lot of guys were boob men. Why she cared if Joe was one of them was beyond her. Matt was. She frowned. At least, he had been at one time. He'd told her himself. But Nadia wasn't very big in that department.

Her attention was immediately back on Joe when he chuckled.

"They're part of the whole curvy package," he said. "But with your energy and confidence and just...*you*." He shook his head like he couldn't find the words.

"Just *me*?" she repeated. "I don't know what that means."

"There's something about you. Something about...everything about you...makes a guy want to spread you out and enjoy you like a buffet of all the best sweet, colorful, soft, warm things ever made..."

Holy crap. Her entire body felt soft and warm and *that* was not at all how this was supposed to be going.

Geez.

Phoebe sat up quickly, almost clocking Joe in the chin with her head.

"This is crazy."

Joe got up slower. "Yeah, see, I told you."

"This is what you meant about the men in your family going crazy? Like you are seriously crazy? Diagnosed and medicated and the whole thing?"

He actually laughed. "Nah, there's no cure. Well, except for willpower. We got blessed with an abundance of abilities—"

"Spouting sexy bullshit for one," Phoebe muttered.

He gave a short nod. "Oh, yeah, we never run out of bullshit. But willpower was not one of the things readily passed on to the males in the Spencer family."

Phoebe took a deep breath. Okay, this was about Joe, not her. He was nuts. She could forgive that. It would be Nadia's problem, not hers anyway. And if Nadia had known him her whole life, she probably knew about the mental instability. Good. This was fine. Her warm, tingly feelings about Joe were just a mixture of him being damned sexy, the liquor and the late night. Lord knew, lots of interesting things happened in Sapphire Falls when the moonlight and Mary's concoctions were combined.

"I'm torn between being irritated that my effect on you is just a product of being a woman within ten feet of you and relieved that's all this is," she told him.

He frowned and shook his head. "No, that's not what I'm saying. I don't go crazy over all women, or even most women. But there is this certain mixture of characteristics that is my weakness."

She should ignore this whole thing. She should take him to Adrianne and Mason's, dump him on the porch, ring the doorbell and run.

Instead, she took a big gulp of strawberry booze, tossed the bottle toward the bucket in the back of the truck that was there to collect bottles and cans from parties, and leaned in, bracing her hand against the truck bed next to her hip.

She couldn't help it. She'd never been the prettiest, the smartest, the funniest or the sweetest. She'd never been the *est* anything, ever. Except the best friend.

The idea that a guy like Joe—even drunk off his ass—was attracted to her was too fun to not delve into a little. She could be forgiven for that, surely. And he might not remember the conversation tomorrow anyway.

"What characteristics?" she asked.

Joe fingered one of the curls that had come loose from

her ponytail. "Your mouth."

His gaze dropped to her lips again and Phoebe fought the urge to lick them.

"And I don't mean your physical mouth—that's a whole other discussion—but your mouthiness."

Yeah, too bad he wouldn't remember saying that. Most people chalked her mouthiness up in the negative column.

But he wasn't done. "The way you make everyone light up when you're around. The way you laugh out loud—like you've never heard anything funnier each time. How you sing loudly to your favorite song even though you're terrible."

She cocked an eyebrow. That didn't *sound* like something that would be attractive, but he was looking at her like it really was. This was getting weirder and weirder. He'd been watching her at the bar for like an hour. Clearly, he'd been paying attention. Why?

"The way your eyes sparkle when someone flirts with you. The way you twirl your hair when you're flirting with them."

"I don't—"

"You do," he said. "And I also like that when you flirt, you don't think anyone notices."

"But—"

"I like that you treat everyone like they're your best friend. No matter who it is or what they want, you treat them like you're happy to see them and that everything they say is witty and brilliant."

"I...do?" She didn't think she really did that. Not on purpose anyway.

"You treat all those poor guys who are madly in love with you like they're all special." He frowned.

She opened her mouth to reply when he went on.

"No, actually, that irritates me. I don't like that part."

"Nobody's in love with me," she said. Then thought about who she'd seen and danced with earlier. "Okay, John might have a little crush."

Joe laughed. And it wasn't one of his usual chuckles. This was an outright laugh. "I do like that, though," he said. "That you're completely clueless about the fact that every guy there tonight wanted you."

She shook her head. "We're all friends." Then she sighed. "I'm everyone's friend."

"See, you make all guys crazy. I mean, they must be crazy to be around this amazing woman for years and not do a damned thing about it."

For just a moment, she didn't care that he was a virtual stranger, or that he was in town for another woman, or that he was a Borcher's Booze virgin and was definitely feeling the effects. He had been watching her and thought she was amazing for some pretty…amazing reasons.

She leaned in, grabbed the front of his shirt and pulled him close. Then she kissed him. Not because she wanted to get him naked, not because of the liquor, but because he'd made her feel kissable for the first time in a while and she really liked kissing.

And she didn't think he'd mind.

There wasn't even a second of hesitation on Joe's part. He tunneled his fingers into her hair, tipped his head one way and hers the other and completely took over the kiss.

His mouth was hot and hungry. He slicked his tongue along her bottom lip and then sucked it lightly into his mouth. When she moaned, he took advantage and boldly stroked his tongue along hers. He tasted like strawberries and sex. Two of her favorite things.

Joe cupped her jaw gently but firmly, making it clear that he was in control of everything from the angle of their lips to the pressure to the pace of the strokes of his tongue. And she loved it. Which she would never have believed.

She wanted to strip her clothes off and climb up on top of him, rub herself all over him, tell him a thousand dirty things she wanted him to do to her. Better yet, she wanted to ask him what dirty things he wanted to do to her and then, and this was important, lie back and let him take over.

This was completely unlike her. She was used to being the one in control. It seemed that the guys she hung out with needed her to make the first move. And the second and third. She led the way, gave the signals, determined the pace of the whole damned relationship, not to mention what was happening with the lips and hands. She was so used to it, in fact, that Joe's dominance surprised her. And made her really hot. Which downright shocked her.

He trailed his lips over her jaw to her earlobe, down to the side of her neck where he kissed, flicked his tongue and then bit down gently.

"I can feel that everywhere." She gasped when he did it again. "It makes my whole body tingle."

"Wait 'til I get down lower," he said huskily against her neck. "I want to suck on your nipples and lick your belly button and put my tongue against your clit and make you scream."

Her whole body was burning up. Nobody had ever talked to her like that.

"Keep going," she said breathlessly, sliding her eyes shut as he licked across her collarbone. He cupped her breast, rubbing his thumb over her nipple with the perfect amount of pressure to make every muscle below her waist clench. Every one of them.

"Keep going with telling you what I want, or with doing it?" he asked, rolling her nipple between his thumb and finger.

She forgot the question.

"Tell me what you want," he said when she didn't answer.

"Keep going," was all she could manage.

"Tell me where you want my mouth."

"Anywhere."

He chuckled softly. "Tell me, Phoebe." He squeezed

her nipple gently. "Here?"

"*Yes.*"

"Tell me."

"You want to hear me say 'suck on my nipple'?"

He groaned and pinched again a little harder, making heat zing straight to her clit. "Yes. God, yes."

Telling him what she wanted was difficult when she couldn't even remember to keep breathing. But she definitely wanted to tell him what she was feeling in full technicolor detail.

And he'd like it. She knew it. It wouldn't scare him off like it might with the nice boys from Sapphire Falls. Like it might with Matt.

Suddenly she froze. Her hands went to Joe's head and held him when he dipped to take her nipple in his mouth.

"Wait. No. Wait."

Dammit, dammit, dammit. This was Joe. *Joe.* The guy that was going to help her break *Matt* and Nadia up. Because they wanted to be with Matt and Nadia.

Dammit.

Joe's head came up and he pinned her with another intense look. "Wait? No? Seriously?"

She nodded. "Seriously. We can't do that."

"Oh, I promise you we can."

She took a deep breath, stoically looking him in the eye instead of looking at the mouth that had been making her feel…things she hadn't felt before.

Dammit.

"We can't. We need to focus on Matt and Nadia. Remember?"

He didn't answer right away. Then he put his forehead against hers and pulled in a long breath.

"Fuck."

"Yeah."

Joe pulled back and straightened slowly. "In my defense," he said, clearly trying to sound normal when his voice was still scratchy. "I warned you. And you kissed me."

She liked that he was struggling to pull himself together too.

"I did kiss you," she acknowledged.

"And I warned you that the Spencer men tend to lose their minds easily when it comes to certain women and sex."

She liked that she was one of those women and simply couldn't work up any regret about that. Maybe tomorrow, but definitely not while even her bones were tingling.

She finally sighed. "This whole night might be the craziest I've ever had."

He nodded. "Told you. Crazy. We should stay far away from crazy."

"Probably." Though if what they'd been doing was crazy, she was kind of a fan.

"Which would mean I should stay away from you," Joe said.

But he didn't sound like he really liked that idea. Phoebe didn't, for sure.

Great. Within a few hours, she'd already come to hate the idea of not hanging out with him.

Crazy for sure.

"You need me," she said. "If you want to win Nadia back, you're going to need my help."

"I'm not sure I'm totally clear on that plan."

Phoebe glanced at the bottle of booze sticking up out of her recycling bucket. "Yeah, tonight might not be the perfect time to go over the details."

Joe nodded and winced. "I would have to concur."

"Tomorrow. We'll go over everything tomorrow. I'll take you for breakfast."

"Okay."

With no idea what she should do or say after that, Phoebe jumped down off of the tailgate and tried to forget the fact that her nipples were big fans of Joe's—which was difficult with them still sending happy signals to the rest of her girl parts. Joe followed and they got back into the truck without a word.

In fact, they made it all the way to Adrianne and Mason's place without a word. Fortunately, her friends only lived three miles away and she could get there on a back gravel road.

"Need help in?" she asked as she parked in front of the big old farmhouse Mason had inherited.

"I got it." Joe more or less slid from the truck seat to the ground.

"Go in the back door. Watch out for the table just inside the door and walk along the wall in the hallway—the floor creaks if you walk in the center," Phoebe said. "Oh, and shut the door quickly or it will squeak. But don't let it slam."

"Got it."

"And you should probably take some ibuprofen and drink a couple glasses of water before you head up to bed."

"Got it."

"Make sure you have your phone by your bed and the ringer turned up. I'll call you and wake you up in the morning."

"Phoebe?" he said, leaning in the truck door.

"Yeah?"

"Stop bossing me around."

She pressed her lips together. Yeah, she did that. In a couple of days, the mouthiness that he'd mentioned earlier as attractive might move down that list a ways. A long ways.

But she couldn't help but smile at the memory of the things he liked about her.

As he gave her a wink, slammed the truck door and headed up the path to the house, she also smiled at the khaki pants he was wearing. Turned out Joe Spencer wasn't quite as buttoned up and conservative as she'd first thought.

She turned the truck for home, replaying the night from the first time she'd seen those khakis to the last time.

Crazy.

That was the best word.

And it looked like maybe crazy was contagious.

ৎৣৣৣৣ৶

"Good mornin', sunshine," Phoebe greeted as Joe pushed Adrianne and Mason's front screen door open.

"This is really early."

"This is the country."

She'd called his cell to wake him up when she'd gotten out of the shower at five thirty. She wanted to get him going so he'd be ready when she got here. It looked like it had worked. He was dressed in light gray dress pants and another white button-down shirt. She was sure there was a jacket and tie around somewhere, but he didn't have them on. Yet.

He looked good...and like he didn't feel so good.

"I need coffee."

"Mason didn't make any?" Phoebe asked. She was sure Mason was already out in the fields or down at one of the greenhouses. He didn't have to be, but he really liked to play farmer. Adrianne was probably still in bed. She also wasn't a country girl at heart. She was a transplant and loved Sapphire Falls, but she believed the day started at nine. Phoebe on the other hand had a deep love for the early morning. She was up at five a.m. and going full steam ahead by six.

"I have no idea," Joe replied.

She bit back her smile. "Then it's a good thing we're going for breakfast."

He groaned a little. "What the *hell* was in that wine from last night?"

She turned and started down the porch steps. "I don't know that I'd call it *wine*."

"What would you call it?" The screen door slapped shut behind him as he followed her down the steps.

She turned back to look at him. Sure enough, he had a jacket and tie in one hand. "I guess I'd call it alcohol."

He was squinting in the early morning light and slowly pulled sunglasses from his pocket, slipping them on. "Alcohol? That's it?"

She shrugged. "It's…locally made. Homemade even."

His eyebrows appeared above the top edge of his glasses. "Moonshine?"

She laughed. "That's a bit dramatic. And probably not all that accurate. Aunt Mary just makes her own wine and brandy and hard ciders. Sometimes they come out a little strong."

Joe swallowed. "A little?"

Phoebe wasn't as good at hiding her smile that time. The city boy was going to have to learn to drink country style. Wait until he tasted the local beer.

They got into her truck and Joe flinched as she slammed her door. Phoebe leaned over to grab him some ibuprofen from the glove box. Her elbow hit the truck horn and the compartment door dropped open and whacked him in the knee. "Sorry." She grabbed the bottle and shook some into her hand. He even grimaced at the sound of the tablets rattling in the plastic bottle. She held the medication out for him. He took it without a word.

She handed him the half-full bottle of water in her cup holder. "Sorry. Best I've got at the moment."

He took it, tipped it back and swallowed the tablets along with the rest of the water.

She started the truck and immediately music blasted from the speakers. Wincing, she reached to turn Brad Paisley down. "Sorry."

"You're saying that a lot this morning," Joe said,

leaning his head back against the truck seat. His eyes slid shut.

"I didn't know you'd feel *this* bad."

"If you'd known, would it make you quieter? Or less bossy? Or at least loud and bossy at a decent time of morning?"

She glanced over at him with a smile. Okay, Joe wasn't a morning person. He had, however, figured out her personality pretty quickly. "Probably not. Loud and bossy, even early in the morning, is just kind of who I am."

"I figured."

"But I would have brought you some Gatorade or coffee if I'd known how bad you felt." She was all of the things he'd said, but she'd also been hungover herself enough to know that he'd be easier to boss around if she made him feel better.

"You didn't give me a chance to tell you anything on the phone. Including the fact that I never get up before seven."

She thought back over their conversation. He'd answered on the sixth ring, she'd said "Hey, it's Phoebe. Get up. I'll be there in thirty minutes." Then she'd hung up.

"Sorry about that too," she said with a shrug. She hadn't needed or expected a long, drawn-out exchange. They were going to do that over breakfast.

"Would you have let me stay in bed if I'd told you?" he asked.

"Nope." They had stuff to do.

"Then I'm blocking your number from my phone."

"Oh, you'll feel better about all of this…and me…once you've had some hash browns, black coffee and pancakes."

Joe groaned. "Don't talk about food."

She rolled her eyes. What a baby.

Ten minutes later, Phoebe pulled into a parking spot in front of Julie's, the only clothing store in Sapphire Falls.

Joe sat forward and peered through the windshield.

"What's this?"

"We're going shopping."

He turned to her. "Here?"

"It's the only option." And Julie had exactly what they needed.

"It's also just after six a.m."

"I have a key." Phoebe opened her door, hopped to the ground and rounded the truck to meet Joe as he got out, much slower.

"You have a key to this place too?"

"Julie's my aunt. I told her what I needed and she said to go ahead. She'll put it on an account."

Joe just frowned down at her.

"What?" Phoebe finally asked.

"You're related to the entire town?"

"About twenty-five percent. A little more by marriage."

"So hanging out with you will get me anything I need, huh?"

"I told you that last night. Stick with me and you'll go far." She turned on her heel and headed for the door to Julie's. "Come on. We need to get to the diner by six-thirty."

"The diner?" But he followed.

Phoebe unlocked the door and held it open for Joe to precede her into the store. This time, he did go in ahead of her, even though it was a dark place. That made her smile. Then again, a lot of things about Joe made her smile.

"Wait here, I'll get the lights." She crossed to the switch on the other side of the room and flipped it on. She turned to find Joe looking around with a combination of disbelief and concern.

"You've got to be kidding."

"Not kidding." She came to stand in front of him. "You want to fit in here, and you can't do that in a suit and tie."

"Then I might want to rethink the 'fitting in' thing."

She laughed. "No, you don't. This is minor stuff for the

love of your life. And who knows," she said, tossing him two pairs of jeans, "you might end up wondering how you've lived this long without denim."

"I've worn denim before."

She lifted an eyebrow.

"Just not for, you know, work. Or in public much."

She grinned. "Well, Toto, you're not in Chicago anymore."

Fifteen minutes later, Joe stepped out from the dressing room and thrust a pile of jeans—minus the pair he was wearing—at her.

"Here. These fit."

"Awesome. Try this on."

Joe looked with clear disdain at the black T-shirt she held out. "Just this one?"

"Well, if it fits we'll just get the different colors."

"The same shirt? Times five?"

Phoebe propped a hand on her hip. "Says the man who wears a white button-down shirt every day?"

Joe sighed. "With a different tie and jacket. It's not the same thing."

"Whatever you say." She shook the shirt. "Try it on."

He narrowed his eyes and something she couldn't quite name flickered in them. "Fine." He started unbuttoning the white shirt he wore.

Phoebe's eyes widened. He was gonna do it right here instead of in the dressing room? Huh. Well, hell, she wasn't going to complain. She leaned back against the counter behind her and crossed her arms.

Joe shrugged out of his shirt and tossed it over the chair next to him.

Phoebe forgot to take her next breath. Or swallow. Or blink.

Okay, wow. Maybe they should just do away with shirts all together for all occasions.

He was toned. Not huge and wide, but definitely solid.

Smooth, tanned skin stretched over the firm muscles of his chest, shoulders and *abs*. Oh, yeah, there were abs. Holy schmoly.

"Phoebe?"

She jerked her eyes from his six pack up to his face. Where he wore a half grin. "The shirt?"

The shirt…oh, right. "Here." She thrust the black cotton at him, making herself meet his eyes and not blush.

"It's okay. If you took your shirt off, I'd be staring for sure."

She shook her head. He was trying to fluster her. Not cool. She was trying to help him. He couldn't walk around Sapphire Falls—he absolutely couldn't walk into the diner—in a suit and tie. Well, she wasn't easily flustered. "Let me just say, thank you for spending all that time in the gym. That chest and those shoulders are exactly why you should be wearing cotton T-shirts. Show some of that off. It's a shame to cover it up with a jacket."

He chuckled. "Thanks. I guess." He slipped the T-shirt on, muscles rippling all over the place.

As he pulled it over his head, obscuring his view for a moment, Phoebe leaned to the right, checking out the hard planes of his back as well. *Damn.*

Joe pulled the shirt into place, then shrugged his shoulders and flexed his trunk. "Fine. Yeah, this fits."

"Great. We've got gray, blue, red and green too."

"Oh, good."

Ignoring his sarcasm, she grabbed another of the black—there was something about Joe in that black T-shirt that did something to her.

He now had four pairs of jeans and six T-shirts.

She sat him down to try on leather work boots while she picked out a couple of caps.

"You can't be serious about these boots."

"What are you gonna do, wear your Prada dress shoes with your new jeans?"

Muttering under his breath, Joe stood and paced the length of the store and back in the boots.

"How are they?" she asked.

"Hell if I know. Are they supposed to make me feel like I'm wearing five-pound weights on my feet?"

She smiled. "Probably. They're sturdy."

"Then yeah, they're fine."

"Okay, let's go. We've got a breakfast date."

On the way to the truck, she stopped him with a hand on his arm. "Hang on." She kept hold of his arm longer than she really needed too, telling herself that she didn't want him bolting when she kicked dirt on him. Truth was, touching him just seemed like a good idea. "Your boots look too new."

"They are—hey!"

She used her foot to scoop the soft dirt around the parking lot onto the tops of the boots, then put her heel on his right foot and ground it in.

"Shake it off."

"What the hell?" he grumbled as he picked his feet up one at a time and knocked the loose dirt off.

"There, that's better," she said. The boots had lost a lot of their shine.

"You're a nut, you know that?" he asked.

"Oh, you ain't seen nothin' yet." She finally let go of him and started for the truck again.

She couldn't keep touching him. Probably. That didn't make any sense. Yeah, he was hot. Really hot. And warm and hard and…yeah, she couldn't keep touching him. They were cohorts in a plan to break up Matt and Nadia—the people they *wanted* to be with. Touching Joe didn't really figure into that plan very well. Or at all.

Probably.

Joe kept his head back and his eyes closed on the drive to the diner. When they'd hit a bump or pot hole in the road, he'd groan, but he didn't say anything more.

They pulled up in front of the diner that was referred to simply as *the diner*. She wasn't sure it even had another name.

"Let's go, big guy. I'm buyin'."

"You sure as hell are," he muttered as he slowly lifted his head and made it out of the truck without falling or puking.

He winced even as the bell over the door tinkled.

Phoebe was almost starting to feel sorry for him.

"Hi, Dottie!" she called to the owner and primary cook.

"'Mornin', Phoebe," Dottie greeted with a wave of her spatula. "You need coffee?"

"Yep. Lots of it." She glanced at Joe. "Strong."

Dottie regarded Joe through the window in the wall that separated the front from the kitchen. "Looks like a big old bacon sandwich too."

"Tomato juice," Joe spoke up.

Dottie cocked her head. "You want a shot of Tabasco in that?"

Joe nodded and Phoebe said, "This is Joe Spencer. He works for Mason and Lauren."

"Nice to meet ya, Joe." Dottie pointed to the booth by the window. "You might as well sit there. Everyone's gonna want to know who you are and they can get a good look if you're near the door."

Joe groaned as Phoebe led the way to the booth.

He was so not at his best right now. Meeting the town did not seem like a good idea at the moment. Or any of the moments in the foreseeable future.

But Phoebe stopped before they slid into the booth and called out—loudly of course, "Hey, guys, this is Joe." The woman even walked loudly. She was wearing flip flops that slapped against the tile floor as she walked. He could only imagine how noisy she'd get in heels.

There was only one other table occupied this early and it was actually made up of four tables pulled together. The chairs haphazardly circling the tables were filled with men who looked like they ranged from old to damned old. They all wore jeans, T-shirts, dirty work boots and caps.

Joe sighed.

"Hey, Joe," several of them called back. He also got saluted with a couple of coffee cups. Then one yelled, "Whatcha doin' here, boy?"

Joe didn't think he could yell loud enough to be heard without his head exploding. He braced himself and opened his mouth, but Phoebe pushed him into the booth. "He's workin', Frank. Leave him alone. He doesn't feel so good this mornin'."

"He get into Borcher's Booze or somethin'?" the guy called back.

Phoebe snickered. "You got it."

"Good for you, boy, way to jump right in with both feet."

Joe gave him a weak smile and a wave. If he felt better after breakfast, he'd go over and try to make nice, but right now he needed to hydrate.

Phoebe took a seat on the bench across from him and crossed her arms on the table top. "You gonna make it?"

"Yeah."

"You sure?"

He lifted a shoulder. "I've been worse off than this. But it usually involves way more liquor, a couple cigars, staying up until the sun comes up and—" He caught Phoebe's wide eyes and shifted on his seat. Maybe that was too much sharing too early on.

"And a couple of blonds and brunettes on the side?" Phoebe asked.

He cleared his throat. "Past life. That's over. I'm turning over a new leaf."

Phoebe gave him a knowing look. "That's not a denial on the multiple girls."

"Past life," he repeated.

"Ah." She nodded. And certainly didn't seem shocked or disgusted. "Well, you're gonna have to change your ways if you're gonna live here," Phoebe said. She was studying the back of the booth beside his shoulder with a frown.

"What do you mean? If Borcher's Booze is a regular thing around here, you're all way wilder and tougher than me," he said lightly.

Phoebe looked up. "Well, there is that."

"Then I should be fine."

"Sure, as long as vanilla is your favorite flavor, you'll be great."

He leaned in. "Are we talking about vodka, ice cream or sex?"

She leaned in too. "Do you like vanilla in any of those things?"

"Nope. Vodka isn't my drink and I like some flavor and even a few add-ins with both ice cream and sex."

"Add-ins?" Phoebe repeated.

"Like crushed up Oreos and colored sprinkles." Joe made note of Phoebe's bright blue sleeveless top. He also knew that her capris were yellow, as were her flip flops, though they had blue rhinestones that glittered from the straps.

He really did like colored sprinkles.

"You use Oreos and colored sprinkles during sex?"

He grinned. "Sure. Or chocolate syrup. Or edible body lotion. Or other add-ins. You know…toys, handcuffs, naughty costumes. That kind of stuff."

Phoebe licked her lips and Joe couldn't look away from the shine on her bottom lip. "What kind of costumes?" She was practically whispering now.

Phoebe Sherwood never whispered. He'd known her

fewer than twenty-four hours and he knew that.

He liked this. He lowered his voice too. "I've always been partial to naughty teachers."

Phoebe blushed.

He liked that too. It was probably almost as rare as the being quiet thing. But he didn't know why she'd be blushing. "Do you have a naughty teacher costume?" he asked, so hoping the answer was yes.

"I am a teacher."

He thought about that, his grin growing. "And here I was gonna say that I thought my new favorite might be a naughty farm girl."

She blushed brighter at that and he laughed.

"You shouldn't be flirting with me," she finally said.

He sighed, his smile fading. "Yeah, you're right."

"You can't really help it though, huh?"

"It tends to get the better of me."

"You're gonna have to tone it down."

"Hanging out with you isn't going to help me there."

They sat looking at each other. Joe honestly didn't know how he should feel at that moment. Maybe apologetic, but that didn't seem to be sinking in.

Phoebe opened her mouth, snapped it shut and pressed her lips together.

Yeah, Phoebe biting her tongue also didn't likely happen often.

"What?" Joe asked.

"Nothing."

"You were going to say something."

"Nah, it was nothing."

"Phoebe, come on. You can say it." He dropped his voice again. "Especially if it's something dirty."

She took a short breath. "There you go again," she said.

"Told you I can't help it with you."

She closed her eyes and sighed. "I'm going to ignore that, because it's trouble." She opened her eyes again. "I shouldn't say what I was thinking. It's none of my business. We barely know each other. And it probably doesn't matter."

Ignoring the attraction between them was a good idea. "I have a feeling that not saying something you think is pretty hard on you."

"Incredibly hard."

He smiled at her quick admission. "Then just spill it. If it doesn't matter, then it still won't matter after you say it out loud, right?"

That seemed to be enough permission for Phoebe. "I can't see Nadia dressing up in naughty costumes or using toys," she said in a rush. "I mean, she's let her hair down and loosened up some since being here—it's hard not to around our gang—but she's still pretty buttoned up."

Joe wasn't sure how to respond. Phoebe was right. Unless Nadia had undergone a personality transplant, she was far from spontaneous or daring. She'd grown up around the wild and crazy like he had and gave anything too risqué a wide berth. As a scientist, she was all about predictability and controlled environments. Of course, that was before she'd gone to Haiti for six months. He knew she'd been pushed outside of her comfort zone there and she'd changed from the experience. Maybe that had made her more willing to try new things.

"Maybe she just hasn't been with the right guy so far."

It was a long moment before Phoebe responded to that. "Yeah, maybe. I know that things with her and Matt are pretty…"

"Vanilla?"

She nodded.

"How do you know?"

"Girl talk."

"Girl talk?" He leaned in. "What kind of girl talk?"

"Exactly the kind you're thinking of. We drink margaritas and talk about everything, including men and sex."

"And Nadia told you about her sex life with Matt?"

"Yes. And that it's good. But she's never mentioned toys or handcuffs or food."

"Maybe she just didn't want to tell you."

"Well, it's definitely come up. Why wouldn't she say anything? The rest of us have talked about what we're getting and what we *wish* we were getting."

Joe knew that he should be more interested in what Nadia had said—or hadn't said—but he couldn't help but ask, "What are you getting and, more importantly, what do you wish you were getting, Phoebe?"

Phoebe narrowed one eye. "I don't see any margaritas here and you're definitely not a girl."

"I'm happy to tell you all about what I wish I was getting. And some of the stuff I've gotten in the past."

"We really should not have that conversation, Joe."

"Probably. But you want to, don't you?" He felt it every time her gaze drifted to his mouth, and he noticed every time she pulled her lower lip between her teeth. If he wasn't mistaken, that was her tell for when she was getting turned on. "Don't you, Phoebe?" he asked.

"I—"

"What can I get ya?"

The moment was interrupted by the gray-haired waitress who'd shown up next to the table, and Joe knew he wouldn't get it back. At least not during breakfast. The waitress set two empty cups down along with a carafe of coffee and a glass of tomato juice.

"Wheat toast, butter on the side, and whatever fresh fruit you have," Joe said.

Phoebe kicked him under the table.

"Hey!"

She was frowning at him but said quickly, "That's for me, Viv. My stomach's a little funny this morning. He'll take the number two."

"Fried or scrambled?" Viv asked.

Fine, he'd play along. He assumed they were talking about eggs. "Scrambled."

"Bacon, sausage or ham?"

He glanced at Phoebe who mouthed, "Bacon".

"Bacon."

Viv turned and left them.

"Fitting in around here requires giving myself heart disease?" he asked, sipping the tomato juice.

"Fitting in around here means being a man. Here that means bacon and eggs. Especially Dottie's. And you'll thank me after eating the pancakes. They're awesome."

"I'm not a big breakfast eater."

Phoebe poured coffee for both of them. He waited for her to add cream and sugar, but she took a big drink of the straight black brew. "You said you realized that you have to change your ways. You're living in the middle of the heartland, and here people eat a big breakfast at the crack of dawn, a big lunch at noon straight up, and a light supper after the sun goes down. Oh, and the men who have been doing that their entire lives commonly live into their nineties."

"None of these guys eat fruit?" Joe groused. It wasn't that he didn't like bacon. Who in their right mind didn't like bacon? He just tried to eat healthier than that.

"Sure, they eat fruit. And veggies. Most of it is stuff that's grown right here. Most of them have big gardens or they exchange with neighbors and friends. They also drink real milk straight from the cow and eat real butter and bacon and beef. Along with fish and chicken. And homemade bread. And, of course, dessert."

"Is there a local gym?" Joe took a drink of coffee and found it to be quite good.

"The local gym is all the farmland and fields you see around here. These guys—and girls—work hard and play hard. Sunday afternoon, they might lay around in front of a football game or nap in a hammock, but cows and corn don't take days off, so most people work seven days a week."

He hadn't thought about that, but it made sense. His world was as different as it could get. Not only did he work Monday through Friday—with the exception of weekend receptions and parties—but most of the politicians he interacted with didn't work holidays and had long recesses. He dealt with other special-interest groups as well, but they also tended to work nine to five, five days a week. The media was a little different, but the information he shared with them was not exactly hard-hitting breaking news.

Joe finished his tomato juice and first cup of coffee and was well into his second when Viv set their plates down.

He had to admit that the bacon smelled amazing and it had been years since he'd had pancakes.

He gave in and slathered on the butter and started to pour the maple syrup.

"Uh, hang on there, big guy," Phoebe said, reaching to grab the bottle.

"What?"

"Those are *my* pancakes that you're messing with, and I like blueberry syrup."

"Yours?"

She put a piece of wheat toast on the plate in front of him. "Uh huh, you ordered toast and fruit."

"But—" He looked down at the bacon.

"I was saving your manhood by saying this was for me, but I'm not eating dry toast and fruit only."

"If we switch plates everyone will know—and ostracize me," he pointed out, taking a piece of bacon and eating it before she could stop him.

She grinned. "I fully intend to leave that plate in front of you and sneak bites from it, but make no mistake that those pancakes are mine."

"I'll give you one," he said agreeably, cutting off a

piece of pancake and putting it in his mouth.

Damn, that was good.

"I'll give *you* one," she said, tugging the plate closer to her and pouring blueberry syrup over half the stack.

He grabbed another piece of bacon while she cut off a wedge of pancake.

They just chewed for a few minutes, eating quickly as they shared the breakfast. It turned out that he got all the bacon, but she got three-fourths of the pancakes. They shared the hash browns and Phoebe only took two bites of the eggs.

When the last of the potatoes had disappeared—her half with ketchup, his half without—Phoebe sat back with a groan. "Ugh, eating that much that fast can't be a good idea."

"The fruit's good," Joe said, taking a huge square of cantaloupe from the bowl in front of Phoebe.

She plucked out a strawberry. "I guess it's safe to say that next time you'll be ordering the number two on your own?"

He grinned. "I might try the number one. It has more pancakes and includes bacon *and* sausage."

She shook her head. "You're gonna be just fine here, Joe. It only took twenty minutes to convert you to a real breakfast."

"I'm going to have to get a job on one of the farms to work it off though."

"You usually go to a gym?"

"Yeah. I do some weights, but mostly I run."

She looked at him funny. "You go to a gym to *run*? How much does that cost?"

"About a hundred a month."

She put down her fork. "You spend a hundred dollars a month so that you can *run*? You can do that anywhere. Why do you need a fancy gym?"

Because working out was a very small part of why

people went to the posh gym he belonged to. It was a status symbol for one thing, and it was a great place to network with the rich and powerful in Chicago. But he didn't say that out loud. "You don't have to worry about the weather or what time of night it is." Both true statements. Neither of which had ever been a factor in his running routine, but still.

"You're gonna have to lace your shoes up on the gravel roads around here, I guess," Phoebe said. "Because Dottie's breakfast is only the beginning of the great food you're gonna get here, and we definitely don't want you gettin' fat."

"You don't think Nadia would still want me if I put on a few pounds?" He stubbornly refused to wonder if Matt worked out or if Phoebe would still want Matt if he got pudgy.

"Still?" Phoebe asked. "You say she wants you now, but she isn't here to prove or disprove that claim."

"It will be obvious once she's back," he said.

Though he had no idea if that was true. In the past, once a friend of his had pointed out how Nadia acted around him, it had been easy to tell that she had a crush on him. But that had been before she'd gotten confident enough to do things like get on a plane to a third-world country—no first-class seat, no five-star hotel waiting on the other end. She'd decided to change her life, do something meaningful, and she'd done it. Leaving him behind to his year of freedom and debauchery.

So did she still have a crush on him? Maybe not. But he needed her. He needed to marry her. She'd keep him sane and on the straight and narrow, just as she'd promised to do before she'd left for Haiti.

And she was the one woman in the world who he genuinely liked and could spend time with, but who didn't make him crazy in the way that he and all the men in his family tended to go crazy over women.

She wasn't a bright, bubbly, loud bundle of energy that made him smile and want to make her blush constantly. She wasn't the type of woman who would make him do stupid things to prove his feelings, like risk his neck jumping out of an airplane, or blow a ton of money buying a billboard on the interstate, or mess with the law by conning a night watchman at the art museum out of his keys.

Dr. Nadia Simonsen was a sweet, conservative woman who would keep him from giving in to his base desires to go completely over the top and out of control.

She was not Phoebe Sherwood.

CHAPTER FOUR

"Okay, then let's talk about the plan." Phoebe poured the remainder of the coffee from the carafe into their two cups.

"I thought we did that in the back of your truck."

Sure, like he'd remember it right now if they had.

"We talked about the general concept, yes," she said, "but I figured out the specifics last night."

He looked at her with surprise. "You dropped me off at like one a.m."

"Yeah."

"You were up and perky at five thirty when you called me."

"Five actually."

"When do you sleep?"

She shrugged. "When I get my stuff done. I don't need a lot of sleep."

Joe sighed. Perky and energetic and a morning person. He definitely didn't want to get involved with Phoebe. He was more of a night owl, but he needed a solid eight hours of sleep. Nine was even better. "Okay, what are the specifics?"

"There are four general groups of people that have to like you for you to be included and liked in Sapphire Falls."

"Should I be taking notes?" He sat back in the booth and draped his arm along the back of the bench.

"Yes," Phoebe told him.

"Okay, hit me."

"The young guys, obviously. They're our age and are the ones you'll be hanging out with, the ones that Nadia knows and likes."

"Seems easy enough."

"They're going to want to talk about farming, football, NASCAR, WWE, farming and football. In that order."

Joe stared at her. He didn't know much about most of that and didn't even know what a couple of them were for sure. "NASCAR?"

"Car racing."

"WWE?"

"Wrestling."

He dropped his arm off the back of the booth and crossed his arms over his chest. "That's it?" He had access to Google on his laptop. He hoped. Actually, he had no idea if Mason and Adrianne had Wi-Fi at their place.

"That's what they'll want to *talk* about. They're also going to expect you to be able to build a bonfire, drink beer and booze and play poker."

Now that all sounded better. "I can drink and play poker with any of them. Guaranteed."

"Well, you can't outdrink them and you can't beat them in poker."

"Ever?"

She thought about that. "Not more than two out of ten times."

"I'll have to hold back." Seriously. He'd been playing poker since he was eight, and doing it well since he was thirteen. He'd been winning big bucks at it since he was old enough to get into the big games.

"That would be a good idea." Phoebe took another drink of coffee. "Any chance you know what you're doing with a bonfire or know anything about football?"

"I'm going to need some help," he admitted.

"I'll make some flashcards," she said. "The other group you need to impress is the girls our age."

"I'm feeling better about that group," he said with a grin. He'd been charming women as long as he'd been playing poker. He'd been good at it for longer than he'd been good at poker.

"Are you?" Phoebe gave him a mischievous smile. "I know that you've got the looks and the charm, but this group requires some skill too."

He cocked an eyebrow. "I have some skills, Phoebe."

That cute pinkness tinged her cheeks even as she said, "You're going to have to country dance."

His cockiness disappeared. "Dance?"

"*Country* dance," she corrected. "That's an important distinction."

"Maybe I'll just buy them plenty to drink and they won't be able to dance."

"They will," Phoebe assured him. "And unless you plan to keep Nadia drunk for your entire relationship, she *will* want to dance. She loves it."

Joe groaned and ran a hand over his face. "I'm going to need help with that too."

"I know. Good thing I'm good at everything and I'm nice to new guys."

He really wanted to make a crack about her being good at *everything* but he was too busy worrying about the stuff he didn't know how to do. "What else?" he asked with apprehension.

"The other two groups are easier. One is those guys." She gestured with her thumb toward the older guys still drinking coffee and trying to talk over one another.

"How do I impress them?"

"Never talk politics, check the Weather Channel every morning before you come in, come in here for breakfast every morning, and, oh, football."

"Football again? Thought you said this was easy." And not talking politics? That was basically his job. "And what if they ask what I do for a living?"

"I said *easier* not easy," she pointed out. "You just tell them you work for Mason and Lauren. They don't need specifics, and they all really like Mason so that will be enough."

He glanced at the group. "And the football?"

"They want to talk old school Nebraska football. I can

fill you in on the highlights, but here's the key with this group versus the young guys—you admit that you're not from Nebraska so didn't grow up with it, then you tell them you're a convert, love the Huskers and want the guys to tell you all about the glory days. One, they won't blame you for not being from here, since that's your parents' fault. Two, they'll love that you've converted. Three, they'll get so busy telling you stories that they won't have time to grill you about what you know."

Joe looked at her with wonder.

She not only knew every in and out of this town and its people, but she really was trying to help him.

Because of Matt.

He had to remember that. She was doing this because she wanted Matt.

But Joe liked having her on his side. In fact, the idea of spending time with her learning all this stuff was more and more appealing all the time.

"Okay, I've got all of this so far," he said. "What's the last group?"

"The older women. These guys' wives, the moms and grandmothers of the younger guys and girls you're going to hang out with."

Typically, Joe would have felt quite comfortable interacting with that group of people too. He was charming and had kept his own mother and grandmother wrapped around his finger for twenty-nine years now. But he would have also typically thought he could get along with men his age—he could drink and gamble and talk sex all night. Women his age—he had charmed more than his share of classy women out of their panties. And men in their sixties to eighties—he talked politicians into things on a daily basis.

Sapphire Falls and Phoebe Sherwood were changing all of his ideas about everything he thought he knew.

"Okay, what do I do with the older gals?" he asked.

Phoebe grinned. "Be yourself."

He blinked at her, waiting for the rest of whatever she was going to say. "Huh?" he asked when she said nothing more.

"Just be yourself. Your big brown eyes, your politeness, your great haircut, your smile, your charm—yeah, you'll be fine."

He sat back, absorbing the compliment—perhaps the first from Phoebe other than the non-verbal ones in the form of the hot kiss the night before and the ogling of his naked chest and stomach that morning.

"Let's start with that group," he said.

She laughed. "You want the secret weapon?"

"Don't tease me, Phoebe."

"Okay." She sat forward. "Wear one of your jackets and ties to church on Sunday. Stay afterward and eat cinnamon rolls and gush about how great they are, chat and charm them for an hour and you're golden. You'll have all the older ladies firmly in your camp. Then they'll tell their husbands, sons and daughters all about how wonderful you are. You'll be that much further ahead all the way around."

Joe felt his mouth lift in a half smile. "I get to wear my jacket and tie?"

"Definitely."

"And eat cinnamon rolls?"

She grinned. "Yep. Of course, you'll have to run an extra mile or two to work them off."

He could absolutely wear a jacket and tie and eat a dozen or so rolls. No problem. He leaned forward too and put his hand over hers where it rested on the tabletop.

She tensed but didn't pull away.

"Thank you," he said sincerely. "You're kind of busting my balls here, but I trust you on all of this."

She swallowed hard and concentrated on their hands. "Sure. I mean, you really want Nadia back. And this is the way to do it. Spend a week the way I just described and you'll be in the running for festival king by the time she's back in town."

Joe stroked his thumb across the back of her knuckles. Her skin was so soft. He wanted to stroke his hand up the length of her arm, across her shoulder and up her throat to her face. Then he wanted to cup her cheek and lean in…

"Matt."

Startled away from his thoughts of kissing her, Joe focused on her eyes. "What?"

"I said, of course you'd be running against Matt."

"For what?"

"Festival king."

"What festival?" He felt foggy. What were they talking about? And why did he want to kiss this woman who was bossy and loud and bright instead of concentrating on the sweet introvert he wanted to marry?

"The Sapphire Falls Festival," she said. "It's our annual town celebration. We're a hundred and thirty-two this year."

"And Matt's up for king?" Of course he was.

Phoebe nodded. "For the third year."

Uh huh. Well, maybe he should give Mr. Matt some competition. Apparently, none of the guys around here were much of a rivalry for the favorite son.

Maybe it was time for some new blood.

"I suppose all of those people—those four groups you mentioned—all love Matt," Joe said.

Phoebe grabbed the check Viv had just laid on the table and slid out of the booth. "Well, yeah," she said, as if that answer was obvious.

Which, come to think of it, it was.

Joe slid out of his seat as well. As Phoebe paid the bill, he headed for the big table of what were essentially the elders of Sapphire Falls.

"Hey, guys," he greeted when they noticed him.

"Joe," the man at the head of the table gave him a nod.

"I was hoping maybe you'd all be here tomorrow morning."

They looked at one another and then back to him. "Where else would we be?" one of the guys answered.

"Great. I'd like to buy you breakfast and have you fill me in on a few things."

"Things?" another man asked.

"Well, I'm new here. Obviously. I'd love to know more about the history of Sapphire Falls."

One of the guys looked suspicious. "What for?"

"If I'm going to be living here, I'd like to know everything there is to know."

"You're going to be living here?" another one asked.

"Yes. It seems like a great place."

"You know anything about farming?" someone asked.

"I work for Mason Riley," he said with his most charming grin, "what do you think?"

The guys all nodded. It was inconceivable—apparently—that someone would work for Mason and *not* know farming. And they had a point.

It made complete sense—Nadia and his desire for a simpler life notwithstanding—for Joe to actually be here to learn more about farming, considering the company that paid his salary was one of the largest and the most respected agricultural research companies in the world.

"You know anything about Nebraska football?" one of the men asked.

Joe hid his grin. Phoebe was good.

"I'm a new fan," he said spreading his arms wide. "I'm hoping you won't get frustrated when I ask you a million things about the Huskers, especially the glory days."

"Well, pull up a chair," another said, offering the one next to him.

"He has to go to work now," Phoebe said, coming up beside Joe. "You guys remember work, right? That stuff you did before you decided to spend all your time drinking

89

coffee and bullshitting."

They all grinned at Phoebe.

"You look good together," one told them.

"She's a firecracker," another told Joe, "but worth it."

"If you can keep her tied down, you're quite a man," someone else added.

Phoebe was grinning and rolling her eyes. "Okay, enough, Joe's a friend. I'm helping him get settled in town, that's it."

"Well, what the hell's wrong with you?" another guy asked Joe. "They don't come sweeter than Phoebe."

Joe looked down at her and had to admit, though sweet wasn't one of the first adjectives that came to mind, it did fit. Like those candy sprinkles. "Maybe that booze killed off some of my brain cells," Joe told them.

They all laughed at that while Phoebe looked up at him in surprise.

"What? You know that I've noticed you're pretty awesome," he said.

She smiled sweetly but slid closer, sneaking her hand down to pinch the back of his thigh. "We have to go," she told the guys as Joe jerked.

"What was that?" he asked as she turned him toward the door.

"Don't go giving them ideas about us, Joe. They'll end up pissed at you when you get together with Nadia."

Ah. Joe glanced back. "They're protective of you?"

"Yes. Especially my two uncles and my grandpa." She shoved the diner door open and stepped through.

Joe almost got hit in the face as he glanced back at the older guys again.

He saved his nose just in time. "You're related to three of those guys?"

"And I've known the rest my whole life. So be careful with the flirting." She unlocked her truck and climbed up onto the running board but paused to look at him over the hood. "In fact—" she pointed her keys at him, "—be careful with the flirting anyway. That's *not* a good idea."

"I know." He climbed into the truck. He did know. He really did.

He just couldn't seem to help it with her.

ڲ؎ڲ

Phoebe couldn't wait to get Joe out of her truck.

She didn't take a deep breath until he got out at the field where Mason was working.

She even resisted watching him walk away.

But she had to close her eyes to do it. Instead of watching Joe, she breathed deeply, wondered what the hell was going on and prayed a little.

Flirting with Joe was exhilarating and tempting. And a big problem.

He was the first guy to make her heart race and make her aware that even her ears could tingle.

And he wasn't Matt.

So this had to end now. She needed to see Matt. That would help.

She was going to see Joe again that night. They needed to work on his country dancing and find out if he knew anything about sand volleyball. They needed to do it alone too, so that everyone believed that Joe was a natural when they met him. If she was going to spend time alone with Joe, she was going to need a shot of Matt to get her through.

Twenty minutes later, she'd tracked him down. At his mom's. Which was even better than finding him alone. She knew that sounded dumb, even in her mind, but she loved Matt's family and already felt like a daughter to his mom and dad. She let herself in through the front door.

"Hey, anybody home?"

"Phoebe, darling!" Matt's mom, Anita, called from the

kitchen. "Come in here."

Phoebe made her way through the house that was nearly as familiar to her as her own. "It smells amazing in here," she said coming through the door. Matt wasn't in the kitchen with his mom, but Anita was baking, which was always a good thing, even at seven thirty-two a.m. "I have perfect timing."

Anita enfolded her in a hug and then put her in a chair. "I'm trying something new." She set a plate in front of Phoebe. "What do you think?"

The plate was covered with what appeared to be tiny cakes. Matt and his family were morning people too, and Anita had clearly been up as long as, or longer, than Phoebe.

"They're for the bridal shower," Anita added.

Phoebe froze with one partway to her mouth, her gaze flying to Anita's face. Matt's mom was fifty-three but could pass for forty-three. She was a warm, soft-spoken woman that Phoebe considered a second mother.

But she had just caused a huge ball of ice to thud to the bottom of Phoebe's gut.

"Bridal shower?" Phoebe asked. Oh, God, had Matt proposed over the phone? Or via Skype? Not super romantic or classy, but maybe he couldn't wait.

And for just a moment, it flashed through her mind that she could spend all the alone time with Joe that she wanted to if Nadia had said yes.

"Yes, what do you think?"

Phoebe made herself nibble the corner of one of the tiny pastries even though her stomach was sure to rebel. It was, of course, delicious. "Perfect, Anita."

"So you think Carrie will like them? She wasn't sure she wanted cake, but she didn't want cupcakes. We thought about truffles or cheesecake. But then I thought we could combine the cake and truffle idea."

She had lost Phoebe right after she'd said "Carrie."

Phoebe felt relief flood through her. The bridal shower was for Carrie Harder. She knew that. She'd known about it for a month. She had a gift for Carrie sitting on her dining room table.

She needed to pull herself together.

"I think she'll love them," Phoebe said. She put the rest of the cake in her mouth and picked up another, her stomach now completely calm. They tasted much better when they were intended for Carrie—or any woman other than Nadia. "Matt's truck's out front. Is he here?"

She needed to see him. Quickly.

"He's up fixing the sink in the guest bathroom," Anita said. "Here, take him a couple."

Phoebe climbed the stairs to the second floor and followed the sound of metal tools on metal pipes. She saw his work boots first. There was no question that those were not brand new. Her gaze traveled up the denim-clad legs to the ass she'd been studying for years. His jeans were also well worn. They were soft and faded and molded to his thighs, hips and butt like a glove.

Yep, that was all very nice. And he could fix stuff. She sincerely doubted that the khaki-and-Prada-wearing casino kid had ever applied a wrench to a leaky pipe.

"You're already going to be king of the festival, you have to be son of the year too?" she asked, nudging his foot with hers.

He looked over his shoulder. "Hey, Phoeb. What's up?"

"Cake, I guess." She held out the two cakes Anita had given her.

He pushed himself up from his hands-and-knees position and wiped his palms on the thighs of his jeans before reaching for the treats. "Thanks."

"So, Matt, I was um…thinking about you."

"How come?"

It was one of those openings that he'd inadvertently given her many times over the past few years. Why not just tell him what she was really thinking? That she was wondering if Nadia could really appreciate that the way to Anita's heart was to clear the table after a meal—Anita's least favorite chore, or that Matt's dad, Ray, needed someone who would talk NCIS with him, or that Matt was happiest when his mom and dad were happy. Did Nadia understand his older brother's strange sense of humor? Would she buy everything she saw with the Muppets on it for his nephew?

"Just because," she said with a shrug. "I think about you a lot."

He grinned. "That's sweet." He put an entire cake in his mouth.

He stood chewing, watching her as if he was waiting for her to say something more. There was a smudge of frosting on his lower lip.

She hadn't gotten too far with saying—or not saying—things up to that point, and frankly, she was out of ideas. Other than the blatant truth, of course. Which she could sure try.

Still, the words wouldn't come.

Maybe it was time she *did* something.

She stepped close and drew the pad of her thumb across the frosting on his mouth, taking it from his lip.

His eyes widened.

Then she put her thumb to her own mouth and licked the frosting off.

His eyes widened further.

Then she licked her lip. "Yum."

Matt's gaze dropped to her mouth.

But he didn't do anything. Just stared at her.

Of course, he also wasn't trying to get away, or stammering some excuse about getting away or demanding to know what the hell she was doing. He just stared.

She wanted him to *do* something. To *say* something.

But it was clear the next move was not going to come from

him.

Fine. She was going to have to get gutsy here. Sure, he was with Nadia, but he wasn't married to her—or even engaged *yet*. And all was fair in love and war. And she'd seen him first.

Comfortable that she had a good case here—or could at least justify it later when she thought about it—Phoebe took his hand in hers and lifted it to her mouth, bringing the remaining cake from his fingers to her lips. She pulled the cake into her mouth, sliding it over her lips before biting into it. She could feel that there was frosting on her bottom lip now too.

Matt's gaze went directly to the streak of sugar and she saw him swallow hard. But he didn't move. So she licked her tongue over the tips of his thumb and forefinger where he'd held the cake. He drew in a quick, surprised breath.

Still, he did nothing else. She lifted her finger to her lip, wiped the frosting away slowly and sucked it from her finger—also slowly—swirling her tongue around the tip.

"Phoeb?" Matt finally said, gruffly. "What're you doing?"

Her heart began to race. What was she doing? Making a move, she supposed. "Isn't it obvious?" she asked instead of being blatant. Again.

"Not exactly." He took a step closer. "What're you thinking about right now?"

That she had just opened a big frickin' can of worms. "That I wish I knew what *you* were thinking."

Tears pricked the back of her eyelids. She could tell Matt anything, always had been able to. She knew him so well that he usually didn't have to tell her what he was thinking, she just knew. But at that moment, she felt like she was looking at a stranger. She could tell that his mind was working hard, trying to figure out what was going on, but she couldn't tell how he felt about it. He didn't look happy, but he wasn't mad either. He didn't look confused, exactly. He also didn't look excited or intrigued or turned on. Her throat froze as the heat of the tears built in her eyes.

"I'm thinking that this is…strange."

Okay, that was not the word she'd been going for.

"Strange?" She backed up and bumped into the shelving unit where Anita had bottles and knick knacks displayed. Everything wobbled—including her heart.

"You're just not…the frosting and the licking…that's just…unusual."

She tried to keep it inside, but the bubble of laughter escaped and sounded a bit hysterical. Yeah, she and Matt had certainly not done a lot of licking around one another, frosting or not. "Unusual. Yeah, it is that," she said, her voice pitched higher than usual.

"I'm not sure what to think," he told her, tucking his hands into his back pockets.

She really wanted those hands to grab her, press her against the vanity and kiss her silly. But in that moment, she realized that that wasn't Matt. He was laidback, steady, up front. He wasn't spontaneous, he wasn't intense.

And those were things she really liked about him. He was predictable. He was sweet. He was, she realized, one of those manageable guys she was used to.

Whatever happened from here was up to her.

She was used to being upfront. She didn't mind telling a guy what she wanted and needed.

The stuff Joe had wanted to hear from her last night was not a problem—unless the guy had her thoughts so jumbled she couldn't actually come up with the words. Though before Joe that had never happened.

Now, with Matt, she felt jumbled. But not at all for the same reason.

She'd never dated a Sapphire Falls guy. She stuck to the guys who lived in small towns around Sapphire Falls. She'd never dated someone who'd known her since she was born—and who she'd know for the rest of her life. She was going to run into the guys in Sapphire Falls at the grocery store, the bar, at the school where she taught. She'd teach some of their kids in the future.

It just felt weird to date one of them. It would feel even weirder to have sex with one of them. Especially sex where she got a little bossy.

But she was in love with Matt. Nice-guy, unassuming, laidback Matt.

If she was going to get sexy with Matt, she was going to have to take control, make the moves, be the one to tell him what she wanted. Exactly what she wanted. What she wanted was to dress in a naughty-teacher costume. She wanted him to rip her clothes off and cover her in colored candy sprinkles.

However, once she said the words 'colored-candy sprinkles' to Matt, she could never take it back. She could *not* do that. At least not at seven-thirty a.m. in his mother's bathroom without any preparation or practice.

"So don't think about it," Phoebe said in a rush. "Just…forget it. It was a stupid, spontaneous thing that I did without thinking."

"It seemed more than—"

"Lack of sleep," she blurted. "And I had about half a bottle of Borcher's last night."

He frowned. "Wow, what was the occasion?"

"Nothing." For some reason, she didn't want to tell him about Joe. He'd meet Joe eventually. Eventually he'd become aware that Joe was trying to steal his soon-to-be fiancée. But at that moment, she didn't want Matt to know that she and Joe were…whatever they were. "So I'm gonna go." She backed toward the door and hit the shelves with her elbow, causing the bottles to rattle again.

She gritted her teeth and inched toward the doorway. "I'll see you…when I see you."

"Right." Matt looked like he wanted to say more but like he had no idea what it would be.

She could relate.

She turned to go and nearly ran into the doorjamb.

"Watch it," Matt said, reaching for her.

She dodged his touch, not sure she could handle it right then. "I'm fine." She got into the hallway and then turned back. "I'm having a party Saturday." She needed to introduce Joe to the gang at some point, and Saturday made sense. They all got together every Saturday.

"I'll be there."

Of course he would be. That's what they did. They'd sat at the river drinking and bullshitting too many times to count.

And now that things were a little awkward between them, the river would be the place that would make it all okay again. Or so Matt would assume. They'd laughed together, confided in one another about their frustrations with their mothers and their dreams for their jobs there. At the river he'd felt safe enough to confess he still liked watching Looney Tunes when he was sick and she'd admitted that once a month she made brownies and ate the entire pan by herself. It was an eight-by-eight inch pan, but still.

It was the place they'd been the happiest and most comfortable together, where their relationship was absolutely simple.

So she was a little sad as she made her way down the stairs, called goodbye to Anita and headed for her truck, because she knew that things at that river were never going to be the same.

It was time to shake things up.

As soon as she figured out how. And got the guts to do it.

"I licked Matt."

Adrianne choked on her tea and had to cough for a moment before she looked up at Phoebe. "You *what*?"

"Licked Matt."

"That's what I thought you said. That's great! Why? Where? When?"

Phoebe laughed and appreciated the tension release. "In his mom's bathroom. This morning."

Adrianne wrinkled her nose. "Okay, licking and bathrooms aren't giving me the best visual here."

"You've never licked Mason in the bathroom?"

Her friend immediately grinned. "I guess the shower is in the bathroom."

"Right."

Adrianne leaned in. "You licked Matt in the *shower*?"

"No." She laughed again. This was why she'd called Adrianne and begged her to come to lunch. She needed to tell Adrianne about her mixed-up feelings and have her sort them out for her. And give her some perspective by making her laugh.

"We were in his mom's bathroom where he was fixing a pipe and—"

"How can anyone like dirt that much?" Lauren slid into the seat across from Adrianne. "These farmers are going to be the death of me."

Adrianne rolled her eyes at Phoebe. Phoebe grinned. Lauren was great. She was incredibly intelligent, upfront and honest—painfully so sometimes—and completely cool. They loved having her around and, well, Phoebe had been half-expecting Lauren and/or Hailey to find out what Adrianne was doing for lunch and show up. Or just show up. There were only three places in Sapphire Falls for lunch. One sucked and one was full of the farmers that were driving Lauren crazy.

All the women in town were thrilled that Adrianne had expanded her gourmet candy shop into a coffee shop, bakery and luncheonette. She was about two months away from adding ice cream and an old-fashioned soda fountain—two months was how long it would take Mason to talk her into it.

"You're referring to the farmers who have helped make you rich and famous?" Adrianne asked.

Mason and Lauren were the leading experts in…almost everything agricultural. At least as far as Phoebe knew. Until Mason, Lauren and Innovative Agricultural Solutions had come into Phoebe's life—or near her life anyway—she hadn't thought that much about the farmers she'd grown up around. But once they'd brought more of their operations to the fields around Sapphire Falls and gotten some local guys into the business of innovative farming practices, she'd gained a new appreciation for farming and farmers. Along with learning some terms that she'd never heard. And that someone could actually get famous from what was essentially growing stuff. Of course, it was amazing stuff and they were growing it in innovative ways.

"I'm not famous." Lauren smiled at Claire, Adrianne's waitress. "Peach tea. Chicken salad."

Claire moved off to fill the order.

"You've been featured in like twenty magazines," Adrianne said.

"Didn't you fly to Europe twelve times to present at conferences?" Phoebe asked.

"And the president has your number in his cell phone," Adrianne pointed out.

Lauren leaned back in her chair and crossed her legs. "The magazines were agricultural magazines, the conferences were agricultural conferences and the president only calls me when he needs me to explain something Mason said or emailed." She sipped again. "That's not *really* famous."

Adrianne and Phoebe looked at one another and then burst out laughing.

"Sorry, you're right," Adrianne said. "That's not really

famous."

"Exactly. It's not like the Queen is calling. It's just the president," Phoebe said.

"Let's talk about something else," Lauren said as her tea arrived. "As long as it's not farmers or farming or anything farming related."

"What is your problem with farmers?" Adrianne asked. "You don't like getting dirty?" She gave Lauren a wink.

"I love getting dirty," Lauren said, "with guys who can clean up at least once in a while. These guys are scruffy and wear *jeans* all the time—" She glanced at Adrianne who was not only wearing jeans at the moment but wore jeans most of the time. "No offense. Your jeans are cute. They're stylish and not streaked with dirt and don't have holes in the butt."

"They have bling on the butt," Phoebe added. Adrianne loved denim and was a completely down-to-earth girl, but she did like jeans with rhinestones and other decorations. She had, after all, been a fashionista before she'd come to Sapphire Falls to simplify her life.

"No offense taken." Adrianne motioned for Lauren to go on. "And I thought you were more into *girls* anyway?"

"I am. Because guys have bad attitudes," Lauren said.

"Bad attitudes?" Phoebe asked.

She had to be talking about the Bennett boys. Travis, Tucker and T.J. Bennett owned one of the biggest family farms that had partnered with IAS. Their crops were now entirely converted to IAS seeds and they were participating in regular trials and studies with Mason and his team.

And they definitely had attitude.

"The attitude that they're so amazing and so funny and so great and so sexy. It doesn't even matter what they wear—we're all supposed to just swoon when they walk by. Or worse, we're supposed to assume that dirty, torn-up jeans are sexy just because they wear them."

Cocky being the best word to describe the Bennett

boys' attitude.

"Did you just say *sexy*?" Adrianne asked with a grin.

"Twice," Phoebe said.

"I said they think they're sexy," Lauren corrected.

"They?" Phoebe asked. She knew very well that Travis was the cockiest of the guys, especially when Lauren was around. There was something about him that pushed her buttons, and Phoebe had suspected for a while that he did it at least partially on purpose.

"Travis," Lauren clarified.

Uh huh.

"Please change the subject," Lauren said, lifting her tea glass.

"Okay," Adrianne said. "Phoebe licked Matt."

Lauren paused with the glass partway to her mouth. She looked at Phoebe. "Yeah?"

Phoebe nodded. "Yeah."

"Well, it's about time."

Phoebe shrugged. "It sounds more exciting than it was."

"Then you must have done it wrong," Lauren said.

Adrianne laughed. "How do you lick someone wrong?"

"Well, how did you do it?" Lauren picked up a pickle spear and paused with it in front of her lips. "Eye contact is important, for one thing." She slowly slid the pickle between her lips and into her mouth and then drew it back out. "And taking your time." She licked her tongue up the length of the pickle.

Phoebe stared. "First of all, I didn't lick him *there*. And second, wow, I don't even have…one and you make that look good."

Lauren gave her a wicked grin and bit off the top half of the pickle. "Don't tease me, Phoebe," she said. "I'll take the curiosity seriously sometime and you'll never be the same."

She was quite sure Lauren was right about that.

"*Anyway*," Adrianne said. "She didn't lick his…pickle.

She licked his…" Adrianne glanced at Phoebe.

"Finger," Phoebe supplied.

Lauren frowned as she chewed. "That could have totally worked."

"It didn't," Phoebe told her.

"What didn't work?" Hailey Conner slipped into the fourth chair at the table.

Phoebe huffed out a breath. She was *never* going to get any advice this way.

But she sat up straighter as she looked at Hailey. A year ago, she would have never wanted to have lunch with Hailey. She was one of those gorgeous, popular, everything-always-goes-right-for-her women and she'd driven Phoebe crazy since second grade when she'd had the perfect long straight blond hair, the thin, willowy body and the cute little laugh that Phoebe had always wanted. As a kid, Phoebe had been chubby and loud with wild red curls and the inability to sit still for long.

It hadn't been ADHD. Her mother had insisted on getting her tested. It was just her—how she was *wired* according to the school psychologist. She was just going to always be a little more energetic than everyone else.

Hailey, on the other hand, had always spoken politely, waiting her turn, chosen her words carefully and impressed everyone with her…everything.

Phoebe had never liked her.

Until she'd finally really gotten to know her.

Since Adrianne had moved to town to work for Hailey, Phoebe had gotten close with Adrianne, which meant she'd spent at least some time with the town mayor. Adrianne had seemingly grounded Hailey some. Phoebe suspected it was Adrianne's easy way of just accepting people for who and how they were. Hailey had always been number one, but Phoebe suspected that it was a little lonely at the top of the heap. As her assistant, Adrianne had seen her behind closed doors and at a few not-so-flawless moments, and

Phoebe figured Adrianne had shown Hailey that she didn't have to be perfect to be liked.

That was Adrianne.

So Hailey Conner had grown on Phoebe as well.

And now she could be a lot of help. She'd dated more men than anyone Phoebe knew.

"I licked Matt. On the finger, this morning. And he didn't do anything about it."

Hailey swung to face her. "You *licked* him?"

"Let's get to the part about him not doing anything," Lauren said.

"I think I shocked him," Phoebe admitted. "That's the first time my tongue's ever touched him."

"What got into you?" Hailey asked, pointing to the grilled brie on sourdough for Claire.

Phoebe sighed. It was so unfair that thin and tight Hailey could eat grilled cheese.

"I don't know," she said honestly. "He was looking good and there was frosting and it just…happened."

"Frosting in the bathroom?" Adrianne asked.

"We were sampling his mom's cakes. I took some up to him while he was fixing the pipe. That's not the important part," Phoebe said. She related the entire incident, right up to realizing that telling Matt her fantasies seemed weird.

"What does that mean?" Hailey asked.

"It's…complicated with Matt. I'm used to being in charge, and Matt's used to that too, but for some reason, I feel like when it comes to sex, it might freak him out."

"You're absolutely right," Hailey said.

Phoebe looked at her in surprise. "I am?"

"Of course." Hailey sipped from her ice water. "Matt's used to being *the man*. Everyone listens to Matt and wants his opinion and puts him in charge of things. It's one thing for you to take the lead in your friendship—he'll let you order the pizza and choose the radio station—because you have the same tastes. You're not going to do something he doesn't like. But sex is different. Matt's going to want to be the dominant one. Why do you think he's head over heels for sweet, accommodating Nadia? He wants to call the shots. If you get all in his face and bossy, it's going to be a turn off."

"Phoebe and Matt talk about everything," Adrianne said. "Why can't she just say, 'Matt, I love you and want you. Take me to bed'? All guys like *that* kind of bossy."

Hailey shook her head. "It'll be too much of a shock. She has to ease him into it. And she has to make him think it's *his* idea."

"What are you talking about?" Lauren asked.

"Seduction," Hailey said with a smug smile.

They all sat looking at her for a moment. Lauren finally said, "More."

"She needs to flirt, tease him and subtly make him start thinking about her as a woman, not just a friend."

"I don't do subtle very well," Phoebe admitted.

Hailey nodded. "I know. You need to work on that. You'll either go overboard and intimidate him or you'll be *too* subtle and he won't get the message."

"How do I work on it?"

"Practice," Hailey said.

"Practice?" Phoebe repeated.

"Yeah. Practice flirting, feeling and acting sexy without being blatant about it."

"How is she going to do that?" Adrianne asked. "Like with other guys?"

"Yeah."

"Okay, who?" Lauren asked. "We can pick the guy and—"

"I kissed Joe."

And yeah, she'd felt sexy doing it. Then there was the way she'd felt flirting with him in the diner earlier. And when he'd taken off his shirt this morning. He'd been thinking about her covered in crushed Oreos. At least, she was pretty sure he had been. He'd said he couldn't help flirting with her anyway.

"You *what*?'

"When?"

"You've been busy."

She refocused on the women with her. They were staring. Again. She was causing that a lot lately.

"I should practice with Joe." He made her feel tingly in a way no one had for a very long time. He seemed perfect.

Lauren was the first to nod. "Actually, he's probably perfect."

He was. He was sexy, he was a hell of a kisser and she liked being around him. And he was sexy. And a hell of a kisser.

Adrianne looked worried. "I don't know. You don't know him very well."

"But that makes it good," Phoebe said, sitting forward as the idea sunk in. "Flirting with and seducing any of the guys I know too well would be potentially awkward. Which rules out all of the guys here. And really, it's not fair to practice seducing someone when it's not going to go anywhere—when really it's for another guy." Yes, this was making more sense all the time. This was good. In fact, this made perfect sense. "But with Joe, it's great. Not only does he know I want Matt, but he wants Nadia. I'm helping him, so he can help me. And with Joe, no one has to know."

Adrianne chewed on her bottom lip. "It still doesn't seem quite right."

"Well, it's not like it's cheating," Hailey said. "I mean, they're both single."

"But they're supposedly in love with Matt and Nadia."

Hailey laughed. "And it's not like Matt and Nadia are sitting around at home, pure and chaste waiting for Phoebe and Joe."

Adrianne's frown didn't lessen and Phoebe reached for her friend's hand. "What's the worst that can happen?"

"What if Matt sees you with Joe and thinks you're together?" Lauren said. "Maybe it would make him jealous? That might be good."

"I don't think it will make him jealous," Adrianne said. The three other women looked at her. "You don't?" Lauren asked. "Why not?"

Phoebe frowned. Yeah, why not? There was major chemistry between her and Joe. And Joe was very different from Matt. That should make Matt pay attention.

"Because he's never jealous," Adrianne said. "Most of the guys in town are a little in love with Phoebe, and she spends time with them—dancing, drinking, laughing—and Matt just smiles through it all. It's like he knows he's got no competition for her."

Phoebe's frown increased. "Most of the guys in town are a little in love with me?"

Adrianne laughed. "Yes, sweetie. They are. They're friendly and act like gentlemen around you. I know they don't really hit on you or ask you out, but they've all got little—or not so little—crushes."

Joe had said the same thing. What the hell was everyone talking about?

"So why don't they do anything about it?" she asked, really wanting to know.

Adrianne shrugged. "I don't know. They don't want to ruin your friendship? They think you're not interested?"

"They know you're in love with Matt," Hailey said.

Phoebe looked at her. "They do?"

"They do."

"Well...crap." She didn't know what else to say to that.

Before she could come up with a reply, Lauren asked, "How was the kiss with Joe?"

Phoebe had to swallow as the memory hit her. "Um, good. Really good."

Lauren raised an eyebrow. "Really good?"

"Awesome. Amazing. One of the best—" she thought

about that and amended, "—*the* best ever."

"Then you definitely need to practice with Joe," Lauren said.

"Why's that?" Not that she was opposed. At all.

"Because he already knows you're in love with Matt and he clearly doesn't care. He'll still kiss the hell out of you. That's what you need. Practice being flirtatious and seductive and *subtle* with Joe.

Sounded good to Phoebe.

"Will he do it?" Adrianne asked.

Phoebe's thoughts immediately went to the night before when Joe had said that she needed to *not* turn her big blue eyes on him. He'd also said something about doing something stupid for her... The memory was fuzzy, the combination of the booze and the late night and the unexpected chemistry, but it was there. He'd felt something when they were together.

"I think so. I know he can give me some tips about being seductive and flirtatious anyway. I'll just straight up ask him for help."

Adrianne looked intrigued. "You've known him for less than twenty-four hours. You already feel like you could confide something like this?"

It felt like more than twenty-four hours, was Phoebe's first thought. "Yeah, I do. Plus, he's got this confident, sexy, been-there-done-that vibe about him. I think he has a lot of experience with women. Both seducing and being seduced."

Lauren laughed. "I think you're right," she said. "I feel that vibe about him too."

"Kindred spirit?" Adrianne asked with a smile.

Lauren grinned. "Something like that. Plus, I've heard some talk from some of the aides and lobbyists he's hung out with in DC. I think Joe has some interesting stories in his past."

Phoebe thought so too from the hints he'd dropped so

far.

"Really? Like what?" Adrianne asked. "When we're together he's always completely professional and polite and classy."

Lauren nodded. "Yeah, but just like we have girl talk, there's guy talk, you know. I've heard something about him having one wild year before he settled down and got serious about his career and everything. He's from big money, and I guess he was given unlimited spending and no ground rules but to have a good time."

Oh, yeah, Phoebe was *definitely* going to get some of Joe's stories out of him.

Along with some more kisses…and maybe a lot more.

She knew she shouldn't be excited about being able to give in to the flirting and maybe see how and if she could affect Joe Spencer. But she was.

It was harmless though. It was like she felt prior to girls' night out or before going on a big vacation—it was going to be fun and the regular rules didn't apply. Not only was it temporary, there was a specific timeline. The real world, the normal routine and expectations would be back in place when it was over. When the clock struck midnight, it was all done and the fantasy became nothing more than a memory.

Their midnight would be the last night of the festival, when Matt planned to whip out that ring and pop the question.

Or maybe an hour before that so he didn't actually get that far.

"So you have a plan?" Lauren asked her.

"Yep." Dance lessons were on the agenda tonight. Dancing could be very seductive.

"You need any help from us?" Lauren asked.

"I'm going to need full access to all of your closets." It was easy since she already had keys to both Adrianne's and Hailey's houses and Lauren stayed with Hailey when she needed to come to town for work. Hailey had made the offer one night when Lauren had been bitching about the bed and breakfast in town not having reliable Wi-Fi. It surprised everyone, maybe Hailey and Lauren most of all, that they got along well. Not that they hung out in their pajamas and talked about boys, but they co-existed peacefully for a week or two at a time.

"I don't have much with me," Lauren said. "But help yourself."

"Promise me you won't take anything purple," Hailey said. "That is *not* a good color for you. Or navy. Or bright red."

Phoebe sighed.

"I have a great green top you should try," Adrianne said. "The tags are still on it. Be sure to grab that."

Having girlfriends was good.

Unable to concentrate on the conversation that turned to festival events, Phoebe left Adrianne's shop a few minutes later with her mind spinning. She had a few hours before Joe would be over. Plenty of time to prepare.

Besides, it wouldn't take a lot of preparation. And she was *not* nervous. It was simply practice for the main event. A trial. Rehearsal. Nothing more.

CHAPTER FIVE

Feeling sexy wasn't as easy as it sounded. Or as easy as it should be.

It was five minutes until Joe was supposed to show up, her bed was covered with nearly every item of clothing that she owned and several that her friends owned and she still had no idea what to wear.

Phoebe glared at her image in the mirror.

She was sure that Hailey and Lauren didn't have any trouble looking or feeling sexy.

Dammit.

She had her hair swept up, which required nearly fifty bobby pins to put the thick, heavy mass of curls that typically did whatever the hell it wanted into some semblance of a style.

She had applied her makeup—three times.

And she'd tried on everything from jeans to the only thing she had that was even close to a little black dress—a little black skirt.

At the moment, she had that skirt on, along with one three-inch black wedge and one bright-pink pump, and a tight orange shirt that she did *not* remember buying. Because why would she buy this? Orange was absolutely not her color and for this to fit comfortably it needed to be a size bigger or her breasts needed to be a cup size smaller.

It was official. She had absolutely no idea what was sexy.

Of course, Joe arrived five minutes early.

He rang the doorbell just as a hank of hair fell from the bobby pins that finally gave up the fight.

"For fuck's sake."

Screw it. She was planning to use him to figure out how to do the sexy, seductive thing so maybe they'd just start with the clothes. She grabbed her short, silky purple robe, shoving her arms into it as she walked. She didn't need to impress him. And she clearly couldn't handle this on her own. Hailey and Lauren could help, but hey, Joe was a man, a man who happened to be attracted to the same woman Matt was. He could probably be a lot of help.

She swung the door open. "Remember what I said earlier about not flirting with me? Forget it. Flirt away."

"Okay. No problem."

She rolled her eyes. Even that was a little flirtatious.

His gaze traveled over her ridiculous ensemble. "What's going on?"

It hit her that with any other guy—friend or acquaintance—she would have felt awkward and shy. She would have been too aware of what was wrong with her hair, her hips, her lipstick. She would have never been willing to let one of them see her like this. But with Joe, she just felt like grinning.

"I'm having a bit of a crisis."

He smiled. "Oh, good, so you know that outfit is—"

"Stupid? Crazy?"

"Interesting."

She laughed and motioned him in. "Very political answer, Mr. Spencer."

He shrugged. "It's what I do."

As she shut the door behind him, she said, "Then we need to get that out of the way right now. I need your complete honesty. No spinning, no sugarcoating. Got it?"

"Yep, got it."

She peered at him. "Promise?"

"Sure. What are we talking about?"

"You have to tell me what's sexy."

"A woman getting wet making out in the rain without worrying about her hair. A woman grabbing me by my tie, pulling me into a corner and saying fuck me. And I believe I've mentioned the colored sprinkles."

She was staring at him, her mouth literally open.

"What?"

"You just rattled those off without thinking."

"I can give it some thought and add to the list," he offered.

Her heart was pounding and she was a lot warmer than she had been two minutes ago. "No," she said quickly. "That won't be necessary."

He lifted a hand and flipped the curls that had fallen from her sad up-do. "What's going on?"

Too bad he wasn't wearing a tie. She was tempted to try that second thing on his list. But he was dressed in one of the T-shirts and pairs of jeans she'd helped him buy.

Speaking of clothes... She pulled herself from the lusty haze he seemed to create so effortlessly.

"Go sit on the couch. I have to show you something. Some things."

"No dancing?" he asked, already moving to the couch.

"Later."

"No arguments here." He sat on the middle cushion and stretched his arms along the back of the couch.

Damn, he looked good. The soft gray cotton pulled tight across his pecs, shoulders and abs. The denim of his jeans wasn't worn enough to really mold to him yet, but it still showed off the firm contours of his thighs.

Then she lifted her gaze to the picture window behind the couch. It wasn't dark enough outside to turn it fully into a mirror, but she caught her faint reflection and remembered that she looked like a mess.

"I'll be right back." She spun and headed for her bedroom.

She slipped into a soft black top with the short skirt, kicked the pink pump out of the way and replaced it with the other black wedge. She jammed five more bobby pins into her hair to keep it up and then strode back to the living room, not giving herself too much time to think.

"How's this?"

Joe blinked at her. "How's that for what?"

"Is it sexy?"

He tipped his head to one side. "Turn around."

She did a full three-sixty.

"It's kind of sexy."

She arched an eyebrow. "It's *kind of* sexy?"

"Yeah."

Well, she had asked for honesty. She looked down and smoothed her hands over the skirt. "Then let's break this down. What's sexy and not sexy about it?"

"Phoebe, what's going on?"

There was something in his voice, a firmness that said he knew this was about more than looking nice to go out and that he was determined to know.

Yeah, okay, maybe it would help if he knew what she was going for here. "I need the guys around here to look at me differently. So I need to literally look different."

"You look great the way you always do. I liked the flip flops this morning."

She couldn't help but smile. That was sweet. "Thanks. I love those shoes." Then she shook her head. "But I have to do something different to get their attention on me as a woman, one they want to sleep with, not just a girl they've known forever and who they respect because I cheat at poker."

"And when you say *they,* you mean Matt," Joe said, with a frown.

She sighed. "Yeah."

"He doesn't think of you as a woman?"

"Not as a *woman*. When the guys here think of me, they think of their good friend, Phoebe." She didn't care what Adrianne had said about their crushes. If one of them really wanted her, he would have made a move. "I'm the one who's helped them ask girls out, who's helped them get girls back after they've screwed up, who's helped them understand what happened when a breakup sticks. I've helped them write love letters and plan romantic dates, and I've helped a few break up with girls without hurting their feelings."

"You're like their own personal Dear Abby," Joe said.

She smiled. "Something like that." And it sucked when it came to her own love life.

"And Matt sees you this way too?"

"Worse. I've given him plenty of girl advice too, but Matt also sees me as the girl who could always kick his ass at video games, who likes to go fishing, who wasn't afraid to pick up snakes and bugs and frogs. He knows about the time I wrote a sappy poem for a guy I liked from another town and how he passed it all around and I was turned into some kind of crazy stalker. He knows about the time I was going to ask a guy to Homecoming and ended up puking on his shoes instead. He knows about the time I was going to someone else's prom and twisted my ankle on my high heels in the parking lot and ended up in the emergency room with a broken ankle and ruining the guy's prom."

Joe's elbows were propped on his knees and he was staring at her, a slightly horrified look on his face. "Wow."

"I know. So you can see why Matt might not look at me romantically and sexually."

Joe scoffed at that. "Phoebe, I promise you that most of the guys in this town, and probably all the others, want to take you to bed. Even Matt. Maybe especially Matt. He knows you so well, gets to spend all that time with you—"

"No," she cut him off. "I appreciate your flattery, but I *know* he doesn't think of me sexually."

"Trust me," Joe said firmly, "that isn't true."

"It is," she insisted.

"Phoebe—" Joe started to argue.

"He could have licked me this morning and he didn't," she said quickly.

Joe's face was a hilarious combination of confusion and intrigue. "What?"

She slumped down on the coffee table facing him and told him about that morning at Matt's mom's. "So there I was with frosting, ready and willing, no one else around, and he didn't do *anything*."

Joe sat looking at her for several seconds before he sat back and draped his arms along the back of the couch again. "Fine. Turn once more."

Relieved that he was finally listening, she stood, moved behind the coffee table and executed a smooth pivot. He looked her over from head to toe and Phoebe fidgeted under his concentrated gaze.

"You look fantastic," he finally said.

"I don't know about fantastic but—"

"That skirt says, 'run your hand up here and see if I'm wearing panties or a thong.' And it shows off legs that make me think about how they'd feel wrapped around my waist."

She sucked in a quick breath. That was…not what she'd been expecting.

"But," Joe went on, still studying her with a strange objectivity in spite of his words. "Something's not right. What else do you have?"

Phoebe couldn't stop thinking about wrapping her legs around his waist. "Um, yeah, okay."

She came back out a few minutes later. "Better?"

She stopped by the coffee table and twirled.

Again, Joe took his job seriously and checked her over inch by inch.

She worked on not shifting her weight from foot to foot, but she felt very exposed under his careful examination. "Nice."

The white top was Lauren's and it hugged Phoebe's breasts fondly. The bodice sparkled with tiny shimmering threads and plunged between her breasts and also past her shoulder blades in back. She'd paired it with black capris that flared at mid-calf but left her feet bare, unable to figure out which of the shoes she'd pilfered from Hailey's closet would be best. Shoes were so not her thing.

"You like this better?" she asked, smoothing her hand over the soft fitted bodice.

"Well, the top will make the guys wonder if the material is stretchy enough to pull down to get to your nipples."

Heat flooded through her even as she scowled at him. He was teasing her.

The top was pretty, but her breasts were *so* on display she felt like she needed to stand with her arms crossed over her chest. The black capris were cute and short, but she felt like maybe it seemed she was trying too hard.

"Stop it," she said firmly. "That's not helpful."

He met her gaze. "I thought you wanted me to be honest. That is honestly what I thought when you walked out here."

She propped her hands on her hips. "It is sexy or not? Seriously. No teasing."

Joe looked annoyed. "It's sexy. But still not right."

"Fine."

She stomped to her bedroom and stared at the bed. Some of it was absolutely not going to work. Hailey and Lauren were both taller and slimmer than she was. She finally pulled on a chocolate-brown dress that was as fitted as the white top but fell farther down her thighs than the black skirt. One shoulder was left bare but the cleavage display was modest and it zipped up far enough that she could wear a strapless bra for support.

Joe was already nodding as she took her place in front of him. She turned around and then stood watching Joe's gaze travel over her. Again, she was barefoot because she didn't know what to put with it other than something brown—and she hadn't grabbed anything brown from Hailey.

"I like that too."

"Gee, it doesn't make you want to rip it off of me?" she asked dryly. Imagine that.

"It makes me want to bend you over the back of that couch."

Phoebe felt that sudden wave of heat wash over her again. "It's…" She had to clear her throat. "It's a loveseat, actually." He was sitting on the couch.

"Trust me, it'll work."

She could feel that her cheeks were hot. She wasn't sure what was going on with Joe, but she wasn't sure this was helping. He was messing with her, and she was now thinking things about her furniture she shouldn't be thinking and was no closer to knowing what to wear Saturday than she had been before he'd showed up.

She coughed lightly. "Maybe we should just do the dance lesson and I'll get Hailey and Lauren to help me with this."

"I don't think Hailey can help you with this. Lauren maybe…but not as well as I can."

She frowned at him. "What are you talking about?"

"What you wear won't matter," he said simply.

She grimaced and reminded herself that she had asked for his honesty. And she knew he was right. Some women had sexy and some didn't, and it didn't matter what they wore. Hailey could make anything look sexy, for instance. She was a hot blond with perky boobs. Of course she could pull it off. Lauren too. Adrianne had a cute-girl-next-door thing going on that lots of the guys in town found appealing.

Phoebe was just Phoebe.

"So if what I wear won't matter, what do I do? Besides getting a few cats, a lot more ice cream, a bigger vibrator and calling it all off?"

Jesus, Matt Phillips was a dumbass.

Joe had been gritting his teeth and clenching and unclenching his hands since Phoebe had told him about the frosting incident. He wanted to go find Matt and ask him what in the fuck was wrong with him.

But Phoebe needed him more right now.

He needed to calm the hell down though, so he could tell her—even show her—that she was driving him crazy without scaring her.

What he wanted was to do exactly what he'd just told her—bend her over that couch-loveseat whatever and show her sexy in a way he knew no man ever had.

"A bigger vibrator is never a bad idea," he said, pleased that he sounded rational and even in control. "But I wouldn't give in to the cats or ice cream urge just yet. You do have to forget about the clothes though."

She looked frustrated and, worse, deflated.

He *hated* that. Deflated didn't fit this woman. She was supposed to be full of brightness and energy.

"Take your hair down."

She frowned. "What?"

"Take your hair down." He knew how to do this—how to convince Phoebe that she should feel sexy and daring and empowered—if he could just keep himself in check.

That was going to be a problem.

He was notorious for getting swept up in the moment and letting women jumble his thoughts—especially the rational thoughts. With Phoebe, he felt like he was not only willing to do *anything*, but like he was on the verge of doing…something really stupid. But great. He definitely had a feeling it would be great. Like regretting it wouldn't even be possible.

But it was going to be stupid.

Whatever *it* was.

The fact that he couldn't even fully define it was as disconcerting as feeling it.

She didn't look necessarily compliant, but she did reach up to her hair and began pulling pins out. There were a lot of pins too. As the twentieth or so hit the coffee table in front of him, Joe began smiling. Why would she do that to those fabulous curls? He had a huge grin going on by the time she let the last one drop.

"I'm sure *that's* sexy," she said, ruffling her hair.

It was. Very. It was *her*. But he knew she wouldn't believe him, or even understand him trying to explain it.

"Now take the dress off."

Her eyes widened. "What?"

"The dress, Phoebe. Lose it."

"But—"

"You want my help?" he asked, battling to stay seated on the couch. "I know exactly what you need, but you have to do what I say."

He could see she was breathing faster. The rise and fall of her breasts was making him grip the couch cushion. He had to do this for her. Yes, he wanted to grab her, press her up against the wall and run his hands and tongue all over her body, but he had to be sure she absorbed every second of being wanted, so he had to go slow.

If the idiot men in this town weren't going to make sure she knew how amazing she was, then he'd happily step up and do it.

The hands-and-tongue-all-over-her-body thing *was* going to happen.

Finally, whatever she needed to think over or decide clicked into place and her fingers went to the zipper along the side of the dress.

The soft hiss of the zipper releasing filled the air as he watched her. The dress gaped and then she slid the one strap from her shoulder and it fell to her feet.

She was left in a beige strapless bra and silky beige bikini panties. They weren't leopard print, they weren't see through and it wasn't a thong, but Joe was as hard and ready to go as he'd ever been.

He took a deep breath in through his nose and swallowed twice to make sure his voice would sound normal when he said, "That's better."

"I can't exactly show up at the party on Saturday like this," she said.

Her voice sounded normal despite the fact she was nearly naked in front of him. Hmm. Interesting. She was feisty rather than discomfited. He liked that.

"No, you can't," he agreed. And not because it was socially unacceptable, but because he rebelled at the idea of other men seeing her like this. "But the point is, the dress doesn't make you sexy or not sexy. Now go put on your grubbiest pair of sweats or shorts or something and an old T-shirt and come back out here."

The thing that Phoebe needed to understand was that a woman's sex appeal came from her confidence, her attitude and her desire. A woman who knew what she wanted and knew that the guy in front of her could—and would—give it to her was the biggest turn-on Joe had ever found. Phoebe was almost there. She had the confidence and attitude—at least in every other aspect of her life. As soon as she figured out what she wanted and how to get it from the men around her, they'd better all look out.

She frowned at him. "I'm almost naked here and you're telling me to go get dressed? Thanks a lot, Joe."

Again, he gripped the couch to keep himself in his seat. She'd see soon enough what she was doing to him. When he left here tonight, she would have absolutely no doubt about how sexy she was.

"What would you rather I do?" he asked.

He hoped that she'd tell him, in graphic detail, step by step.

She crossed her arms over her stomach and rounded her shoulders slightly. "Whatever you want."

She had no idea what all *that* entailed.

"Tell me what *you* want me to do," he encouraged. Not just because he really did want to hear her tell him where exactly she wanted his tongue, how hard, for how long, but because, while he knew she bossed everyone around, he was sure she'd never told anyone else that.

"Well, there's that couch thing you mentioned," she said, her attention on his chest rather than his eyes now.

"Which couch thing?" he asked, already picturing it.

She huffed out an exasperated breath. "You know exactly what I'm talking about."

"But you're *not* talking about it," he said. "You're *hinting* about it. And you're hoping I'll take the reins."

"Yes, exactly," she said, nodding. "It was your idea."

This was so unlike the feisty girl he thought he knew. "But you liked it."

"Yes, but—"

"What?"

She let out a deep breath. "You want to know what I'd *really* like? A guy who just *does* it. Who doesn't need any direction. Who doesn't worry about being a gentleman or saying please. Who is so consumed by passion that all he can do is grab me and press me against the wall and kiss me until we're both about to lose our minds. Then I want him to spin me around and bend me over that damned couch without me having to *tell him to*."

Joe stared at her for a moment. Then he swallowed. Then he took a deep breath. Then he took another. Finally, he said, "That was pretty good. Telling me what you want is important."

"You're driving me crazy," she muttered.

Well, that made two of them. Joe stood swiftly. He could be patient, he could be encouraging, he could certainly take his time—when the situation called for it. But Phoebe Sherwood was stubborn, and her continued reluctance to take some control here was pushing his buttons.

"Come on." He grabbed her hand and tugged her down the hallway to her bedroom.

"That's more like it," she said from behind him.

He turned and looked down at her. "You like this? Tell me what you want."

She stared up at him and shook her head. "You're doing just fine."

He sighed. "So you're fine with whatever I do? You'll just follow along?"

She nodded mutely.

Mute was the exact opposite of what he wanted from her.

He liked being in control sexually. He loved nothing more than when a woman turned things over to him and put him in charge of her pleasure. But the women he did that with knew that's what they wanted and that they would enjoy it. They gave him control because they wanted him to have control.

Phoebe was giving him control because she wasn't confident enough to take it for herself.

Phoebe Sherwood, the most popular woman in town, the one who wore bright colors and had a mouth that never stopped moving, was an introvert when it came to sex. And worse, she didn't think the men here wanted to have sex with her—not to mention any kind of hot, unconventional sex she might ask for.

Well, that was going to change. Right now.

"You're the bossiest woman I know," he told her. "That shouldn't change when it comes to sex. In fact, that's the best time to be bossy. You should—"

"Dammit, Joe." She yanked her hand from him. "I'm trying to be submissive here!"

He froze. Except for the frown that grew deeper and deeper. The words replayed in his head over and over until he finally turned and said, "*What?*"

She sighed. "I'm trying to practice being *submissive.*

Subtle. Sweet."

He couldn't help it. That made him hard. The idea of a bright, energetic, loud, demanding woman like Phoebe letting him have his wicked way with her...yep, very, very hard.

"And when you say *submissive,* you mean..." He trailed off wanting her to fill in the blank. Was she talking about floggers and safe words here? And if she was, was he up for it?

Yes. Absolutely. It would be new territory for him—though he did have those silk ties—but he'd never shied away from any promise of pleasure before.

"Submissive. Giving up control. *Not* bossing the other person around," Phoebe said.

Ah, okay, no floggers. Got it. "Maybe we should use a different word," he suggested.

She raised an eyebrow. "You don't like submissive?"

"It just brings to mind...other things."

Now both eyebrows went up. "Other things?

He coughed lightly. "Probably not where you were going with this."

"Like whips and leather and blindfolds and gags?"

He coughed again when he nearly swallowed his tongue. "Uh, yeah."

She gave him a sly grin. "A gag might be a good idea if you want me to keep my mouth shut. I have trouble with that."

He leaned in. "I do *not* want your mouth shut." In fact, there were all kinds of wonderful things he wanted her to do with that mouth. None involved keeping it closed.

This time, she had to cough. "Okay, what word do you like?"

Joe thought for a moment. "Acquiescent."

She looked impressed. "I can go with that."

"I don't know if you can, actually," he teased. "It means to do what another person wants."

"I *know*," she said. "I'm asking you what you think of everything so I can get an idea of what guys want from me without *talking* about it all directly."

He pulled in a long breath and nodded as he let it out. "Well, I don't know if subtle is really the right choice for you."

She huffed out a breath. "No shit."

He had to laugh at that. "So why are you trying to do it this way?"

"I can be a little...in your face."

"Uh huh."

"That doesn't work for...all men."

He caught her hesitation and wanted to swear loudly. "It doesn't work for Matt?"

She shrugged. "I told you, he's pretty vanilla."

"And that means he likes to be in charge and the woman is supposed to just follow his lead?"

"I don't really know how he is. I just don't want to scare him off."

"Scare him off? By telling him what you want and need?"

She nodded. "I tend to get a little—"

"Bossy?" he suggested with a grin in spite of being extremely annoyed.

"Yeah."

Joe looked at her for a long moment. She was gorgeous and sassy and full of life. Why a man wouldn't want to surround himself with all of that—loudly, brightly and *often*—was beyond Joe. "Damn, he's a dumb ass."

Her eyes widened. "Hey, you're the one in love with the submissive, I mean, the *acquiescent* woman he's having vanilla sex with now."

He didn't reply right away and her eyes widened farther as her grin grew.

"I saw that," she said, pointing her finger at his nose.

"Saw what?"

125

"That flicker in your eyes. You like the idea of a submissive woman."

Upfront and honest. He could do that. "I don't own a flogger, but I don't *hate* the idea of a woman being so into me that she'll totally trust me to give her what she needs. But," he added when Phoebe was about to respond, "I want it to be real and natural. *She* has to be turned on by letting me be in charge. She can't do it just for my sake. I have no problem with a woman telling me exactly what she likes and wants either."

She pressed her lips together.

He moved in closer. "But you did say earlier you wanted a guy who would be so overcome he'd just take over."

Her cheeks got a little pink at that. "Yeah."

"So you might have a little bit of submissive in you after all."

She bit her bottom lip and then asked, "You think so?"

Submissive. That wasn't a word he thought he'd be associating with Phoebe much, but he couldn't help but be interested in how far she'd let him go before she wanted control again.

He leaned in. "With the right guy, I think maybe you could pull it off."

She looked up at him with those big blue eyes. "Maybe we should see if you could be that guy."

Oh, he was that guy. He gave her a slow smile. "Now *that* was seductive."

She grinned.

"So you want to try this out? I get to be bossy for a while?" he asked.

She perked up at that. "Yes."

He appreciated her enthusiasm. "That means you do what I say."

"Right." Her eyes were wide…with interest.

He liked that. A lot.

"Acquiescent doesn't necessarily mean quiet," he told her.

"Okay."

"If I ask you a question, you answer it."

"Okay."

He almost laughed at how eager she seemed. Almost. But he couldn't quite get enough air into his lungs.

This was going to be fun.

He pulled her into her bedroom and looked around. It looked like her closet and dressers had exploded.

"Find a T-shirt and shorts," he said. "Now." His tone was clipped and firm because his mind was spinning so fast with all the things he wanted to show and prove to her that he couldn't really focus on the details of things like conversation.

Phoebe went to the dresser. He couldn't pull his eyes from her sweetly curved ass in those plain-Jane panties until she pulled open the second drawer and took out a pair of cutoff sweatpants in neon green and a hot-pink tank top. "Like this?" she asked.

"Yes, exactly." That's what had been missing from the outfits she'd been showing him—the color. She needed vibrant colors, not brown and white and black. This was Phoebe.

He took the tank and shorts from her and moved in to face her.

Without a word, he reached behind and unclasped her bra, letting it fall to the floor.

He took in the sight of her bare breasts, the nipples instantly hardening to perfect points.

Her breathing shifted, becoming ragged and she parted her lips.

But he just looked at her, aching, tempted but determined to make this about her. His hands itched to touch her, to cup those beautiful weights, to tug and suck and pinch the tips and see how sensitive she was.

Instead, he slipped his fingers into the sides of her panties and slid them over her hips, letting them drop away as well.

Even the little bit of skin he felt along her hips with the backs of his fingers was warm and soft, and he decided he would most definitely lick her there later for a very long time.

Knowing he was only torturing himself but unwilling to do it any other way, he knelt in front of her.

She gasped, barely loud enough for him to hear. He intended to make her gasp a lot louder before the night was over.

The soft auburn hair at the apex of her thighs was trimmed neatly, but the little pink nub of her clit peeked through, testing every fiber of his willpower.

And then his gaze dropped lower.

"Holy crap," he breathed.

He heard her give a soft laugh. "It was a crazy, spontaneous night in college."

He drew the pad of his thumb over the tattoo high on Phoebe's inner thigh.

"They're paw prints." He looked up.

She nodded. "Cat prints."

"Cat prints," he repeated. His eyes went back to the ink—little cat paw prints in a pattern that made it look like the kitty had climbed right up her thigh. "That's—"

"Silly."

"Hot."

She didn't say a thing, didn't make a sound, and he looked up. Her lips were parted as she breathed, her hands clenched at her sides, and she was staring down at him.

"Really hot." So hot he was having a hard time remembering what he was doing down here. He held open one leg of the shorts. "Here."

She lifted one foot and then the other, putting them through the openings. He pulled them up into place as he stood, his eyes taking in the creamy expanse of her thighs, the pale skin of her stomach, the sweet indentation of her belly button—another place he intended to put his tongue— and then the tempting valley between her breasts and the glorious mounds themselves. Her chest was a light pink that led up her throat to her cheeks, but he knew the color wasn't from embarrassment. It was pure desire.

He held the tank open and Phoebe ducked her head. He slipped it over her curls and she lifted one arm at a time to pull the shirt into place.

The tank covered her but molded to the delicious shape of her breasts, and her nipples were prominent against the cotton, begging him to taste.

A very good place for his tongue to start, come to think of it. As if there weren't about a hundred other spots just as tempting.

He stepped back and took in the woman in front of him. Sexy as hell.

She looked down. "I'm confused."

He chuckled. He had a painfully hard erection, his hands were shaking with the need to touch her and his mind refused to focus on anything but that she smelled like green apples everywhere. But he still chuckled.

"Let's go." He couldn't stay in her bedroom. Not because he didn't like sex in beds—he most definitely did—but because he didn't know that he'd ever leave Phoebe's. This was supposed to be helping her with another man. Hell, *he* was supposed to be here about another woman.

He grabbed her hand and tried to decide if he should feel guilty.

He didn't...but maybe he *should.*

Nah. Nadia was cozying up with another guy every night she was in Sapphire Falls and—he glanced back at the woman he was towing into the living room—there was no way he was going to be able to leave Phoebe alone now.

"We're going *out* like this?" Phoebe asked, tripping along behind him.

"No, we are most definitely not going out."

"But I'm dressed now."

"You're covered up, not really dressed. And that's because we're going to work up to the naked thing."

"You mean work *back* up to the naked thing."

Yeah, she'd been naked. Very naked.

"Okay, back up to the naked thing."

"Which seems like a waste of time since I was already naked."

The moment they stepped into the living room, he spun her and backed her up against the nearest wall. "You weren't naked the right way."

She stared up at him. Her breath came rapidly and he could feel it warming his lips.

"The right way?"

"You took someone else's dress off after trying it on for another man's sake. I want you, the real you, taking *your* clothes off for *me*."

Phoebe licked her lips. "Okay." She reached for the hem of her shirt, but he caught her hands.

"Not yet."

He pressed her hands over her head and held her wrists against the wall.

"Joe." But she didn't say anything else.

She blinked up at him, those big blue eyes trained on his. And just as he'd suspected the first night—he was in trouble.

This might be the stupidest thing he'd done yet.

The best stupidest thing.

She must have read the conflicting emotions on his face because she frowned slightly.

"Joe?" She looked worried.

Fuck. That was not what he'd meant to cause. The only thing to worry about right now was if he had enough condoms in his wallet.

He grasped both her wrists in one hand, grabbed her hip with his free hand and pulled her fully against him. "I'm going to kiss you until we're both about to lose our minds. Then I'm going to spin you around and bend you over that damned couch."

"Loveseat."

He captured her lips with his, covering her gasp and noticing that it took only one second for her to kiss him back.

Their lips moved hot and greedy against one another. She strained against his hold on her wrists, but Joe knew that he couldn't let her go yet. She'd take over and she'd want to rush things. He could feel that about her. She'd start touching him, thinking they'd get right to the good stuff, and he wouldn't have the chance to show her how amazing and sexy she was and, well, show her all the other good stuff she'd been missing.

"Take it easy," he said, huskily against her lips. "Let go. Let me do this."

"Joe," she said again.

He ran his hand from her hip up under the tank top, desperate to finally feel her nipple pressing into his palm. "Do you like having your nipples played with?" he asked. "Because I could happily spend an hour here." He cupped her left breast, imprinting the feel on his hand.

She simply gasped.

"Phoebe, you have to do what I say and answer my questions," he reminded her, making his tone firm.

She moaned. So she really did like having someone else take control. That was going to work out very well for both of them.

"Answer me."

"Yes," she answered, breathless against his lips

He took her nipple between his thumb and finger and plucked gently. "Like that?"

"Yes."

"That's all? Exactly how you like it?"

"No. Yes. No, more," she mumbled.

"Tell me, Phoebe. I'll give you anything, but I have to hear it." It occurred to him that this giving-her-anything-she-asked thing was exactly what he'd felt a flicker of from the very beginning and what he should be concerned about. But at the same time he felt the ah-fuck-it that he was sure had echoed in the hearts of Spencer men for generations. This just felt too damned good to care about anything else. Like sanity and his future.

"I want more," she whispered.

He slipped his hand from her shirt, even as everything in him protested it.

Her eyes flew open. "Hey."

He shook his head. "You have to tell me what you want. Exactly."

"I said more."

"More what?"

"Of what you were doing."

"Kissing you? Feeling you up?" He slid his hand back under the tank top and cupped her breast again. "Like that?"

"More," she said through gritted teeth.

"I need specifics."

"Why?"

He grinned. This was the craziest seduction he'd ever been a part of. He had his hand on her and she was sassing him. "Okay, *you* need to be more specific. I want you to ask for what you want."

"Joe," Phoebe said tightly, clearly irritated. "Either pull harder on my nipple or get out of my house."

Triumphantly, he pressed his hips against hers and tugged on her nipple, "Oh, I'm not going anywhere."

She arched into his hand. "Like that, but harder."

He complied and she moaned.

"Keep talkin', darlin'," he said against her ear.

"I want your mouth on my nipple now."

"You're catching on." He drew her shirt up, exposing both breasts, her left nipple a darker pink than the right from his stimulation. He bent his knees and licked her neglected right side.

She whimpered softly and arched closer. "Again."

He did, adding a swirl and then blowing softly, loving how the bud drew tight.

"Suck on me, Joe," she rasped.

"That a girl," he praised gruffly and took her nipple with a long suck, swirling his tongue and feeling hot blood surge through his cock as she whispered his name.

"Harder. Suck harder," she urged.

Gladly. Joe sucked as he drew on the other nipple with his fingers, relishing how she writhed against him. When her moans grew longer, he lifted his head. For a moment, his breath stuck in his chest as he looked at her. Her skin was flushed, her eyes were closed, her fingers curled into fists above where he held her wrists captive. She looked incredible, and knowing he'd caused it made something very primitive and male inside him want to shout.

"Now what?" he asked softly.

"I want your hand in my pants."

She was catching right on.

"Where? Specifically?" he teased as he straightened. "Come on, you've loved telling me what to do since I met you."

Unable to resist, he took her mouth in another hot kiss before she could answer. He didn't hesitate to stroke his tongue along her lip, demanding entrance and then slid possessively against hers when she obediently opened.

When he finally lifted his head, breathing as hard as she was, she met his gaze directly. "I want your fingers inside me. Now."

They were definitely on the same page.

No man had made her talk like this, he knew, but he'd never had a woman talk quite like this to him either. He'd heard plenty of "deeper, Joe", "harder, Joe", "fuck me, Joe", but those women had been seasoned. They'd known how and when to say it to urge him on, had placed those verbal commands perfectly. There was nothing calculated or practiced about Phoebe's demands. She was saying it because she wanted it. He was making her say it out loud, but this wasn't about turning him on—it was about her and what she needed from him. Other women needed orgasms from him, pleasure, a good time. Phoebe needed to know who she was and that she had all the power she wanted. That he could give that to this woman made him feel...humble.

Which was a really stupid thing to feel when a woman was asking him to put his hand in her pants.

He didn't need any further instruction with that last request. Palm flat against her stomach—which she sucked in quickly at his touch—he slid his hand past the elastic waistband of her shorts until his fingertips brushed soft hair.

"Don't," he whispered. "Breathe. Trust me. You're gorgeous." He paused.

Still her stomach didn't relax.

"Relax. Let me feel the real you," Joe said. "I want every inch of you."

He felt her sigh.

"I must be out of my mind," she muttered, but her stomach did relax.

"You're beautiful," he told her, rubbing his hand over the softness of her belly.

"Yeah, yeah. Keeping it moving, Joe." She went up on tiptoe, bringing his fingertips closer to where she wanted him.

He chuckled lightly. Keeping her hands trapped was a great idea. "I want to hear you say that you know you're beautiful."

"What, are you writing a Hallmark card here?" she huffed.

He grinned in spite of how seriously he took this. That mouth of hers never quit.

He'd never worried so much about the woman in one of his escapades. They kept up just fine and had a great time. But with Phoebe, he wanted to be sure that everything was focused on her.

"I want you to strip me down and put your tongue on me and in me."

He immediately lost all lightheartedness as lust crashed through him. Screw acquiescence and submission and all of that. Hearing this woman tell him how she needed him was the hottest damned thing he'd ever experienced. "Where?" he said gruffly, already yanking the tank top over her head. "I'll put my tongue anywhere, everywhere. Just tell me."

"On my clit and in my pu—"

He cut her off with a rough kiss.

"Like here?" He slipped his hand lower, sliding his fingers into her wet heat.

She gasped. "Yes. More."

He paused, straining to keep his hand still when he really wanted to dip and stroke and flick until she was calling his name. "Be specific," he said through gritted teeth.

She shifted against the wall, widening her stance. "Another finger. Deeper."

He did as she asked, sliding two fingers into her, stretching her and reaching to stroke her deep.

"Faster."

He did as she asked, along with adding the brush of his thumb over her clit.

She moaned and arched. "Wait 'til I get my hands on *you*," she promised breathlessly. "You're in so much trouble."

He grinned, pressing more firmly against her both inside and against her clit. "You're so mouthy."

"My mouth will definitely be involved."

His cock jerked and he increased his rhythm, no request necessary. "You drive me crazy."

"Good." It was a whisper as her head fell back against the wall.

He felt an internal tremor begin and had to bend to take her nipple in his mouth again. As he swirled his tongue, he moved his thumb and felt her entire body tense. She went up on tiptoe and then pressed down against his hand. Just like that, she came apart, gasping his name.

They stayed like that for several seconds until she slumped against the wall.

Joe focused on his breathing, finding himself as spent as if he'd been the one to climax. He leaned to rest his forehead against the wall next to her, slid his hand from her body and rested it against her hip.

He also let go of her hands. Which had the exact effect that he'd expected. Her fingers went immediately to his fly. She cupped and caressed the hard length of his erection as he struggled to stay standing. When she popped the button open, he jerked his head away from the wall.

"Phoebe—"

She gave him a mischievous look that summarized everything he was worried about getting addicted to. This woman was fun. And sweet and smart and sexy—the trifecta of things that made him into a worry-about-everything-later idiot. Add in the fun, and there might not be anything he wouldn't do.

Before he could talk more sense into himself, Phoebe pushed the shorts from her hips and let them drop.

The trifecta, plus fun, plus naked.

Oh, and he liked her.

Fuck.

He thumped his head against the wall as he grabbed her

greedy hands.

He had the nearly overwhelming urge to whisk her off
to Paris. Or Monte Carlo. Or Rome. Phoebe would be a lot
of fun traveling the world. He could spoil her, show her all
kinds of new things, take her to his favorite places and
discover some new favorite places.

She'd have to quit her job of course. And leave
everyone she knew and loved. But it would be a lot of fun
making it worth it to her.

Which was about the craziest thing he'd contemplated
in a really long time.

And for the first time in years, he was glad his
grandfather was a prick—and specifically that Joe had
recently told his grandfather he was a prick—because he'd
never let Joe take the family jet to Paris.

But he still wanted to.

That was the problem.

He could not whisk Phoebe off to Paris—or anywhere
else, of course—even if his grandfather were the nicest man
on earth. That would fall solidly under the heading "stupid
things Spencer men do when they think with their dicks
instead of their brains."

But Phoebe would really be a lot of fun in Paris.

"You ever been to Paris?" he heard himself ask.

He felt her hesitate in surprise. "No."

"Monte Carlo?"

"Nope."

"How about Buenos Aires?" he asked as another
fantastic city came to mind. He'd love to take her there. He
didn't know how to country dance, but he did know how to
tango. That would probably shock Phoebe. Which would
also be fun.

She pulled back to look at him with a funny smile.
"Never been anywhere really. Why?"

"Because I…" He trailed off. Was he really going to
ask her to go to Paris? He didn't have to use the family jet.

He could buy two regular plane tickets after all.

Or maybe he was going tell her that he thought they were moving too fast? Or that he didn't think they should do this after all? Or that he intended to do this over and over again all night?

None of those were good ideas.

He was so screwed.

"Because you what?" Phoebe asked, putting her lips against his.

It only took two seconds for Joe to sink into the kiss that was as hot as before but now held a sweetness that was addicting. She moved her lips and tongue against his and Joe realized he was an idiot for ever having assumed this woman was shy about anything.

He pulled back, his hands on her shoulders. "Would you go to Paris with me?"

Phoebe blinked up at him. "Now?"

That wasn't a no.

And he really needed a woman who would simply say no without hesitation.

Even better, a woman who would roll her eyes, say no and then add something like, "Don't be ridiculous," or call him a dumbass. Which he was for even thinking about it.

Someone like Nadia. She wouldn't call him a dumbass. She was too classy for that. But she would definitely roll her eyes. Definitely. And she'd laugh it off. Definitely. Not because she wouldn't want to go to Paris with him, but because she would know that he shouldn't take her to Paris on a whirlwind trip and she would want him to think it through, make some plans, pay attention to the details, weigh the pros and cons.

Nadia was his personal twelve-step program sponsor.

But maybe Phoebe wasn't dangerous. Maybe she didn't know he was serious. And maybe he wasn't. He never doubted the women he made his outrageous offers to, but he wasn't sure of her. Maybe he was just testing her.

"Yes, now. By the time we drive to Omaha, I could have our private jet ready to go."

Phoebe tipped her head to the side. "I've never been to Paris."

Still not a no.

"Everyone should go to Paris. As often as possible."

"Will there be more of this?"

She rose on tiptoe and kissed him again. Hot and sweet. That was how he was going to think of Phoebe from now on.

When she pulled back, he pulled in a long breath. "Yeah. If you go to Paris with me, there will be more of that." And God knew what else.

The problem with his spontaneous trip was that there was always…a problem.

And it was always for the woman he was involved with. Not that it slowed him down. He still did stupid impulsive things. It wasn't like anyone died. They just were…inconvenienced, sometimes embarrassed, maybe a little achy in the morning. But where his grandfather, father and brother had ended up screwing *themselves* with their stupid decisions, the *women* were the ones who suffered the consequences of Joe's decisions. He definitely suffered hangovers, got issued unlawful conduct tickets and often lost lots of money. But he didn't mind. The girls he was with, however, did sometimes mind the things that happened—like losing an engagement ring in a poker game or ending up on YouTube skinny dipping in a fountain or waking up naked in a strange city…next to another girl. Come to think of it, the women *often* regretted things the next day.

"Then I'm in. I just have to be back by Saturday."

He looked at her closely. That hint of mischief was there, but that was a constant with Phoebe it seemed.

It was still damned appealing.

He could push. He wanted to push. He could have her

throw a bag together and start out for Omaha. How far would she let them get before she called a stop to it? Or would she?

If she didn't, how would he feel?

Joe was torn. Not only did he want to see if Phoebe meant yes when she said yes to him even about crazy plans, but he really did want to take her to Paris. On the other hand, he was trying to turn over a new leaf.

No one had any lasting injuries from his escapades, no one had a permanent record, and Hilary had managed to talk her fiancé into taking her back in spite of her wild weekend with Joe in LA.

There had been no irrevocable damage done.

Yet.

Deep down, he knew he had to stop doing stuff like this.

He took a big step back.

Even more, he didn't want to mess with Phoebe.

He took another big step back.

"What are you doing?" she asked with a frown.

"Backing up."

"Why?"

"Because it makes it harder to kiss you."

Her frown deepened. "Let's try this again...*why* are you backing up? Especially if it's harder to kiss me from there."

"Because I want to stop kissing you."

She raised an eyebrow this time. "Here, in Paris, or both?"

He even wanted to kiss her eyebrow. "Both. All of it. Anywhere."

"You want to stop kissing me anywhere?"

Hell, no. But he *needed* to stop kissing her. Anywhere. But especially in Paris. Or New Orleans—which would also be a really fun city with Phoebe, come to think of it. "Yes. No more kissing."

He loved the kissing. He wanted the kissing. A lot of it.

All over her body. And the kissing itself wasn't the problem. It was all the things the kissing made him want to do too. That *too* was what got him into trouble.

"Joe?"

"Yeah?"

"About ten more seconds of this and I'm going to get really pissed off."

Yeah, that also happened routinely with the women he got involved with. Though it usually happened forty-eight to seventy-two hours after he initiated the hey-let's-do-something-crazy conversation. After they'd had fun...and the consequences had set in.

"Sorry, but no more kissing."

Phoebe crossed her arms over her breasts and started looking pissed as promised. "Why?"

"I...can't explain it."

Her jaw tightened. "Try."

"No." It didn't matter. Besides, it sounded stupid when he explained it to anyone but his brother. Levi totally understood. His hey-let's-do-something-crazy conversations always led to trouble too.

"Joe," she said warningly. "You're past the ten-second limit."

He sighed. "I know."

"So, we're not kissing anymore and you're not going to tell me why other than to say that you don't want to anymore? Suddenly? Right after asking me to go to Paris?"

He *really* wanted to kiss her. In Paris. He took one more step backward. "Yeah. It's complicated. But important."

"It's important that you not kiss me anymore?"

"Yes. Very."

"And Paris is off too?"

That was for the best. It was. But there was always Madrid. Or Aspen—they could get there really quickly.

No. Dammit.

Joe nodded. "Paris is off too. So is Monte Carlo. And Buenos Aires. And *Aspen*."

She was looking less pissed and more confused now. "You hadn't mentioned Aspen."

"I had in my head."

"You had thought about asking me to go to Aspen?"

"Yes."

She looked at him strangely. "I would have said yes."

"Exactly. That's the problem."

She sighed. "I'm confused."

"I know."

He sounded like a crazy person. But he didn't want to explain it to Phoebe. Being described as a millionaire playboy had been fun and even flattering—in his mind anyway—in his early twenties. And his mid-twenties. But now he was trying to be a grown-up, and that's all Phoebe needed to know about him. If she saw him that way—mature, responsible, conventional—then she wouldn't look at him with interest or passion or excitement. In fact, if he pissed her off now, she would probably stop talking to him and he wouldn't be constantly confronted by how fun and sweet she was and could ignore all the things he was so tempted by. And he wouldn't whisk her off to Paris. Or Aspen.

Or her bedroom.

"I need to go." He took one final step back and ran into the desk she had against the far wall. Which wasn't far enough.

"That's probably a good idea," she agreed.

"It's a *very* good idea," he assured her.

He started for the door, determined not to look back at her.

What a fucking mess.

"Look out for the fox, coyotes and raccoons," she called as his feet hit the porch. "They love to eat *chickens*."

Was he chicken? Scared of Phoebe and what sex with

her would do to him? Absolutely. "Ha, ha," he called back. He descended the four steps in one bound. Then he stopped and turned back. "Raccoons don't eat meat, do they?"

The only answer he got was a slamming door and the distinct sound of the lock clicking into place.

He looked around the dark yard cautiously. Yeah, he was relatively certain raccoons didn't eat meat.

But he was equally certain foxes and coyotes did.

He jogged the few yards to his car. Once inside, he locked the doors and pulled out his phone. A few seconds later, Google confirmed that raccoons would, indeed, eat meat.

Great. One more thing that he'd learned tonight. Right up there with the paw print tattoo on Phoebe's inner thigh, the sound she made when she came and that resisting his natural inclination for frivolous spontaneity sucked just as much as he'd anticipated.

CHAPTER SIX

"Joe licked me."

This time, Adrianne wasn't drinking tea. Instead, she choked and coughed over her vodka and orange juice. For Adrianne, it was mostly orange juice, but it still burned more than tea when she choked on it.

"*What*?"

"Joe licked me."

Adrianne opened her mouth, no doubt to ask all the questions like when, where and why, but instead she asked, "Did you lick him back?"

That successfully made Phoebe smile—which was something. She was furious and she wasn't even entirely sure why.

Joe had come over for a dance lesson, things had progressed and he'd pulled back.

Yes, it was the pulling-back part that bugged her, embarrassed her and definitely bothered her self-esteem. But why was she angry?

"I used my mouth on him," she finally admitted.

Adrianne leaned in with wide eyes. "How was it?"

Hot, amazing, surprising, hot and frustrating. And hot. "Good," she said, noncommittally, "right up to the part where he asked me to go to Paris with him tonight, then babbled a bunch of stupid crap about it being important he stop kissing me and then practically fell over himself getting out the door."

Adrianne frowned. "He asked you to go to Paris?"

"Yeah." And that was what got to Phoebe. Not the crazy invitation, but the way that she'd known he meant it. She could tell that he'd wanted her to say yes too. Then when she'd said, "I would have said yes," he'd freaked out.

She felt like she'd failed a test.

And how did saying yes to something someone wanted

her to do count as a failure?

That was why she was mad.

Not because he'd been able to walk away when she wasn't sure she could have. Not that. That didn't matter. They shouldn't have been kissing in the first place.

But that thought was what made her raise her hand to signal for another drink. One that contained quite a lot of vodka.

"Why would Joe ask you to go to Paris with him?" Adrianne asked.

Phoebe frowned at her. "Why not?"

"Uh, two words," Adrianne said, "Nadia. Matt."

Phoebe frowned harder. "Yeah, well Nadia and Matt are not exactly available for sexy trips to Paris at the moment."

"So it was about Paris?" Adrianne asked. "You just wanted a free trip to France?"

Phoebe took a drink instead of answering that no, she would have gone to…Pittsburgh—that was a less-than-exciting-or-sexy-city, wasn't it?—if Joe had asked.

"Or maybe it was just that you were overwhelmed by orgasm endorphins and would have agreed to help him clean toilets if that's what he had suggested?" Adrianne asked, taking a sip of orange juice.

Phoebe took another drink as well, found it didn't help and set her glass down. "How did you know there was an orgasm?"

"I was just hoping, for your sake, that the licking paid off." Adrianne looked smug.

Phoebe found Joe across the bar at the pool tables—as if she could help it.

Yeah, it had paid off.

The guy was nuts. Not the bad he-might-hack-her-up-in-her-sleep kind of nuts, but the what's-he-gonna-do-next-and-will-I-want-to-kiss-him-or-shake-him kind of nuts.

The wanting to shake him was a pretty good likelihood,

but the chance of more kissing was worth the roll of that dice.

And wanting to shake him wasn't all that bad. She was frustrated, confused and a little pissed. But she sensed there was something there, something worth delving into. *Why* had Joe bolted?

She had to know, *had* to find out, like she *had* to breathe.

She shook her head. Speaking of nuts…

"You going to go talk to him?" Adrianne asked.

"No. You run out of my house like I set you on fire for any reason other than me actually setting you on fire and you get the silent treatment."

Not that Joe seemed to notice or care. He was clearly avoiding her as well.

"How long does the silent treatment last?" Adrianne asked.

Phoebe looked away from him, the need to know what he was thinking and feeling burning in her chest. "A week."

"Uh huh," Adrianne said. "How long really?"

Phoebe thought about how shocked and mad she'd been when Joe's shoes had hit the porch. Then she thought about the way he'd kissed her, Paris, Aspen, the sight of him backing up into her desk and sighed. If she'd wanted stories before, now she *had* to have them.

Besides, they'd have a great time in Paris.

"About an hour," she said honestly.

Adrianne laughed.

"Of all the girls in Sapphire Falls, who's most likely to pick up and take off on a long weekend, all-expenses-paid trip to Paris?" At least she assumed it would be all expenses paid.

"You," Adrianne said. "Definitely."

Yeah, and somehow Phoebe thought that was the problem. For some reason. "And if you were on a diet and called me up at midnight and said, 'Phoebe, I want cheesecake. Go with me to get some.' What would I say?"

"You'd say, 'I'll pick you up in five minutes.'"

Phoebe frowned. She would. "I'm an enabler."

Adrianne shrugged. "You're more of a life-is-too-short girl and a good friend. I mean, you'd take me for cheesecake, but you'd cut me off after three or four pieces. You wouldn't let me do something that would actually hurt me."

Phoebe laughed, but she knew, somehow, *that* was why Joe had changed directions so fast.

"So does Matt know Joe's here to steal his girl?" Hailey asked, taking a seat with a glass of red wine—a sign she was at the Come Again for girl-talk only.

For a second, Phoebe thought she was talking about her. Was Joe stealing her? Would Matt even care?

"What?" Phoebe turned to find Joe again. "Oh."

He and Matt were at the pool table but neither was shooting or even poised to shoot. They were talking. Except that it was clearly not casual. They were squared off and Matt looked mad. Matt didn't get mad. He was laidback and easygoing and liked everyone—and vice versa. She couldn't see Joe's face, but he was holding himself stiffly, legs apart, hands clenched at his sides.

Oh, boy. Not good.

And if this was about Nadia, she knew she was going to be really disappointed.

This standoff should be about Nadia, Joe thought briefly as he resisted the urge to hit Matt.

Instead, of course, it was about Phoebe, the woman who had been causing him trouble since he'd come to Sapphire Falls. He shouldn't let her get to him. He shouldn't let her get him so worked up.

But he was still about to get into a fight with the crown

prince of his new hometown because of her.

"I'm not going to leave Phoebe alone," Joe informed her best friend. Of course, he absolutely *should* leave her alone, but he wasn't going to.

"You gonna marry her?" Matt asked.

Joe's heart thumped hard in his chest, but he stubbornly stared Matt down and, instead of answering, asked, "It's because of you, isn't it?"

The other man propped his cue against the table, clearly seeing this conversation was getting serious. Did the other guys just let it go, agree easily, nod and smile when Matt told them to back off from Phoebe as he had to Joe a few minutes ago?

Matt crossed his arms over his chest. "What do you mean?"

"The reason no one asks Phoebe out."

Matt looked around the table. There were several men gathered in the area, watching the game, waiting for their chance to play, drinking and joking. At the moment, however, they were all listening intently to Matt and Joe's conversation.

Matt narrowed his eyes. "All I said was that I didn't want *you* messing with her."

Joe propped his hip against the pool table, faking casual when he was anything but. He spent a lot of time with manipulative men. He knew how to handle them...and when they were trying to handle him.

"The men in Sapphire Falls seem like decent, intelligent, heterosexual guys," he said loud enough for many of those very men to hear him. "There's no way in hell that Phoebe shouldn't have a million guys lined up outside her door. Unless someone—someone they don't want to piss off—is telling them to stay away."

Matt seemed to force himself to relax, or pretend to relax. "I'm her best friend. I've simply made it clear to everyone that if they want to spend time with Phoebe, they need to be serious. No one better mess with her is all."

"So if they're not willing to marry her, they can't even take her out for coffee?"

"All you want to do is take her out for coffee?"

"No."

Matt's expression didn't change, but he straightened away from the table. He was an inch taller than Joe and easily had forty pounds—of muscle—over Joe.

"Then I don't want you messing with her," Matt said.

"Well, see, the thing is," Joe said, "I didn't go to high school with you. We didn't party together. You haven't done me any favors over the years. You don't have any power over me."

His chest felt tight. Matt had been keeping Phoebe protected—and maybe it was well-intentioned—but he'd also been keeping her from being appreciated. And that pissed Joe off. The guys in Sapphire Falls hadn't felt free to show Phoebe how they really felt about her, so she didn't know that they thought she was beautiful and sweet and sexy.

Joe fought a frown. Was that why she was so into him? So hot for him? So willing to pick up and jet off to Paris or Vegas or Aspen? Because no one else had ever even tried to wow her? Because of Matt?

Dammit.

What a fucking mess. A complicated, crazy, emotional, fucking mess.

Not only was Phoebe not seeing how amazing she was, but what was he feeling for this woman? He went for women who were sure of themselves, who had lots of offers, lots of options, because he wanted them to pick *him*.

Son of a bitch.

He wanted Phoebe. It didn't matter why or how. He wanted her, he liked her and he wanted her to know that she was worth every bit of wooing any guy could possibly dream up.

Of course, wooing in Sapphire Falls looked a lot different from what he was used to. And it was what Phoebe would want. And respond to.

Yep. It was a complicated, crazy, emotional, fucking mess.

"I can still kick your ass though," Matt said when he realized that Joe had a point about the power thing. Matt didn't have anything to hold over him or cash in on.

"You could. Maybe," Joe said. "But it wouldn't matter." It wouldn't. He'd still see Phoebe again. He might even ask her to Paris again.

He stoically resisted looking in her direction, but he knew exactly where she was. He even knew she was drinking orange juice and vodka tonight. She was wearing the white top he'd seen earlier—probably on purpose because she knew he was thinking about her nipples—and blue jeans that made him think of all the smooth sweet skin underneath, the beige panties and that damned tattoo. Even now remembering those tiny prints stepping up her inner thigh, like a treasure map, he felt his cock thicken and harden.

Fuck.

"Just leave her alone, Joe. You're not her type."

"Who is?"

"A guy like me," Matt said matter of factly. There was a touch of pride in his voice—as there should be.

"But you're crazy about Nadia," Joe said. It occurred to him that as Nadia's friend he maybe should be irritated by Matt's protectiveness of Phoebe. But it wasn't about Nadia, and Joe realized that whether it was the paw prints or Paris or just Phoebe, things had shifted tonight.

Joe wanted Matt with Nadia so that Matt wouldn't be with Phoebe.

It was a mess.

Phoebe wasn't going to keep his spontaneity and frivolity in check, but they were going to have a hell of a good time before the regrets set in.

"I am crazy about Nadia," Matt agreed.

"If you really *care* about Phoebe," Joe pushed, "you'd let her have some fun, let her feel what it's like to have a guy crazy about her."

"Not you."

"Why not me?"

"You're not from here."

"You won't let any of the guys who *are* from here close to her," Joe said, frustrated. He didn't exactly want to feel this way for Phoebe—the I'll-do-anything-to-make-her-smile-and-think-I'm-awesome thrill that he knew his brother, dad and grandpa were addicted to. But he felt it and it was too much to ignore.

"I don't want them messing with her," Matt said, also clearly frustrated. "If one of them is serious—like long-term, real stuff—that's different."

"So if they promise to marry her, you'll *let* them ask her out." Joe rolled his eyes.

Matt glared at him. "This is none of your business."

Except that it was. Phoebe was his business, strange as that was.

"Wrong, Phillips. I know having someone tell you that is new for you, but you're wrong."

"You don't know her like I do."

"Who cares how well you know her. *You're* not going to marry her—" Joe stopped and stared at Matt. "Holy shit."

"What?"

"She's your backup plan. You kept these guys from getting serious about her because she was your plan B if you never found someone else."

Matt didn't deny it immediately, and Joe did what he'd been fighting since he'd come to Sapphire Falls—he went with his instinct.

His fist connected with Matt's jaw at the same moment

he thought, "Screw being rational."

Everything after decking the man-who-would-be-king was a blur. People shouted, someone—or more than one someone—grabbed him, Matt swore, someone held him back too and the next thing Joe knew he was sitting in the backseat of the Sapphire Falls police car and heading downtown. Which took three minutes to get to.

The bright side of being arrested in Sapphire Falls was that Ed, the town cop, didn't take away his personal belongings, so Joe had his phone. And once the door of the cell was shut and locked, Ed said, "I'm heading to the Stop for coffee and a cookie. Want somethin'?"

Joe blinked at him. Was it possible to get an arrest record and a candy bar at the same time?

"Coffee would be great."

"Back in a minute."

Joe pulled his phone out and dialed his brother. Because any time he did something stupid, he thought of Levi.

And punching Matt Phillips because of Phoebe was stupid. He'd do it again, of course, but it would be stupid the second time too.

"Isn't it past your bedtime nowadays?" Levi answered on the third ring. Wherever he was, it was loud. Music and conversation blared in the background and—yep, there it was—the ringing of slot machines came through the line loud and clear.

Levi loved their family's empire and lifestyle. He loved the constant action and noise of the casinos and he really loved the money, and the women who loved his money. Levi was absolutely not looking to change his life like Joe was.

And yes, Joe almost always hit the pillow earlier than Levi, but nine times out of ten it was because Levi was using his mattress for things other than sleeping.

"Just getting my second wind," Joe said. Levi knew that Joe was trying to turn over a new leaf, trying to be more responsible and serious about life. His career had been the first change—actually deciding on what he wanted to do with the two degrees his father had paid for.

Then he'd moved, gotten a few suits and ties and bullshitted his way into his job at IAS. It wasn't that he wasn't qualified. He had degrees in political science and marketing, but more importantly, he was a charmer. IAS needed someone who could talk to politicians and officials on the local and national level. Charm went a long way. He loved what he was doing with Mason, Adrianne and Lauren, and one draw had been a job where he needed to wear suits and talk about important things with important people.

His next life-changing goal had been about women. Reducing the number and the maintenance level.

"You need money, advice or an alibi?" Levi asked.

Joe grinned in spite of his situation. Levi was only half kidding, he knew. If Joe answered with option one or three, Levi would provide what he needed, no questions asked.

"Advice, actually."

"Well, there's a first time for everything. Hang on."

Joe could tell that Levi was moving somewhere quieter. Loud music and laughter in the background was pretty typical in a phone conversation with Levi Spencer, so Joe appreciated the effort on his brother's part. He heard Levi mumble something to someone—he'd put money on that someone being a built blond—and then heard a door shut and it was quiet on Levi's end of the phone.

"I can't wait to hear this," Levi said.

"I'm doing it again and I don't know how to stop," Joe said.

"Doing what exactly?"

Levi knew where Joe was and why. He also knew that Joe was intent on being a better man. He didn't share Joe's desire to move outside of their family's footsteps, but he knew how Joe felt and didn't try to talk him out of it.

Much.

"I'm about to blow it with Nadia."

"Because of another woman?"

"Of course. Spencer men don't do stupid things that fuck everything up over anything less than a woman."

Levi chuckled. "Do you want me to pretend I'm surprised this is happening to you?"

"You're not at *all* surprised?"

"Nah. You aren't crazy about Nadia. If you were really in love with her, I'd say you had a chance at being responsible and rational, but—"

"I can be responsible and rational," Joe cut in.

"Not when it comes to showing a woman a good time and making her say, 'Oh, Joe, you're amazing.'"

His brother's female voice imitation should have made Joe smile, but instead he turned and paced the length of his cell with a frown. "You're one to talk," he said. "You've never met a damsel in distress that you could resist."

Levi was just like their grandfather—any woman who needed him was like a drug. Whether she needed money, someone to tell her ex to leave her alone, a new car, a new job, anything. Levi and Charles Spencer were hooked the minute they heard that a woman had no one else to turn to.

"Yep," Levi said about his damsel addiction. "And where you like to shock and awe, I like to comfort and protect."

Joe snorted. "Saint Levi, that's you." Never mind that *saving* those women had consequences like black eyes, stolen debit cards, wrecked cars and, oh yeah, a criminal record.

Levi chuckled in his ear. "So you found someone new to impress and it's gonna piss Nadia off?"

Joe was startled to realize that Levi's assumption wasn't entirely accurate.

Yes, Nadia was absolutely *not* impressed by him and he'd figured that would be good for him. He needed a relationship that wasn't about him wowing the woman. A two-way street where they spent time doing things like making dinner and going to movies. Not where he pulled out his private jet or VIP backstage passes or was able to jump the line at the clubs or take her up to the owner's box seats at the game. Maybe even one where she did things for *him* once in a while. Just a normal relationship with a woman who knew his flaws and faults and liked him anyway.

Up until three days ago, the only woman he knew like that was Nadia.

But not anymore.

Phoebe did not think he was perfect. The whole reason she was spending time with him was to give him a complete makeover. Not exactly the actions of a woman who was overwhelmed with how amazing he was.

And he realized that the Paris thing with Phoebe wasn't so much about impressing her—though hearing Phoebe Sherwood say he was amazing would be just fine. No, Paris was about having a good time with a woman he really liked.

"Impressing Phoebe would take a lot more—no, something a lot *different*—from a private plane," Joe finally told his brother.

"Then stick with Nadia. Her family has their own plane so you don't have to worry about her liking you just for that. She's the one to make you stop acting like a spoiled rich kid with an inferiority complex," Levi said.

"Inferiority complex?" Joe said. "Me?"

"All of us. Why else do you think we do all these crazy things?' Levi asked.

"Because it's fun."

And it was. Until he'd started feeling guilty about it, he could honestly say that he'd always had fun. Plus, it was how the men in his family related to women. That was how he'd been raised.

"Some fathers teach their sons to hunt and fish and fix things," Joe said. "Spencer men make sure their boys love women and know how to get their attention."

"Because we have egos in need of stroking," Levi replied.

"Yeah, maybe it started as an ego thing back in the family tree—God knows, Grandpa likes when people think he's important—but I really do think I've just been doing it for fun." And because he didn't have a good reason not to.

Levi laughed. "Well, I sure as hell think it's fun too. But I also know that the harder I have to work for someone's attention, the better it feels to get it."

Oh, yeah, being notable and exciting to women with every option in the world felt good.

Joe thought back over that again.

Oh.

In fact, it was kind of what he did every day at work. His job was to get the attention of important people—politicians, CEOs and other officials—and convince them to believe in and support IAS. And yes, the harder it was to convince them to meet or to get involved, the better it felt when it happened.

He always made it happen.

"I don't think inferiority complex is entirely accurate," Joe said, just because he felt like he needed to.

"I think it's pretty close."

Joe swung around at the sound of a third—very feminine—voice.

Phoebe was sitting, legs crossed, on the bench across from the door of the cell, sipping from a paper coffee cup with the Stop logo on the side.

The strangest feeling of relief and satisfaction hit him.

"Is that my coffee?" he asked.

"Yep. Saw John on my way in." She sipped again.

"Stealing might end up with you on this side of the bars."

"For the moment, I like this arrangement," she said. "We need to talk."

"Is that the girl?" Levi asked in his ear.

Joe kept his eyes on Phoebe. She was watching him with a strange combination of amusement and concern. Yeah, she was the girl. "How could you tell?"

"Your voice changed."

Well, shit.

That was Joe's first thought. But the next moment, he noticed how cute she was when she tucked her hair behind her ear.

"Levi?"

"Yeah?"

"I'm definitely going to blow this with Nadia." And possibly Phoebe.

Levi just chuckled. "Let me know so I can get you drunk afterward."

They'd been there and done that.

"Why'd I call you again?" His brother wasn't being particularly helpful.

"So I could get you the plane. Grandpa won't answer your calls and you won't call Dad because you hate proving to him how much you're like him."

Phoebe simply watched him back as he watched her drink the rest of his coffee.

"I don't need the plane."

"But it'll produce more of a wow factor."

Joe gritted his teeth. Yes, it would, and that was tempting with Phoebe even more than with any other woman.

"Maybe she's already wowed," he said.

Phoebe arched an eyebrow and then launched the now-empty coffee cup into the wastebasket next to Ed's desk.

Levi laughed. "I know you learned from Dad that there's no such thing as *too* much wow."

Yeah, that was pretty much their father's future epitaph.

It was the motto by which he lived—finding beautiful, confident women, charming them, making them fall in love with him and then, when the woman was no longer enamored—or he'd used up his tricks or it just wasn't fun anymore, he found a new woman.

Now, looking at Phoebe as she tucked one foot up underneath her on the bench, eavesdropping unabashedly, he knew two things—Phoebe wouldn't be easily enamored and he'd never grow tired of trying.

"Not sure I can impress this one."

"She a nun?"

Joe snorted. Phoebe Sherwood a nun? "Not exactly."

"She too smart for you?"

"Probably."

"She one of the scientists who are living in Haiti in a hut for a year at a time?"

They weren't really huts, but Levi didn't listen or care about that. "No."

"She's just too good for you in general."

"'Fraid so." He really was a little afraid of that.

Phoebe lived a simple life in a little town, but she was...content. Happy. Sure of who she was and what she wanted. She was so much more than the women Joe generally spent time with. Did he like wooing women and affecting them with his money and connections and coolness? Of course. Would Phoebe enjoy Paris? His plane? The fact that he knew the president? Maybe. But would it make her crazy about him? Not likely. Winning a girl like Phoebe over would take more than having something or doing something.

He'd have to *be* something. Something big and special. If he could pull it off at all.

"I need to go, Levi."

"You know the number if you need the plane. Or anything else."

Maybe that was why he'd called Levi. Because he

needed someone to have his back as he embarked on this adventure. He might not be in the usual type of trouble, there might not be a huge monetary loss or scars, but he had a feeling there was an even bigger risk here.

"You're speed-dial number one."

Joe disconnected the call and pocketed his phone.

"First of all," Phoebe said, stretching to her feet and then dragging the bench she'd been sitting on closer to the cell. "I'm mad about earlier."

"Me punching Matt?" Joe pulled the folding chair in the cell up closer to the bars and sat.

"The disproportionate amount of naked time on your part compared to mine and the orgasm with no follow through."

"Ah." He shifted on the chair as the memory of the orgasm hit him. At least she wasn't mad about Matt. "Isn't the orgasm itself pretty much follow through?"

Phoebe laughed and Joe felt tension wind his spine tighter. He loved making her laugh.

"I'm not complaining about the orgasm itself," she assured him. "Just the not-naked-enough thing and the stumbling-from-the-house-like-a-crazy-person thing. But," she said, crossing her legs, "We can fix all of it if you just realize one thing."

"What's that?"

"That I want to cover you in cherry syrup and suck you like a lollipop."

Joe stared at her. "Holy shit."

She grinned. "Don't you wish you'd stuck around?"

He leaned back on the chair, tipping it onto the two back legs, studying this woman that he wanted with an intensity he couldn't get used to. "Do you have cherry syrup?"

"If not, we'd find something else. Maybe grape jelly. I like all flavors of suckers." She emphasized *suck* and Joe had trouble swallowing.

"So, anyway," she went on as if she hadn't just teased him with a blowjob. "I think it's important that you realize I wanted to do that even before I knew you had a private plane."

Joe cleared his throat, unable to keep from thinking about where he might get cherry syrup at this time, or really any time, of night in Sapphire Falls.

"I'm glad," he said sincerely.

"I'm just curious," she said, "did it ever occur to you that you don't have to try so hard?"

"Try so hard?" he repeated. Maybe the grocery store would have it…but they were only open until five-thirty. After all, everyone in town made dinner by then, so if they were out of something they'd know before that time, or it could wait until the next day.

"To get a woman to like you."

He focused fully on her face. He let the legs of the chair thunk onto the ground.

"What do you mean?"

"You were talking about impressing women and how I might not be impressed. Oh, and that thing about the inferiority complex."

"That was just my stupid brother giving me a hard time." Joe leaned to rest his forearms on his knees.

"Uh huh. Tell me about the last time you took a woman on the plane."

He sighed. He was locked inside a jail cell in Sapphire Falls, Nebraska. He had nothing more interesting to do, and she looked like she'd settled in for the long haul. And he wanted her to stay.

"Samantha. I met her at the casino one night. We flirted, she told me she'd never been to Mexico, so I took her to Puerto Vallarta for two days."

"And was she impressed?"

"Incredibly."

"And then?"

"She missed the first day of school."

Phoebe's eyebrows climbed nearly to her hairline. "Please, please tell me you mean grad school."

"Grade school." He fought a smile. "She was a second-grade teacher."

Phoebe breathed a sigh of relief. "What happened?"

"She sweet-talked the principal."

"That worked?"

"With my large donation to their fine-arts program, it worked like a charm."

Phoebe shook her head as if she didn't know what she was going to do with him.

He hoped whatever it was involved cherry syrup.

"Another one," she said.

Joe thought about it. Not all of his escapades involved the plane. The wildest seemed to, but he'd gotten into plenty of trouble with just a car or his own two feet. "Okay, Stacy was a Red Sox fan, so I took her to Boston and introduced her to their third baseman."

"Nice."

"Yeah, well that didn't work out so well for me. She was a *big* fan of his."

Phoebe smiled. "Ah, you came home on the plane alone?"

"Exactly."

"Poor baby. Hope there was liquor on that plane."

He grinned. "Nah, I wasn't that broken up about it."

"The next blond came along and you were over it?"

Did he detect a note of jealousy in her tone? His grin grew. "I like redheads just as much."

She rolled her eyes. "Sweet talker. Okay, who was next?"

"Melissa was a Disney fanatic, so I took her to Orlando and got her dressed up like Cinderella in one of the parades."

Phoebe just stared for a moment.

"What?"

"I'm actually a little impressed by that."

He grinned again. He had plenty more. "You always wanted to be Cinderella?" He'd buy her the damn castle.

Phoebe lifted a shoulder. "Every little girl wants to be Cinderella at one point or another. But I mean something like that takes some thought and paying attention. You could have bought her a movie or a figurine or something, but you helped her really get into her fantasy."

He couldn't remember who they were talking about. Some girl he'd messed around with once. But when Phoebe said *fantasy*, his brain couldn't get past wondering about what her fantasies were.

"So what happened to Melissa?" Phoebe asked.

"What do you mean?"

"Well, you're not with her now, so something must have happened."

He shrugged. "I didn't expect her to be forever or anything."

"So it's just about sweeping them off their feet?"

He paused. Did he want Phoebe to know this?

"Come on, Joe. Remember the inferiority-complex issue? I need to know how deep it goes."

He sighed. He didn't have an inferiority complex dammit. "Yeah, how come you agreed with that?"

"You're here to win Nadia over and you're willing to let a stranger boss you around and basically change everything about you to do it. You can't be too sure of yourself to let that happen."

He frowned at her. "*You're* the bossy stranger."

"I know." She chewed on her bottom lip for a moment. "And I'm realizing that I should probably just let you be yourself."

He frowned harder at that. "Being myself…might not be quite what Nadia is looking for." And Nadia wasn't the woman he was concerned with anymore.

"You don't need private planes and Disney World, Joe," she told him.

Looking directly into her eyes, he felt a little lost. Without Disney World, what did he have? "I'm not so sure about that."

Phoebe suddenly bounced up from her seat. "Okay, let's go."

He rose, not even sure why. "Go?"

"We have a new project."

She headed for Ed's desk.

"I'm all for going," he said, "but there are these thick metal bars in my way."

Phoebe turned from the desk with a ring of keys in hand. "Not for long."

She came toward him and fit a key into the lock of the cell door.

"You're breaking me out?"

"I'm *letting* you out."

The door swung open and Joe paused, sure that an alarm was about to squeal.

All that happened was Phoebe looked at him as if he was crazy.

"You coming?" She tossed the keys back into the desk with a loud clack.

Joe stepped from the cell cautiously. Still no alarms, barking dogs or cops yelling *freeze*.

"Where are we going?"

"To give you a lesson in wowing on a budget."

He followed her from the building, and when he saw Ed, who was standing outside chatting with a couple of other guys lift his hand in a wave, Joe decided he was a free man.

"Wowing on a budget?"

"Mostly, you'll be spending creativity and time," Phoebe told him.

"I don't get it."

"I know. But you will."

He followed her to her truck and climbed up. "Will there be any cherry syrup involved?" he couldn't help but ask as she started the engine.

"Well, that's up to you," she said with a sly smile.

It was already a great plan as far as Joe was concerned.

Phoebe was pissed.

Watching Joe leave her house after that world-rocking orgasm was nothing compared to how mad she was at all the women who had oohed and aahed over Joe's fancy plane and his willingness to throw his money around.

And Nadia. Why hadn't this woman who was such a good friend to him, who he was supposedly so crazy about, ever convinced him that he didn't need all the overboard gestures and extravagant displays to make a woman fall for him?

Or had she and he hadn't believed her?

Well, screw Nadia. She'd had her chance. The fact that she wasn't sitting around pining for Joe made it clear that she wasn't quite the genius everyone thought she was.

Either way, Phoebe was in charge now. She was going to prove to Joe that he didn't need fancy hotel suites and backstage passes at Disney World to make a woman crazy, and he *was* going to believe her.

Sometimes bossy and in-your-face came in handy.

She pulled up in front of Mason and Adrianne's house. Putting the truck into park, she lifted her butt off the truck seat and dug into her front pocket. She pulled out a twenty-dollar bill and handed it to him.

"Okay, starting tomorrow, you're going to wow me, and you can't spend more than this or leave Woodburn County."

Joe looked from the twenty to her face and back.

"You've got to be kidding me."

"Nope. I want romance, seduction and to be wowed for twenty dollars or less. The further under twenty, the more wowed I'll be."

"And what's in it for me?" he said with a grin.

"You have no idea how much you want me wowed, Joe."

His grin was instantly replaced by an intent look full of heat and promise.

"I'm suddenly inspired."

Phoebe pulled in a long breath, willing her heart to slow. "Great. Can't wait to see what you come up with tomorrow."

"Now."

"Now? What do you—"

Joe slid across the seat until they were hip to hip. He lifted her, dragged her across his lap—which she really enjoyed—and dumped her into the passenger seat.

Then he slid behind the wheel and put it in reverse.

"Joe?"

"Yeah?"

"What's going on?"

"You'll see."

With that look of hot mischief on his face, she could see why women said yes to anything and everything he suggested—even if it risked their jobs, or worse.

Four minutes later, Phoebe wasn't sure if she was more wowed by how great he looked behind the wheel of the truck, that he remembered how to get to the river behind her house, or that he'd taken her there.

"This is a good start," she said, turning to face him. "But wh—"

"Get out." Joe opened his door and hopped to the ground.

She would have asked more questions but he'd already shut the door and, more significantly, he'd pulled his shirt off and tossed it on the hood of the truck.

Phoebe stopped with her hand on the door handle. "Holy—"

Her body flushed with heat as every memory from earlier that night rushed back in full, high-def color and detail. His mouth, his hands, his fascination with the paw prints, the way he'd insisted on undressing her and then dressing her, the...all of it. Joe. All of *him*.

He turned to face the truck when he realized she hadn't gotten out yet.

"Let's go, Phoebe." There was enough light to see that he looked determined and playful, somehow at the same time.

"I, um..." She felt frozen. Frozen by wanting something so much, knowing somehow she should say no, but knowing somehow that she wouldn't say no to this guy.

Hands on the front of his jeans, chest bare—smooth and firm and completely lickable—Joe came around to her side of the truck. "I'm not skinny dipping by myself."

The heat flashed through her again and she tightened her fingers on the handle, but she didn't open it. In fact, she fought the urge to lunge for the lock. Suddenly, she was nervous. Not physically. No, something much worse.

"Skinny dipping?"

"It's inexpensive, in the county and very sexy. And I'm guessing, or hoping anyway, that you're a little tingly thinking about it."

"Well, see? I've already proved my point," she said, trying for lighthearted but aware her voice sounded squeaky. "You don't need to throw money around to make a girl nuts."

He moved closer to the open window, a grin that was almost predatory on his face. "You feeling nuts, Phoebe?"

"Well, I'm thinking skinny dipping sounds like the best idea anyone's ever had, and *that's* nuts."

He lifted the handle on the outside of the door and

pulled the door open slowly. "Why's that?"

Her hand dropped from the door to the seat beside her and her fingers dug into the upholstery. "It's a *river*. Things live in there. And poop in there."

He chuckled and she gripped the seat harder instead of running her hand over his chest.

"I don't believe for a second that you've never skinny dipped, Phoebe."

"My grandpa's pond—manmade, no fish, only for swimming—and Lance Owens's parents' pool after prom senior year."

Joe reached in and, with a big hand on each of her hips, pulled her out of the truck.

"Well, that's okay. I don't think we're going to make it down to the river after all."

CHAPTER SEVEN

He had her shirt up over her head before she could even take a deep breath.

His hot mouth found the spot where her neck curved into her shoulder and she moaned. He moved her away from the truck far enough to swing the door shut and then he pressed close, backing her up against it. She tipped her head so his mouth could keep going along her neck and collar bone.

"Joe," she said breathlessly.

"Yeah?" He licked at the base of her throat and slid his hands up her back to the clasp of her bra.

She felt it give and then his hot hands cupped both breasts, thumbs brushing over the tips that ached for him.

"What were you saying?" he asked against her ear.

She could hear the amusement in his voice. "Something—" She sucked in a quick breath as he squeezed one nipple.

"Sorry, go ahead," he said.

"Bastard," she muttered.

He laughed.

The rumble in his chest made her want to press every inch of her against every inch of him.

"Come on, tell me," he urged. "Because very soon you're not going to have enough breath to do anything more than groan or manage a quick 'yes' or 'harder'."

She was nearly there now. "That's too bad, because I do some great dirty talking. I'd think you'd want to hear, 'You're amazing, Joe.'"

"I think I'll be able to tell." With that cocky comment, he bent and took a nipple in his mouth.

She wanted to give him some smartass comment, but even if she could breathe—which was *not* possible—he really was amazing.

He licked, sucked and nipped gently and she was unable and unwilling to form words—and didn't care.

"I want to hear it," he said gruffly, bringing her hips to his.

She just shook her head. She had no idea what he was talking about anyway. He grinned a knowing grin she hated and found profoundly sexy at the same time.

"Tell me," he commanded.

She arched closer, pressing the fly of her jeans against his.

He dug his fingers into her hips, holding her still. "No, you don't. Tell me, Phoebe."

Tell him what?

"I want you," she managed.

"I know." He grinned again. "Ditto by the way."

She tried to reach his mouth.

He moved so she couldn't.

"I knew that first night that I wanted to tie you up."

She pulled back at that. "What?"

"I knew that first night out here that you like to rush things, go all out, full steam ahead. Slowing you down would be some of the most fun I'd ever have."

Tingles exploded all over her body. "It was the booze."

He shook his head. "This would be easier if it was, but no."

She swallowed. So this was two-sided. That helped. "That's what I was going to say. You're going to have to face the fact that you drive women crazy—not your money and not your crazy ideas."

He didn't say anything for several seconds, and she wondered if she'd screwed up somehow. She didn't want to send him running like earlier. She grabbed the waistband at the front of his jeans and held on. "*You're* a great guy. I'm sure those trips were awesome and I'll never say no to being swept off to Paris, but I'm feeling completely swept off my feet right now, and I'm in my own backyard up against my own truck. I don't need your private plane, but I do need your mouth on me and your jeans around your knees."

Another three seconds—or three years—passed before he gave a low growl and sealed his mouth over hers.

The kiss was hot and aggressive, as were his hands on the front of her jeans, unbuttoning and unzipping before sweeping them down to her feet.

She'd worn sandals that she easily kicked off before her jeans went flying, and then he had his hand wrapped around her knee, bringing it up to his hip as his other hand slipped into her panties.

He slid two fingers inside her without warning, but she was more than ready—hot and wet and welcoming.

"Damn, *yes*," Joe muttered against her lips.

Her head fell back against the truck and she arched closer to his hand, needing his touch deep and hard. He complied.

He stroked her, his breathing as ragged as hers, and she felt that sweet tension pull tighter and tighter deep inside.

"Joe," she gasped.

"God, you go off like a firecracker," he said gruffly. "I love that. I want to make it happen over and over."

She didn't have enough breath to tell him that actually she *didn't* go off fast usually, but she opened her eyes and saw the stark hunger as he rubbed his thumb over her clit and she did go off. And saw fireworks.

The tremors of pleasure weren't even close to quiet when he moved his hands to undo his own pants.

Phoebe realized she still had her fingers tucked into the front of his jeans.

"Let me." She slid her fingers farther into the denim, coming into contact with the silky head of his erection.

Joe sucked in a quick breath. "Phoebe—"

"Yeah, there's no running away this time," she said softly, sliding in along the hot length. "I'm as spooked as you are about all of this, but it isn't going away, and as you've probably noticed, I'm a pretty upfront person."

She tugged, bringing him close and allowing her hand to sink farther into the warm denim and cotton encasing the mouthwatering firmness she couldn't wait to have fully exposed.

Joe crowded in, bracing his hands on the truck behind her. He certainly didn't seem to be planning his escape. In fact, he pressed his cock into her hand and groaned.

"I have noticed that about you, actually."

She grinned. "So, I vote for doing this since we both want it."

"Well, if *this* is me having a chance at every inch of your sweet body, then hell, yeah, I'm on board."

Phoebe laughed and warmth filled her that had nothing to do with where her hand was. She liked this guy, and yeah, they *had* to do this.

"You're overdressed—again," she said. "I'd help you get out of these jeans, but my hand is pretty happy right here."

She wasn't sure how he got his shoes off or his jeans all the way off. There was some wiggling involved, but that just caused more rubbing between her hand and his cock, and she couldn't concentrate on anything beyond that. He was gorgeous. Hot, hard, heavy—three of her favorite adjectives when it came to this kind of thing—and she couldn't wait to put all of that glory to good use.

"Phoebe." Joe was breathless and she glanced up to find his jaw tight and his eyes hot.

"Yeah?"

"How do you feel about sex against a truck?"

"If it's with you, this truck and right now, I'm all for it."

Joe quickly swept her panties down her legs and lifted her leg. "Then move your hand."

She gave him another long stroke and a squeeze that

caused him to hiss softly and then got her hand out of the way. His eyes locked on hers, he lifted a condom package to his mouth, ripped it open with his teeth and slid it on all in under five seconds.

She was impressed.

"How can it possibly feel like this is long overdue?" he asked. "We just met."

She couldn't answer because she had no answer for the crazy notion—that she felt just as strongly—and because he fit his cock against her entrance and surged upward at the same moment.

They gasped together and then groaned. Every cell in her body seemed to start to dance. "This is way better than Paris," she said.

Joe chuckled.

He couldn't believe it. He was buried deep in the sweetest, hottest body he'd come across in as long as he could remember, but the mouth that came with it wouldn't stop.

He liked it.

Not just how wet she was, how great she sounded, how soft her skin was or how delicious her lips were, but *her*. Her humor, her sweetness, how she'd said *he* was driving her crazy. They were standing in a field in the country outside of Sapphire Falls, Nebraska, and she was still crazy about him. He didn't need Paris or Monaco to get on Phoebe's good side. He was enough. Which felt humbling and unbelievable and fricking great all at the same time.

He slowly pulled out, loving the feel of her inner muscles trying to hold him in, and then pressed in again. "You've never been to Paris," he said, watching her breathe raggedly as he stroked long and slow and deep.

"And I don't want to go if it doesn't feel like this." She

dug her fingers into his shoulders as he surged deeper.

"We could do this in Paris," Joe told her, deciding in that moment to make love to Phoebe in every country in the world at least once.

She tipped her pelvis and went up on tiptoe on the foot that still touched the ground. When he stroked in again, he hit a spot that made her say, "*Yes.*" So he did it again.

"It wouldn't really be fair to Paris," she said, somehow using the truck behind her butt for leverage and getting even closer.

"What wouldn't?" Joe asked, trying to concentrate on the conversation—he was having a *conversation* during sex—while also trying to angle just right to get up against her clit when he stroked in again.

"Doing this there," she said. She moaned as he came very close to her clit that time. "Because I'd love it for sure then, but it would have nothing to do with Paris itself."

He gave up and just reached between them, finding her sweet spot with his middle finger.

"Yes," she gasped. She tightened her pelvic muscles and he gasped. "See? We could do this at the circus and I'd suddenly love clowns," she said, moving her knee higher somehow and pressing her heel into his ass to pull him closer.

"Clowns?" he asked, a little lost.

"I hate clowns."

"I've never understood that phobia."

"I wouldn't call it a phobia. I just think they're weird."

And suddenly, Joe stopped thrusting and looked into her face. Her curls were wild, her breathing was choppy, her bare breasts rubbed against his chest. He was inside her—as close as two people could get physically—and they were talking about the circus.

"Are we talking about clowns?" he asked.

"No. We're complimenting your ability to even make me like clowns with your sexual prowess." She wiggled her hips, trying to resume the action.

He gripped her hips with both hands, fully intending to be in charge here.

"I appreciate the compliment," he said. "But the clown thing is a little creepy."

"See? They're weird."

"Not the clowns themselves," he said, torn between wanting to laugh and growl. "*Talking* about clowns during *sex*."

"Oh." She wiggled again with one of her naughty grins. "Well, you haven't made me so breathless that all I can do is moan or say 'yes' or 'harder'."

His eyes narrowed as she turned those words back on him. He should definitely tie her up. With a little growl, he thrust hard and deep. "We better fix that." He thrust again. "Because you're driving me nuts."

Her eyes closed again and her mouth was in a perfect O with only uneven breaths coming faster and faster as he moved in her.

Finally, she whispered, "Faster." Her pelvis, thighs and arms all tightened around him.

Oh, he gave her faster. And a few minutes later, she wasn't saying anything except his name—on a long, loud cry as she came.

He was right behind her, losing himself in her in the hardest, most satisfying orgasm he'd ever had.

She slumped between him and the truck a moment later, and he gently let her down until both her feet were on the ground again. They worked on catching their breaths as they leaned against the truck. It occurred to Joe that he should possibly be worried about mosquitos—or other bigger wildlife with bigger bites.

"Should we get in the truck?"

Phoebe pushed her hair back from her face and gave him a big smile. "You worried about those meat-eating raccoons?" she asked.

He picked up her clothes and tossed them at her. "Raccoons do eat meat."

She laughed. "I know."

"Well, I'm meat."

She laughed harder. "You're *big* meat though. They won't mess with you."

"Well, thank you. Now get in the truck."

Still giggling, she pulled her shirt and panties on and climbed up into the cab. Watching her ass wiggle and her braless nipples press against the soft shirt, he figured she wouldn't have them on much longer anyway and followed her in after pulling his jeans on.

As he nudged her over and took a seat on the passenger side, she said, "You know, it wasn't that long ago you were trying to get me *out* of the truck."

"And look how much you liked that. You should probably just do whatever I say all the time."

She faced him on the seat, tucking her feet up under her. "You got it right earlier—I do go gung ho, full speed ahead."

He reached for a half empty water bottle in the cup holder. "I know. You definitely need to be tied up."

As he drank he noticed that she was watching him closely, barely moving, certainly not talking.

He lowered the bottle and looked at her. "You okay?" Was she afraid he'd do something like tie her up without her wanting it? They were out in the country, very alone, with no chance of anyone coming along. A thought occurred to him. "Hey, you wouldn't come out here like this with anyone else? Anyone you didn't know really well? Right?"

She shook her head. "Never."

His protectiveness toward her felt natural, but he recognized it was strange.

"Have you tied women up before?"

He glanced at her sharply. Was she scared? She didn't

sound scared. She sounded…he wasn't sure.

He reached over and turned the interior light on.

She frowned and blinked at him. "Hey."

"You're not scared, are you?"

"Of what?"

"Me. Me tying you up."

She shook her head quickly. "Of course not."

"I'm a stranger."

"But—"

"A stranger takes you out in the country late at night and starts talking about tying you up? You *should* be scared."

"But it's *you*."

"You need to be careful."

"I am careful."

"And suspicious."

"I'm not suspicious of *you*."

"You should be—"

"I'm turned on."

That stopped him. "Huh?"

"I'm turned on thinking about you tying me up in bed."

His body shifted gears before his brain did. He wanted to tie her up. He'd played with it only a couple of times but had enjoyed it. And with Phoebe he almost *had* to do it.

He wanted her spread out, at his mercy, needing him. He wanted to make it all about her, to possess her and do something she'd remember forever. That would take a lot of trust on her part, and the idea of having that from her was as much a turn-on as anything else.

A wound up, loud, fast-talking girl like Phoebe needed to slow down, to take her time and enjoy, to let someone else focus on her and her pleasure. Of course, that couldn't be just any guy. It had to be someone who—

No, it had to be him. Period.

"We're doing that," he said decidedly, wishing they could go to Mason and Adrianne's right then. He had a ton of neckties they could put to good use.

Phoebe's eyes brightened. "Really?"

"Why would I possibly *not* mean it?"

"Well, just in case that's not your thing."

"Honey, I think everything with you is my thing."

She grinned widely. "*That* is a really good answer."

She scooted close and climbed onto his lap, straddling his thighs. "I have scarves at my house and my house is about a half mile from here."

But even a half mile seemed too far. "That will have to be the third time tonight." He cupped her ass in his hands.

"Third? What do you—oh," she said as he pressed her against his already-rejuvenated erection.

She wiggled deliciously and bent to kiss him just as her phone rang.

"Ignore it," he muttered.

"Okay."

But then his phone rang.

They pulled back, glanced at the phones that sat side by side on the dash and then at each other.

"Adrianne and Mason?" Phoebe asked.

"Coincidence?" he asked.

They both reached at the same time.

The ringing had stopped but Phoebe said, "Missed call from Matt."

Joe read his display. "Nadia." They looked at each other. They were the best friends. They were the first ones Matt and Nadia would call with big news.

"They got engaged," Phoebe said.

Joe nodded. "Probably."

"Over the phone?"

"Maybe Skype?"

"He couldn't wait?"

Joe frowned at Phoebe's frown. Considering what had just happened between *them* and the confession that *he* drove her nuts, was she really that broken up over Matt and

Nadia?

"I guess that's kind of romantic, isn't it?" Phoebe slid off his lap.

Joe's frown turned to a scowl. "Maybe."

Then her phone beeped with a text message. The next second, Joe's chimed with a voice message.

Phoebe read the text out loud. "*Need to talk.*" She frowned. "Well, that's just great."

She didn't sound happy. Maybe she was annoyed about being interrupted too.

"You don't want to hear the news?" Joe asked.

"I don't really want to hear all about the big proposal in person. Then I have to try to smile through it."

"Why would you have to *try* to smile?"

"He's going to expect his best friend to be happy for him."

Yeah. Nadia would expect the same from him and—well, he wasn't quite as disappointed as he would have been a few days ago. Damn, this was complicated.

He looked at Phoebe. Her face was illuminated by her phone in the dark truck as she texted something back to Matt. Her breasts pressed against the soft fabric of the shirt, her bare legs were tucked under her again and her hair was loose and unruly around her face.

She looked adorable.

"What if I asked you to go to Paris again?"

She looked up quickly, her thumbs poised over her keypad. "What?"

"Paris. Let's go."

Her eyebrows rose. "Thought we established that I'm already wowed."

"Which is exactly why I want to take you," he said honestly. "I've never been just for fun, relaxed, been able to enjoy. I've always been working."

"Working?" Her hands and phone went to her thighs, her full attention on him.

"Working to impress, to distract whoever I'm with from what they left behind." For fear the regrets would set in sooner versus later.

Phoebe tipped her head, studying him. "You've always picked women who had a lot to leave behind, huh?"

Joe felt like he should shift or avert his eyes or something when she looked at him so directly, like she knew something he didn't. But he met her gaze. "If jobs and scholarships and fiancés and weddings are a lot to leave behind."

"You made a woman miss her *wedding*?" Phoebe demanded.

"First, I didn't force her onto that plane," Joe said. "Second, it was her friend's wedding. And she wasn't maid of honor or anything."

Phoebe was staring at him, mouth open.

"She had a good time," Joe felt the need to add.

"Where does this come from?" Phoebe finally asked. "I mean, you're an intelligent guy. How do you not realize that this is not normal behavior and that there must be some motivation behind it other than having a good time?"

Of course he knew that. He was intelligent. Regardless of how he acted sometimes.

"Why do you have to be so important to a woman that she loses her mind and makes you the focus of her attention—even if it's only temporary?" Phoebe pressed.

"My dad."

"Your dad?" she repeated. "You think this is genetic?"

Joe sighed. It seemed so, but he knew better. "Role models. My grandpa and dad have been seducing and sweeping women off their feet as long as I've known them."

"Why?"

"My grandmother and grandfather were more or less an arranged marriage, and she has *never* been impressed by him," Joe said, offering the only explanation he'd been able to come up with himself. Of course, watching his grandparents together, it seemed crystal clear. His grandmother wasn't just indifferent to his grandfather, she was downright critical. He could never do anything right. "Finally, he gave up and looked to other women as a way to stroke his ego and prove that he did have something to offer."

Frankly, his grandmother was a witch, and Joe avoided spending time with her as much as possible. Her criticisms weren't reserved only for her husband.

"What about your mom?" Phoebe looked fascinated.

He smiled. It was bizarre. "She was, and is, incredibly independent. My dad grew up watching his father and was a master at romance as well. But my mom was a challenge. He had to really work at it. But once he won her over, it was almost like his interest was gone too. Of course, by then she was pregnant with me, so they got married and stayed together. But he hasn't changed. He still flirts and romances and seduces, and she's so wrapped up in her work and volunteering that she doesn't seem to mind."

"And that's your thing too?" Phoebe asked.

He couldn't deny it. "When you woo a woman who can't be or doesn't want to be wooed it's even more—"

"Of a stroke to your ego?" she supplied.

"Something like that," he admitted.

"So your dad does it too—the whole charm and money and romance thing? Because your mom isn't all wrapped up in him?"

Joe shrugged. "That's how I explain it."

"But your grandma and mom stay with them?"

He nodded. "Another mystery I've pondered long and hard. Grandma probably stays for the money and social status. She's a piece of work. Mom stayed for us initially. I don't know why she stays now, but she doesn't seem unhappy."

Phoebe frowned. "The whole thing is nuts, you know."

"I know."

Her phone beeped again and she glanced down.

He was sure it was Matt again. Well, screw him, Joe had her right now. "Phoeb—"

"That's why you want me, you know," she said, looking up.

His chest tightened. He did want her. But this didn't sound good. "What do you mean?"

"Because I have a lot to give up." She glanced at the phone again. "Even just for a quick trip to Paris."

No. That wasn't what this was about. Joe gritted his teeth. That *probably* wasn't what this was about.

His phone beeped with a text as well. He looked down. *Are you there?*

"Nadia?" Phoebe asked.

"Yeah."

Phoebe bit her bottom lip and he clenched his phone tighter in his hand.

"Listen to the voice mail," Phoebe finally said. "See what's going on."

Joe took a deep breath. "If they're engaged, will you go to Paris with me?"

It was less to leave behind, he figured, if Matt had taken the plunge. She'd then be free of the what-ifs. Unless she intended to still try to break them up...

"Yes."

Her soft answer made his heart thump. "Yes to Paris?"

She nodded. "Yes to Paris...with you."

His eyes locked on hers, Joe lifted his phone, punched in the code for his voicemail and waited, holding his breath.

"Joe." Nadia's voice sounded hoarse. "Call me. I need to talk to you. I don't think I want to live in Sapphire Falls. Being in Haiti again has showed me...well, a lot of things. Sapphire Falls is too...a lot of things too. Something. I don't know." She sniffed and Joe realized she was crying. "I need to talk to you. Matt and I broke up. Please call me."

Slowly, Joe brought the phone away from his ear and pressed the end button.

"What is it?" Phoebe leaned in, clearly concerned by the look on his face.

The scent of green apples wafted to his nose, and his gut—and his heart—clenched.

"They broke up."

Phoebe's eyes widened. "They...broke up?"

Joe nodded.

"Oh."

Yeah. Oh.

Phoebe watched Matt tip back another shot of tequila. It was his fourth. Not that she was counting. Not that she was remembering him streaking down Main Street the last time he'd had tequila. Not that she didn't understand the need for a good shot of tequila once in a while.

"A year," Matt said. "A frickin' *year*. That's...so long."

Phoebe blew out a long breath. A year was a long time, especially when it was how long Matt's fiancée wanted to live in Haiti—potentially without him.

"She's doing important work, Matt," Phoebe offered.

"Of course she is." He stared sullenly at his beer. "But she's doing some of it from here now. Why can't she keep that up? Or go to Haiti, that's great, but how about like a month at a time? Mason said that was possible."

Phoebe sighed. She had so many conflicting emotions swirling right now that she had no idea what to say. Matt was upset and he was her friend. Of course she cared about that. But she couldn't help being distracted by the fact that Joe was on the computer at Mason's, Skyping with Nadia.

She'd dropped him off on her way to meet Matt at the Come Again, specifically so he could get a hold of Nadia. Beautiful brainy Nadia. Who was in a third-world country working to save lives.

Yeah, *that* was helping her mood and confusion. She forced herself to focus on Matt. "What did you say when she told you?" Phoebe asked.

"I told her not to go. That I loved her. That I want to get married."

"And she said?"

"To come with her. That she loves me too, wants to get married but wants to take this chance in Haiti. She wants me to go with her."

"And?"

"Come on, I can't do that. I'm the football coach. What about teaching? I can't take a year off."

Phoebe chewed on her bottom lip, debating the wisdom of ordering a tequila shot for herself. This was the perfect opportunity, what she had been hoping for since Matt had showed her Nadia's engagement ring. They'd broken up. They had a very real conflict. Phoebe could easily side with Matt and assure him that they could never make it work. Nadia was a brilliant scientist. The world needed her. She should go to Haiti.

But for the life of her, Phoebe was thinking of Joe hearing this same story. Sure, it was Nadia's perspective but that didn't matter. The bottom line was that Nadia and Matt were going in different directions suddenly. Matt wanted to stay in the quiet, simple, familiar life of Sapphire Falls. The life Phoebe wanted. While Nadia wanted to up and move to another country.

Then there was Joe. Joe who wasn't opposed to packing a suitcase and flying off at a moment's notice. Who made a habit of it, in fact. Sure, Haiti wasn't exactly the posh location he was used to, but he was clearly a bit of an adventurer. Besides, with a private plane he could easily go back and forth between DC and Haiti. And being up close and personal with the biggest project his company was involved with currently would look great when he walked into the president's office.

Phoebe raised a hand to signal the waitress. When Tina looked her way, Phoebe held up two fingers.

"So what should I do?" Matt asked, looking miserable.

He reached for one of the two shot glasses Tina set down. Phoebe grabbed it from him and tipped it back quickly, then followed it with the other.

She might not be saving the world one starving village at a time, but she could hold her own in any drinking game. She was quite a catch.

She focused on her friend. The man she had thought she was going to spend her life with. The man who had the same background and the same future that she did.

"You love her?" she asked.

"Of course. I mean, I think so."

"Why?"

Matt frowned at her. "What do you mean *why*?"

"Come on, Matt, why do you love her?"

"I love her because when we're together I feel good…right…unlike I do any other time or with any other person. I feel hopeful and happy and excited. Does that make sense?"

He'd had her at the word good. She knew what he meant, because she had felt that too.

"So how are you going to feel about her being in Haiti, while you're here alone? You won't feel good, or right, or hopeful."

Matt nodded. "I know." He looked like someone had taken his puppy away. Heartbroken—Matt's expression was the definition of the word. "So what do I do?"

"I think we have to get you two back together."

Phoebe shook her head as she heard her voice say the words. She was going to help get the guy she thought she wanted to marry back together with Brainiac Barbie.

"I'll have to move to Haiti."

"Haiti would probably be good for you," Phoebe said.

"You've never been to another country. The farthest you've been from Sapphire Falls was the Grand Canyon when you were eleven."

"So? You've never been out of the country. You've never even been to the Grand Canyon."

Well, maybe that was about to change.

"I've been thinking—there's a big old world out there beyond Sapphire Falls. Maybe we both need to see some of it."

Matt blinked a few times and then leaned in. "There's something different about you." He frowned. "You look really good."

"Uh, thanks." She'd barely had time to pull her hair back and put on lip gloss after being sexed up at the river by Joe.

"Yeah. You look...relaxed. Or something."

She did feel a lot less anxiety about the whole Matt-and-Nadia thing, that was for sure.

And if she thought about the sexing, her whole body got warm and soft.

"And you're kind of glowy," Matt said, as if confused.

She blushed at that. Post-coital glow? Still? Possible. The sex had certainly been good enough to have a lasting effect.

Matt lifted his hand and tucked a stray curl behind her ear. "Yeah," he said. "You're all really glowy."

Matt's thumb lingered against her cheek. She stared at him. He was looking at her lips.

Matt was touching her cheek and looking at her lips.

Subconsciously, she licked them. To her utter amazement, his mouth opened slightly as she did it. He took a deep breath and then leaned in.

Oh. Crap.

Matt was going to kiss her. In the Come Again. Where everyone would see. He had broken up with Nadia, so was technically single. But still...oh, crap.

She fought the urge to stop him. It was a kiss. And she was curious. It wasn't an engagement or anything.

Except that it would be for them. They'd been friends for too long. If something happened that didn't typically happen between them—and kissing definitely fell into that category—it would be noticed and would have to mean something.

Oh, boy. Stopping a near kiss was also big. She would never have another chance with Matt if she stopped their first kiss.

At the last second, she put her hand up in front of his mouth.

Lips against the pads of her fingers, he blinked at her.

Having her fingers against Joe's lips would have made her tingle clear to her toes. With Matt, she just felt a lump in her stomach.

"You're in love with Nadia," she reminded him.

He mumbled something behind her fingers. She moved them and he leaned back. "And drunk," he said.

She nodded.

He just looked at her for a long moment. "I still think we should do it," he said.

"Kiss?"

"Yes."

"Why?" Her heart did trip a little though. She'd thought about it, of course. She was attracted to him. If she wasn't, she wouldn't have considered him a potential husband. There had to be a spark. She knew that, felt strongly about it actually.

"We want the same life," he said. "Don't we owe it to ourselves to see how this feels before we both take a huge plunge into a new life?"

Hmm. That made a bit of sense. Of course, she'd had two shots of tequila.

"How about we try this again after a few hours of sleep and some coffee?" If it still made sense tomorrow, she'd try it. Though she wasn't sure why she wasn't a little more excited about the idea.

Matt sighed. "Fine."

"I'll walk you home," she said. He'd had considerably more to drink than she had and the walk would help sober her up too. She'd probably need to call Adrianne for a ride, but at least her head would be clearer.

"Okay." Matt shoved his chair back and stood.

Surprised by his easy agreement, she stood and pulled her purse strap up on her shoulder and followed Matt to the door.

They stepped out into the night and immediately Matt grabbed her arm, spun her to face him and kissed her.

Okay, she'd give him points for style. That was smooth. And he was a good kisser. He moved his mouth over hers, cupped and held her jaw in his hand and everything about it was good.

Except he wasn't Joe.

She pulled back. They both took a deep breath.

Then Matt said, "Very nice."

Nice. Yes, it was nice. She nodded. "Yeah."

"Do you want to do it again?"

Moment of truth. Right now, Joe was talking to Nadia, hearing about her desire to stay in Haiti, probably thinking about what an adventure that would be. Everything that had broken Nadia and Matt up would be a non-issue for Joe. He could be all she wanted.

He might be in the midst of making those plans and promises even as they spoke.

Phoebe had spent years thinking Matt was her perfect match.

She'd just met Joe.

Excuse after excuse tripped through her mind, but she still came back to, "No, I don't think so."

"Okay." Matt stepped back. "Probably a good idea."

It definitely probably was.

"It was nice though," Matt said again.

She looked up into the face she'd looked for that first day of swimming lessons when she'd been terrified, the face she'd searched for in the crowd at their college graduation, and the face she'd most needed to see at her grandmother's funeral.

Matt was her best friend.

If things were awkward now, she'd kill him.

"Nice. Yeah. So what?" she asked. "Chocolate chip cookies are nice too. But you know they're not my favorite."

"Monster cookies," he said immediately.

"Yep. Oatmeal, peanut butter, chocolate chips and M&Ms. The works."

Matt tucked his hands into his front jeans pockets. "So does he have the works?"

Her eyes widened at that. "He who?"

Matt laughed. "Give me a break, Phoeb. Joe Spencer. Does Joe have—and give you—the works?"

She stared at her friend. He knew her well. Really well. But he hadn't been around her and Joe. "Why do you ask?"

"He punched me."

"Yeah."

"We were talking about you."

"What about me?"

"He thinks I'm scaring off the other guys in town who want to date you."

Phoebe didn't know where to start with her questions to *that*. "There are other guys who want to date me?"

Matt looked amused and a little sad at the same time. "Of course there are. Lots. But none of them are good enough for you."

Phoebe crossed her arms and narrowed her eyes. "You're in charge of who I date?"

"I'm in charge of who asks you out."

"So you *have* been scaring them off."

"Yes."

"But…"

He waited, one eyebrow up.

"You shouldn't have," she finally muttered.

"Who from Sapphire Falls are you crazy about and actually are pissed to have missed out on?"

"It's not that." And she couldn't come up with a name anyway. "You were meddling."

"You deserve the best. First, if the guy is easily dissuaded, he's not for you. Second, you would have settled. You love it here. You want to live in Sapphire Falls your whole life, and you would have settled for a guy from here just for that."

Phoebe had to swallow hard after that. Settle? That felt…sad. But could she argue with it? Not when she was looking at the guy she'd been planning to settle with. Matt was good-looking, charming, fun, but most of all, he wanted to spend his life in Sapphire Falls.

"I know you," Matt said after a moment. "If you'd really wanted any of the guys here, you'd have had them, my influence or not."

That felt…true.

She nodded. "Okay. You're probably off the hook. I need to think about all of that, but I probably forgive you."

"So back to my question," Matt said. "Is Joe a monster cookie?"

Phoebe started nodding immediately. "Yeah, I think he is."

"Do you think Nadia thinks he is?" Matt asked.

Now there was a good question. "I don't know how she couldn't. But I might be biased."

"Let's hope he's only sharing his M&Ms with you."

She smiled but her chest hurt. She *might* be biased. But Joe had some damned amazing M&Ms. And most women—maybe even Nadia would think they tasted even better in Monaco or some other exotic city. She, on the other hand, wanted his M&Ms as they were, right here in Sapphire Falls.

CHAPTER EIGHT

"How is country dancing in any way a substitute for scientific research in a third world country that could end world hunger?"

Her words sounded a lot like things he said to the secretary of state, Joe thought. There was no question that IAS was doing amazing, historic things that would change—already was changing the world. And Nadia was certainly part of that.

"It's not a substitute," he agreed. "But that doesn't make country dancing or the fact that you like it a bad thing. In fact—" He had to be careful here. Nadia was the woman he'd assumed would save him from himself. She was level-headed, from his world, aware of his flaws and faults. Plus, she was doing amazing things in Haiti—not just scientifically or agriculturally, but as a humanitarian. All of IAS's leaders were. They were involved. They held the hands of the Haitians, they spent time meeting and getting to know not just the government officials and aid workers they partnered with, but the people themselves— the ones who planted and harvested and directly benefited from the work they did in the lab and fields.

Joe knew all of this well. His job was partly PR. That meant being sure that the government, the media and the public knew all of the good things IAS was doing. And what they weren't doing. There was a lot of drama in the world about genetically modified organisms and part of Joe's job was to educate and answer questions about IAS and GMOs. It took patience and a lot of repetition to assure people that IAS was not involved in producing GMOs. And he texted or called Nadia whenever he got stuck in his explanations. She was always there for him.

Nadia had always been a great friend. Nadia knew where he was from, how his family worked, knew all about the private planes and other luxuries. She'd grown up with all of it too. And she'd shed it to become a world-renowned research scientist who was changing the world.

If he wanted to be a better man, she would be someone who could really help make that happen. If he needed someone to say no to him and his wild streak, she was the perfect one.

So why did his mind keep wandering to the redhead who said yes in such a delicious way?

The redhead who was, at that very moment, with Matt—her dream guy. The guy who knew her and who wanted the same things she did.

Phoebe and Matt were a great couple. They made sense. They'd be happy. She'd say yes to him too, because he'd ask her for all the things she wanted too.

Joe looked at his best friend on the computer screen. Even with thousands of miles between them, he knew she was sad. She had broken up with her almost-fiancé. This was the perfect chance to convince her she was right and that she and Matt were better off apart.

Instead, he was trying to figure out how to comfort Nadia and get back to Phoebe in the next two minutes. That was about as long as he could take it.

"Nad, I'm not good at this stuff."

She nodded. "I know. You're probably trying to think of something to buy me."

He pushed his coffee cup back. "I was specifically trying *not* to think of something to buy you."

"But that was your first instinct."

She knew him, so there was no point denying it. "Yeah."

"If the urge returns, I could use a new watch."

He chuckled. "You go for basic, practical watches." He really liked that about her. Fancy and shiny and sparkly didn't matter to Nadia. "I'll buy you one anyway. There's no wow factor, so it doesn't feed my addiction."

She smiled. "If I'm going to be married to you, I might have to change my tastes."

Joe felt his chest tighten. Married. Yep, they'd talked about doing that, hadn't they? In fact, he'd been the one to bring it up. "Ah, Nadia, don't change anything. You're the best."

She gave him a knowing smile. "And I'm not going to be married to you anyway, right?"

He shrugged. "I think your heart is already spoken for."

"It wasn't about hearts before."

No, it had been a friends-with-benefits proposal. The benefits had been all about keeping him out of trouble and her from being alone with her test tubes for the rest of her life, but it had been a win-win. And there would have been sex. Facing her now, he realized that he'd never really looked at Nadia that way, but she was definitely attractive. Things would have worked out fine.

If they hadn't fallen in love with other people.

"I guess things have changed," he finally said.

"Your heart is spoken for now too?"

It was somehow. It had happened fast, blindsided him really. But it had happened.

Nadia cocked her head to one side. "I've never seen you in love before."

"Nope."

"I've known you for a really long time."

"Yep."

"Hmm."

There was no hmm about it. "It's more of an *oh, fuck*."

"You're not happy about it?" She seemed surprised.

"Considering she's in love with someone else, no." At least he thought she was in love with someone else. He'd come to Sapphire Falls for another woman too, but he'd never assumed that he was in love with Nadia. He loved her, she was good for him, but it wasn't hot passion or even possessiveness that he felt for her. He was protective of her.

He wanted what was best for her. He wanted her to be happy. He enjoyed spending time with her. But he wasn't *in love* with her.

Not like he was very afraid he was with Phoebe.

With her it went beyond protective—it was possessive, she was *his*. He wanted to claim her. He wanted to be responsible for her happiness, to assure her that she was all he'd ever want or need.

Oh, fuck was absolutely the right response.

❧

"How can I get Matt to Haiti?" Phoebe asked, setting coffees in front of Lauren and Mason the next morning at Adrianne's shop.

Lauren looked up from the newspaper she'd been reading. "I'd recommend an airplane. Boats are slow."

"Har, har." Phoebe dropped into the chair next to Lauren. "Seriously. Could you use him there for something?"

"Matt wants to go to Haiti?" Mason asked, not looking up from the notebook he was scribbling in. "That seems strange."

Lauren picked the coffee up and sipped. "I think it's Nadia that wants him to go to Haiti."

"Oh, that makes sense then," Mason said, still writing. "I put her in charge of the soil project. She needs to be there."

Lauren rolled her eyes. "Right. So if someone thought that Matt and Nadia should be together, she would wonder how to make it work for Matt to go too."

Mason shrugged, his attention still seemingly on the numbers and symbols he was writing in his notebook. "Well, he could just go then. They need teachers. Joe could talk to Kate and get it set up."

Phoebe gripped her cup with both hands and tried not to

crush the cardboard.

Lauren nodded with a small smile at Phoebe. "That's right. *Joe* would be able to set all of that up with Kate, our contact with Outreach America. They handle all levels of personnel. Since he's our PR guy, we have him handle those interactions."

It occurred to Phoebe, as it did on a near weekly basis, that Lauren sure didn't look like what she would expect a world-renowned soil and water conservationist to look. In fact, Lauren's salon-perfect hair, manicured fingernails and designer clothes and shoes made her look like she spent a lot of time inside. Being pampered. Which she did, in spite of being a majority partner in a company that was a major influence in global agriculture, of all things.

Phoebe took a deep breath and then a sip of coffee. Her heart had been pounding ever since she'd gotten in her car to head over here. She'd known she'd find them here—Lauren and Mason met every morning at the shop to get their business done before Mason headed to the fields—and they were the ones who could make it possible for Matt to go to Haiti.

And while making her toast that morning, she'd decided she wanted him to do it.

For lots of reasons. For him—what she'd said last night about him not getting very far from home was true. Neither of them had really ventured outside of their comfort zones much. And for Nadia—she was doing wonderful things with Innovative Agricultural Solutions and she should absolutely continue that.

Phoebe couldn't make him go, of course, and she didn't exactly *want* him to go, but he was her best friend first and foremost, and as she'd lain awake until four a.m. that morning, she'd realized two important facts. One, the uncomplicated realization, was that she wanted Matt to be happy. Two, Nadia made him happy, Haiti made Nadia happy and so Haiti could make Matt happy too if he gave it a chance. That was the complicated one.

Now hearing that yes, Nadia needed to be in Haiti and yes, Matt could have work there too, Phoebe's heart was thumping so hard she almost couldn't breathe.

She was going to lose him. He'd be gone for months, across thousands of miles, with another woman. She was probably going to lose him for good.

Still, she said, "So Matt needs to talk to Joe," she said, almost choking on his name. "And Joe can get him set up?"

To leave Sapphire Falls for a country far away for twelve months.

It would be funny if Matt wasn't leaving to be with the woman Joe thought he wanted.

That made it less funny and more ironic.

"He can make the contacts and get the ball rolling," Lauren said. "Matt will have to interview, go through the background check and so on. But yeah, Joe can make Outreach aware that Matt's involved with us. That will act as a reference and definitely get him in the door. His experience and references from his teaching here will do the rest."

It was pretty much a sure thing. Phoebe realized that was what Lauren was telling her. It could happen. It *would* happen. If Matt wanted it to.

Phoebe swallowed a big gulp of coffee.

This was big, no doubt about it. It would be big for a lot of people—Matt, of course, his friends, family, students and Nadia.

Phoebe thought about the big gestures she'd been planning for Matt herself. A big gesture could really show someone he was special, worth an effort and extra thought. A big gesture was exactly what some people needed—both giving and receiving. Not Joe Spencer, of course. He was the king of the big gesture. He'd gestured for the wrong reasons and to the point it didn't mean anything anymore, and for the wrong people. But people like Matt, for whom things had always come relatively easily—putting forth some time and energy could be important.

She sighed, suddenly tired, not just from tossing and turning until the wee hours, but from trying to prove to one guy that he didn't have to try so hard while trying to convince another that he needed to step it up a bit. Or a lot.

"Do you really think he'll do it?" Lauren asked.

"He better. I can't have my project lead distracted, and Nadia definitely sounded distracted when I spoke to her," Mason said.

It was a little freaky how he could do heavy-duty scientific analysis while still following a completely unrelated conversation.

"He and Adrianne were getting it on in the kitchen a little bit ago, so he's got all kinds of stuff running through his head," Lauren said, smiling at the top of Mason's head with a combination of affection and exasperation.

Phoebe grinned. It was common knowledge among their friends that Adrianne was Mason's best muse. Often when they were getting sexy together, formulas or solutions would come to Mason and he'd have to stop to take notes.

"To answer your question," Phoebe told Lauren. "Matt needs to do this."

"Are you going to tell him that?"

She was going to have to. Who better to convince him than his best friend?

This whole thing was really getting out of hand.

"Don't worry. I think Haiti's gonna get one Brainiac Barbie and one Teacher Extraordinaire."

"This town really has its entertaining moments, you know that?" Lauren saluted with her coffee cup.

Yep, it really did. Phoebe just wasn't so sure this was one of them.

∞

Joe followed Adrianne through the swinging door that divided the back office from the front of her shop. There was a tiny kitchen too, but Adrianne preferred to do most of her candy making at home in the huge kitchen of the old farmhouse where she and Mason lived. He knew that both Mason and Lauren were out front as they were every morning. That was why he'd gone in through the back to talk to Adrianne.

Mason was hard to talk to because he really wanted to only talk about plants, and Lauren was a little intimidating frankly. Adrianne, on the other hand, was a nice balance. They'd become friends during their travels to Washington DC and other meetings needed to educate stakeholders in what IAS was doing. And she didn't think that him contacting Kate at Outreach America about Matt teaching with them in Haiti for the next year made Joe an asshole. Which was exactly what he'd wanted to hear.

No, sending an exceptional teacher to a poor country in desperate need of help of all kinds didn't seem like an asshole thing to do. But his motivations were less than pure and—surprise, surprise—his conscience did work after all.

He pulled up short as Adrianne moved out of his line of sight and he saw a bubbly redhead sitting at the table with his bosses.

She saw him immediately too.

She looked like she'd just swallowed her coffee wrong.

"Hi, Phoebe."

"Hi," she squeaked.

He smiled in spite of the chance that she'd possibly aspirated French roast into her lungs. Was it really just last night that he'd done her up against her truck at the river? Or had she done him? Either way, it had been too long since. He wanted her again. Now.

But he had to know what was going on with her and Matt. What, if anything, had happened last night? What had they talked about? Had Phoebe finally told Matt how she felt about him?

Surely not. It was nine a.m. If Phoebe Sherwood had confessed her undying love and devotion to *him*, she wouldn't be getting out of his bed for a good forty-eight hours.

Would she be pissed that Joe was instigating a plan to ship Matt off for a year? And worse, if he hung out with her while Matt was gone, would he ever know for sure if he was her consolation prize just because Matt was out of the picture?

He decided he really needed to know. Before he made a complete ass out of himself.

"I made contact with Outreach America. They need teachers in Haiti and they're interested in Matt," he said, moving around the front counter so he could get a closer look at Phoebe's face.

Her eyes widened. "How did you know about that?"

Well, that wasn't what he'd been expecting. "What do you mean?"

Phoebe looked at Lauren, who leaned back in her chair, crossed her legs and said, "Definitely entertaining at times."

He wasn't sure what that meant either, but he couldn't concentrate on Phoebe's words, how much he wanted to kiss her, how much he wanted her to not want Matt *and* what Lauren was saying all at once.

"We were just talking about seeing if Outreach America could help get Matt to Haiti. How did you know?"

He looked over at Adrianne with confusion. "You were already talking about that?"

She shook her head. "Not me. Must have been these three."

"Phoebe wants to get Matt to Haiti," Mason said, not bothering to look up from his notebook.

Joe focused on Phoebe. "*You* want to get Matt to Haiti?"

She pulled her bottom lip between her teeth and nodded.

Joe's heart turned over in his chest. But he made himself calmly lean against Adrianne's front counter and cross his arms. "But that would mean Matt and Nadia would be together."

"I know," Phoebe said.

"And that's okay with you?"

She nodded. "Yes."

Joe cleared his throat instead of blurting out *let's go get naked.* But he still thought it and needed a couple of seconds to reroute his thoughts. "Did you tell him…everything?" he asked.

Maybe she and Matt had done the heart-to-heart-thing last night. Maybe it was over.

"I, um—" She frowned. "Everything?"

"How you feel?" Joe was certain that the two women in the shop knew about Phoebe's feelings and plans for Matt, and if Mason didn't know, he probably didn't care.

"About him?" she asked.

Joe glanced at everyone else. Adrianne was watching with fascination, Lauren with amusement, and Mason flipped to the next page in his notebook and kept writing. The make-out session with Adrianne that morning must have been a good one, Joe thought distractedly. Then he focused in on Phoebe again. "Yes. About him. That you're in love with him."

Phoebe's cheeks got pink but she raised her chin. "No, I didn't tell him that."

"Don't you think you should?" he pressed.

"Do *you* think I should?" Her eyes narrowed slightly.

Did he think she should let Matt know he could have her forever? Or at all? Hell, no. But…"Yeah," he said heavily. "You should take the chance to see what might happen before he's gone. You don't want to wonder what if." *He* also didn't want to wonder what if.

He wasn't sure that Sapphire Falls had enough vodka to get him through Matt realizing that he could have Phoebe and doing the obvious thing and marrying her before she changed her mind. But they did have Mary's booze. That stuff *might* be enough.

She shoved her chair back and stood. "Well, he kissed me and all I could think about was you, so I figured the "what if" was taken care of." She stomped to the trash can in the corner and threw her cup in.

By the time she spun toward the door, Joe had processed her words. He grabbed her arm as she reached for the handle. "He *kissed* you?"

"Yes." She met his gaze. "Did you hear the part about me thinking about you?"

"Yeah." He had.

"You sure?" she asked. "When he had his *lips* on me, I was thinking about *you*. Got it?"

Joe felt his heart try to turn again, but his chest was too tight. "Yeah."

"So I'm definitely okay with him going with Nadia."

"He *kissed* you," Joe said again. What the hell had they been talking about? Or doing? Where had they been? How much kissing had there been? Did she kiss him back? The thoughts rolled, unstoppable, through his mind.

"Yes," she said, exasperated. "How does that make *you* feel?" she said directly.

"Like punching him again." Hard. And repeatedly.

She looked at him for a few seconds before her mouth finally curled up. "Okay, that's better."

"Does Matt know about your paw prints?"

Her eyes widened. He heard a choking sound behind him that he assumed came from one of the girls, but he didn't take his eyes off of Phoebe.

"What paw prints?" Lauren asked.

So it was Adrianne who knew.

"She has three little cat paw prints tattooed on her inner

thigh," Adrianne said.

"Inner thigh?" Mason echoed.

Joe grinned. So there *were* things that could pull the genius out of his equations.

"Four actually," Joe said, watching Phoebe's cheeks get redder.

"Four prints?" Lauren asked.

"Yep."

There was a pause and Joe knew that Lauren was about to say…

"Damn, that's hot."

"It is," he agreed. Then he bent his knees to stare directly into Phoebe's eyes. "Does Matt know about them?"

"He knows about them," she said. "But he's never seen them."

Joe let out a relieved breath. "So I only want to punch him for kissing you."

She gave him the biggest, most surprising smile he'd ever seen. Then she stretched up on tiptoe and kissed him.

After only about a minute, she started to pull back, but Joe cupped the back of her head and the warm silky strands of hair curled around his fingers as if to hold on to him. He tipped her head and deepened the kiss, gratified when he felt her press closer to him, chest to toes.

He lost himself in the taste, feel and smell of her for another minute that was completely satisfying and much too short at the same time. Then the door to the shop opened, bumping Phoebe from behind and startling her enough to break the kiss.

"There you are," Hailey said, stepping through the door with a frown at Phoebe. "You ready?"

Joe leaned in before Phoebe could answer her. "What was that kiss for? I want a repeat later."

She grinned. "For wanting to punch someone for me. No one's ever done that before."

Dammit. He pulled back, making himself maintain his smile. This woman should have men slugging each other constantly. "Can I punch just anyone, or does it need to be Matt to get another one of those kisses?" He'd happily punch Matt, but there were clearly other idiot guys in Sapphire Falls, and he might run into one before he saw Matt.

She laughed and he felt some of his tension ease as he smiled back.

"You don't need to actually punch anyone. It's the thought that counts."

"Then you should be all over me. I'm wanting to punch people kind of regularly around here."

She gave him a quick peck on the cheek and then said in his ear, "I'm happy to get all over you."

Heat surged through him and he grabbed her hand, intent on heading straight for her truck, then her house, then her bed.

"Hold on there, Slick," Hailey said, stepping in front of him. "I need her."

"Ditto."

Hailey smiled but shook her head. "Festival starts tonight. Phoebe's setting up the haunted house."

Phoebe groaned softly. "That's right. I am."

"The haunted house?" Joe asked. "It's not Halloween."

"It's festival tradition," Hailey said firmly. "And it's going to take all day."

Joe felt Phoebe's hand slip from his. "It's true."

"I'll help. It'll take half the time." And he knew exactly how he intended to spend the other half.

"We have to get to the fields," Mason said behind him.

Joe looked back to see Mason closing his notebook and rising.

Sure, *now* he pulled his nose from his book. Dammit.

"I'll see you later," Phoebe said when she heard Joe's low frustrated growl. "And I'll let you in on *all* the festival traditions."

She said it with just enough flirtatiousness in her tone that Joe looked down. "Yeah?"

"There's the Ferris wheel, the haunted house and then Klein's Hill."

"The haunted house is my favorite," Mason said.

The look he gave Adrianne and her resultant giggle gave Joe a pretty good idea why.

Oh, yeah, Joe was going to learn every one of Sapphire Falls' goofy traditions. And he was definitely going to make Phoebe giggle like that.

"I'll see you later," he told her with promise.

"Definitely." She said it breathlessly.

He was also going to hear more of that breathlessness. A lot more.

৩৯৶

It was the longest, most frustrating day Joe had had at work to date. And it had nothing to do with the work he was doing. Or, to be more specific, the work he was *watching.*

Mason Riley had a thing about people messing with his plants.

Which was fine. Joe wasn't a scientist, and after he'd stepped on a seedling whose net worth was around three thousand dollars on the very first day, he'd stayed far out of Mason's way.

But he was still observing, watching how the team worked together, watching them getting their hands dirty, listening to their strange scientific language and noting the smiles that said they loved what they were doing.

In fact, he was working on an article he hoped to get the Associated Press interested in and taking photos of the group in action. It really was fascinating.

Joe had heard Adrianne describing the work and the

team and had found it interesting even through her eyes, but experiencing it in person was amazing.

The group was made up of some of the most brilliant scientific minds in America and some local farmers who had been born, raised and intended to die within a twenty-mile radius.

But they talked and laughed and worked alongside one another like lifelong friends who had everything in common. Kind of. That was the most interesting part. To look at the group, he couldn't have pointed out the scientists from the farmers. They were all dressed in blue jeans, T-shirts and work boots. Dirty blue jeans, T-shirts and work boots. But if he was close enough to listen to them talk, he knew who was who within a few words.

The scientific team used terms like dimethylformamide and alpha-helix-hydrogen bonding that made the farmers laugh and shake their heads. The farmers told lewd jokes that made the scientists laugh and shake their heads. It was a beautiful thing.

But doing only observations gave Joe more opportunities for his thoughts to wander.

They always wandered to Phoebe, but today was worse than usual.

Phoebe wanted Matt to go to Haiti. She'd thought of Joe as she'd kissed Matt. That was something.

Something big, he'd like to think.

But there was still a nagging doubt at the back of his mind. He couldn't quite put his uncertainty into words, but there was something holding him back from being completely ecstatic as he drove into town for the first night of the big Sapphire Falls Annual Festival later that night.

He was going to see Phoebe and he felt like a teenager heading for his first date. He welcomed the excited, jittery feelings though. He hadn't felt this way about a woman in a long time. For him, it was usually about making a major impression on the woman, thinking about how she would feel and react, not so much about how *he* felt about things or a matter of his being excited about their plans.

Tonight he was excited about Phoebe. The evening was in her hands. She was in charge. That alone was completely unusual for him. He was always in control. But this was her turf, her traditions, and he was looking forward to every second.

There were so many people in town that he drove eight blocks from the town square before finding a parking spot along the curb. As he walked back toward the lights and noise, he noticed how peaceful Sapphire Falls was. The sidewalks were lit by old-fashioned street lamps and those were muted by the leaves of the big, established trees that lined the streets. Many of the houses had their front porch lights on as well, casting warm, welcoming glows onto the perfectly trimmed lawns surrounded by—no kidding—white-picket fences.

A dog approached one of the fences. He, or she, didn't bark but stood wagging its tail and watching Joe pass. Joe imagined the animal had learned that from its humans who probably sat on the porch swing and watched the neighborhood go by.

It was a nice town. But he found that he actually preferred the country. The full dark, the quiet, the wide open spaces. Like at Phoebe's place.

Phoebe.

Joe picked up his pace.

The lights and noise grew steadily as he approached the center of town.

The Sapphire Falls Annual Festival was…something. By festival or county fair standards, it was small, but judging by the excitement level of the people who lived in Sapphire Falls—and for ninety miles in all directions—it was the best thing since Mary and Tex Borcher had turned innocent strawberries into Booze.

Everyone had turned out. Young and old, male and

female, rich and not-as-rich—all walks of life, all social ranks, just *all.*

The town square was packed with people and booths offering everything from homemade soy candles to Christmas ornaments to handcrafted hair accessories. The smell of kettle corn and funnel cakes and deep-fried-whatever-on-a-stick wafted on the light summer breeze, and Joe felt his own smile grow. This was a great way to spend a nice summer night. Only one thing, actually one *person*, could make it better.

He looked around, realizing that finding Phoebe was going to be more difficult than he'd anticipated. The haunted house seemed like the obvious place to start and was easy enough to spot, so he headed in that direction first.

The house was the big, old brown three-story that sat facing the square on one side.

It was complete with a wrought-iron archway over the long walk leading to the ten steps that climbed to the huge old porch. There were tall trees on all sides, the branches arching over the house and yard, casting creepy shadows—if that's what you wanted to see—and the roof had several sharp peaks and dark windows.

He knew that the house had once been a residence but was now used for a variety of things beyond playing haunted on Halloween and at festival time. It was a town museum of sorts and had several parlors that were used for teas, showers, parties and club meetings.

He wondered if there was a dark corner or two inside where he could pull Phoebe for a minute. Or several minutes. He had to get his hands on her again quick.

Halfway across the square, Joe spotted Matt. And he sighed. Matt was with a group of guys, several of whom Joe recognized, including three of the farmers he'd been observing in the fields earlier. He should touch base with Matt. He should ask if Kate from Outreach America had gotten ahold of him. He should offer to answer any questions Matt might have about the organization. And Matt would likely know exactly where to find Phoebe.

That last thought was what made Joe alter his course and head in the direction of the man he still kind of wanted to punch. Maybe if he didn't think about how Matt had kissed Phoebe the night before, the urge would lessen. Maybe.

But as he came up beside Phoebe's best friend, he really did still want to hit him.

She thought of you, he reminded himself. Which helped. In fact, part of him wanted to make sure Matt knew who Phoebe had been thinking of. But he resisted that and just smiled at all the men. "Hi, guys."

"Hey, Joe," several greeted.

Matt gave him a short nod.

"He's sure that he got her pregnant in there last year," Steve Greely said. Steve was one of the guys that had gotten involved with Mason's planting project from the minute Mason had decided to move it to Sapphire Falls.

"No way," Travis Bennett said. "Carly would never do it in the haunted house."

"That's what Wade said," Steve replied with a shrug. "Do the math, it works out."

"At least they're married," Drew said. "Renee Carter got pregnant at the festival two years ago and that was a major oops."

"Women get *pregnant* in the haunted house?" Joe asked.

"Well, not on purpose," Drew said with a grin. "But there's lots of hanky panky in the dark."

T.J. Bennett, Travis's brother, raised an eyebrow. "Who says hanky panky?"

"What should I call it?" Drew asked.

"Fucking, I s'pose," T.J. said easily. "That's what it is."

"In the haunted house?" Joe repeated.

"Oh, yeah. There's a tradition," Drew said.

This tradition thing was *quite* the tradition.

The look on his face made T.J. laugh. "Not of getting knocked up," he clarified. "But of getting frisky for sure."

"Frisky is better than hanky panky?" Drew asked.

"Well, let's face it, fucking is better than any of it." T.J. grinned and tipped back the can of soda he was drinking.

"The house has changed over the years," Steve said, tucking a hand into his front pocket. "I wasn't gettin' that far in the house in high school."

"Maybe that was just you," T.J. said. "Ever think of that?"

The other guys laughed. Steve scoffed. "Sure, you were getting laid in the haunted house in high school. Sure."

"I saved that for Klein Hill. More room to move around on those blankets than you can in those corners in the house," Travis inserted.

"You got *laid* on Klein Hill?" Tim Morton asked.

"You don't believe me?"

"I got to third base, but not laid," Tim said.

"I got a blowjob once," Drew added. "But yeah, not laid."

"Well, the girls were probably thrilled to go up there with me then," Travis said.

"Girls?" Drew asked. "Plural? No way."

"Three," Travis said. "But I'm not naming names, so don't even ask."

"Klein Hill?" Joe asked completely intrigued and a little lost at the same time.

"That's where we take our girls to watch the fireworks during the festival," Drew explained. "It's a tradition. You start on the Ferris wheel, then heat stuff up in the haunted house and then go for it on the hill."

"Except that clearly we don't all think of going for it the same way," Travis said. "There were obviously a lot of sexually frustrated girls around here. Wish I'd known you guys weren't delivering. I could have helped more of them out."

Steve laughed. "You think we were the ones pulling back?"

"I can tell you there weren't any girls pulling back when they were with me," Travis said.

"Me either," T.J. added.

"Bullshit," Drew finally said.

"Guess it's my word against yours," T.J. said.

Joe glanced at Matt who hadn't said a word so far. He was listening, but he clearly knew these stories. Joe looked at Drew. "The girls who got pregnant in the haunted house were in high school?"

Drew's eyes widened. "Oh, no, no. Carly's twenty-six or seven. She and Wade have been married for five years and already had a little boy."

"And Renee's probably twenty-three," Steve added. "That was an oops, but not *that* big of an oops. She was with her boyfriend and they're married now."

"So you all *still* take girls to the haunted house and the hill?" Joe asked. "You haven't outgrown that?"

Drew raised an eyebrow. "Who outgrows making out…and more?"

Okay, that was a decent point.

"Plus, it's such a nice tradition. We'd hate to break it up," Steve said with a chuckle. "Of course, the women are on to us now."

"They weren't on to you back then?" Joe asked, not believing that for a second.

Tim chuckled. "Well, they pretended not to be. That's part of the…"

Tradition Joe filled in mentally as Tim said it.

"It's all about sex?" Joe asked. "Wouldn't a couple shots of peach schnapps and some slow dancing at the Come Again do the same thing?"

Drew hooted at that. "I like you."

"The rest of the year, that's pretty much how it goes," Travis agreed with a grin. "But at festival time, there are new rules. It's nostalgic and different and fun. Once a year, a guy can use cotton candy and the Ferris wheel to show a girl how he feels, and it feels…sweeter or something."

"It softens the girls up," Steve agreed.

"But it's still about sex," Joe said. He needed to find Phoebe and the Ferris wheel ASAP.

"Not just that, actually," Drew said, looking around at the other guys. "I mean, yeah, sometimes it leads there. But it's a little bigger deal at festival time."

"What does that mean?"

"It means that we use peach schnapps and slow dancing the rest of the year," Matt said. "But we save the festival and the Ferris wheel for the special girl. The one we've been afraid to tell how we really feel. The one that we need a big gesture for. The one that's better than schnapps."

Joe turned to look at the other man. "You were going to propose to Nadia on the Ferris wheel, right?"

"Right."

Now that made sense.

And the look of sadness on Matt's face made Joe feel better about the call he'd made to Kate earlier.

A flash of red caught his eye and he immediately homed in on Phoebe moving through the crowd toward the cotton candy. He wanted to buy her cotton candy and yeah, definitely, get her on the Ferris wheel. She was dressed in a white sundress that he really wanted to see lying on his bedroom floor.

"Who took Phoebe through the haunted house in high school?" he asked the group. He wasn't sure if he'd want to hit the guy or shake his hand. Phoebe Sherwood was definitely better than schnapps.

The guys looked at one another and then glanced at Matt quickly before looking away.

"Um," was all Drew could offer.

211

"I'm not…" Steve started and then trailed off.

"I don't…" Even Travis, the lady killer, couldn't come up with anything.

Well, at least she hadn't been one of the three girls Travis had nailed on Klein Hill.

Though part of Joe—a very confused part that was making him stark-raving crazy—wished Travis had taken Phoebe up there and at least *tried* something.

Joe definitely hadn't missed the looks they all shot Matt. "Are you telling me that none of you wanted to take Phoebe to the haunted house or Klein Hill?"

Drew frowned. "Well, yeah, we wanted to."

Steve nodded.

"Hell, yeah, I would have taken her to the hill," Travis added.

Joe looked at Matt. The other man scowled at him.

Joe shook his head. "Unbelievable. And pathetic. A fantastic woman was right in front of you all these years and you all let Matt tell you what to do—or not do—about her?"

"But we…couldn't date her," Drew said, looking confused.

"Why not?" Joe asked. "Because your star quarterback wouldn't throw the ball to you in the championship game? Or because he'd punch you in the face? Or because he'd tell everyone that you still slept with a teddy bear? What did he possibly threaten you with that would be worth more than dating Phoebe?"

Travis looked even more confused than Drew. "What the hell are you talking about?"

"Matt kept you from dating Phoebe."

"Matt was *in love* with Phoebe," Steve said.

The words seem to hang in the air and Joe frowned as they sank in.

Joe turned slowly to face Matt. "What?"

Matt looked pissed. "I told the guys that I was in love

with her and that she and I would end up together. I didn't want any of my friends messing with her because I plan to have these friends for the rest of my life, and I didn't want to have to look at men who'd slept with my wife while we barbecue in my backyard."

Joe stared at him. "You were serious? You were in love with her and thought you'd end up together?"

Matt clenched his jaw and his fist and Joe braced for him to swing. "Yeah. So?"

"So why didn't you get together? She wanted you too."

"Not until about three years ago," Matt said. "And I didn't know it until a year ago."

"So then…"

"Nadia came to town."

Joe had no idea what to say. This was all still very complicated. More so actually. Then something occurred to him. "So you kept everyone else away from her so you could have her. Until a new girl came to town. Then you just…forgot about her?"

Matt's jaw clenched again. "Of course not."

"No. Right," Joe said, anger knotting his stomach as realization hit. "You were keeping her on the back burner. In case things didn't work out with Nadia. And then as soon as things fell apart, you kissed Phoebe to finally get that jump started and…she was thinking about another man."

Matt's eyes narrowed. "What the hell are you talking about?"

"She didn't climb all over you, did she?"

"That's none of your damned business."

"Well, it *is* my business that she was thinking about someone else, because it was *me.*"

Matt took a step forward and Joe held up a hand. "Oh, no. You don't get to be pissed about that. *You* chose Nadia. *You* didn't make a move on Phoebe in all the time you had with her. Forget it. It's over."

Matt gritted his teeth, but he didn't say anything.

Joe looked at the other men. "You hear that, guys? Matt doesn't have a claim on her anymore. There is an amazing single woman walking around here who deserves to be on that Ferris wheel and in that haunted house and up on that hill and Matt isn't going to say a fucking word about it."

Drew, Steve and Tim all stared at Joe, then their gazes swung to Matt, then back to Joe.

"What about you?" Travis asked Joe. "What are you gonna say about it?"

Joe sucked in a long breath. He was definitely wound up and needed to calm down. He'd called Matt off in front of the other guys. Phoebe would soon be aware of her fan club and that's the way he wanted it. She deserved that. She deserved the spotlight, the wooing, the guys competing for her attention.

So what was he going say about the others taking her on the Ferris wheel?

He wanted to warn them to be careful. To be damned sure that they were ready to be the men that Phoebe needed them to be. To be committed to making her happy and keeping her safe.

And just like that, he understood Matt.

Awesome.

He wanted Phoebe. He did *not* want anyone else taking her on a Ferris wheel, or buying her fried food or even holding her hand in the haunted house—not to mention all the other shenanigans that went on in that place.

Even as all of those thoughts crystalized, he was dumped right back where he'd been that morning when he'd realized that Matt could be gone for a year. The niggling doubt, the inexplicable hesitation was suddenly clear. With Matt gone, Joe could have her all to himself. And if she never found out that the other guys wanted to take her on the Ferris wheel and kept believing that she was just everybody's best gal pal, he would have no competition.

But did he want to be the guy she wanted simply because he was the only guy she believed wanted her?

Every time he thought this mess was going to get easier, something else came up to make him nuts.

In the end, he couldn't do it. Phoebe was amazing and she deserved to know that he wasn't the only one who thought so.

"I'd say go for it," Joe told the other guys. "In fact—" He had to swallow to get the next words out. "—I insist. Tim's gonna ask her to dance, and Steve's going to win her a big-assed stuffed penguin even if it costs him a hundred bucks, and you're all going to take her on the damned Ferris wheel. On me." He handed a hundred to Steve, one to Drew, one to Tim and started to hand one to Travis but then pulled it back. "It's on me for three of you."

Travis laughed. "No worries. Getting Phoebe Sherwood on the Ferris wheel is worth whatever it costs me."

In that moment, he kind of liked Travis.

And he really hoped Phoebe didn't.

Drew looked at the bill in his hand. "Seriously? You're *paying* us to date Phoebe?"

"No." Joe shifted uncomfortably. "I'm paying for the expenses of the date."

"Because you want us to date Phoebe," Steve clarified.

His throat closed just as he started to speak. He coughed. "Yes."

"All of us?" Tim asked.

"I want you to all ask her. It's up to her who, if any of you, she says yes to."

Drew started to say something and Joe cut him off.

"But you better all *try*. Make her feel special, make sure she knows that you really want her." He stopped and frowned at all of them. "You *do* really want her, right?"

Drew looked skeptical but he nodded. "Sure. Phoebe's great."

She was more than great, but Joe let that go. He looked at Steve.

Steve shrugged. "I think so too. She's really cute."

She was gorgeous—and Joe's gut clenched at the thought of those paw prints again—but he also let that go. He turned to look at Tim. "What about you?"

"Definitely," Tim said, with more enthusiasm than the others.

Joe wasn't sure how he felt about that.

"And I'm all in," Travis added with even more enthusiasm. "No worries there."

Joe wiggled his fingers, determined not to punch Travis. For now.

"Okay, so I saw her over by the cotton candy. Go get her."

"Actually, you won't have to go that far."

Aw, dammit. And of course. And *dammit*.

Joe watched the other men straighten and his eyes slid shut. Great. Just great.

He turned, taking a big breath before opening his eyes. "Hi, Phoebe."

Her expression was easy to decipher, in spite of the fact that there were several emotions there—shock, confusion and definitely hurt.

She visibly swallowed hard, then she focused on the others and clearly forced a smile. "So, who's first? I'm ready to ride."

He didn't like *that* one bit. "Phoebe, I—"

"And we'd better get started," she said. "'Cause I intend to spend every penny of Joe's money."

"He didn't give me any money," Travis told her. "He's less than excited about me getting you in that haunted house." The smile he gave her was full of charm.

Joe gritted his teeth. Fuck. This was his idea. It was good. He had to let it happen and it wasn't fair to punch the guys who were just doing what he'd suggested.

"Then you're first," she said, grabbing Travis's hand.

"Too bad, boys," Travis said as Phoebe led him away. "After me, I don't think you're gonna have a chance."

"He has a point," Steve said.

Joe tore his eyes from the sight of Phoebe holding Travis Bennett's hand on the way to the haunted house. "Then tell you what," he said, once more pulling out his money clip. "Win her over. Whatever it takes. This is just one night." He started handing them bills. "Flowers, gifts, dinner, wine...whatever." He didn't stop until he was down to his last ten dollars. He hoped that was enough for a bottle of Booze.

"But—" Drew started.

"Just give her a lot of attention, make her feel special, spoil her," Matt said.

Joe turned to the other man. Matt met his gaze directly and Joe knew Matt understood what he was going for. And how fucking hard it was on him. He nodded. "Yeah."

The other men pocketed the money without argument, but it was clear they thought he was nuts.

Which was possible. The other option was that he was in love. It seemed there was a fine line between the two.

"How about you and I go get a drink?" Matt said to Joe. "And you can tell me more about Outreach America."

Joe took a deep breath and nodded. Sure, why not? Crazier things had happened.

CHAPTER NINE

"Just so you know, I'm not going to knock you up in the haunted house," Travis told Phoebe as they dodged the foam ax the killer zombie—a.k.a. Jack Swanson, the postmaster—swung at them.

"I wasn't exactly worried, but thanks for that," Phoebe said. She gripped Travis's hand tighter to avoid stumbling over the body parts strewn on the floor that was lit only by a black light.

"Well, I always carry condoms, so nothing to worry about," Travis quipped as they rounded a dark corner.

Phoebe chuckled even as she braced for the freaky witch that was supposed to pop out as soon as they passed the sensor in the wall. "I'm shocked."

Travis ducked under the long cape that hung off the back of the mannequin-turned-witch. "And I also want to be sure to say that I would have gladly used several condoms with you before tonight if I'd known."

They heard the buzz of a chainsaw—and a chainsaw-wielding mummy—approaching, and Phoebe pulled Travis behind a huge wooden coffin propped against the wall.

Travis pressed close as the mummy ran by.

"If you'd known what?" Phoebe asked softly.

Travis Bennett was hot. Period. He was one of those guys who was cocky and charming without being slimy or annoying. Except to Lauren, of course—he drove her crazy for some reason. But he was also a good guy. Phoebe had known him forever and had accepted his hotness as a fact that didn't really affect her one way or another. Kind of like the fact that Mr. Anderson grew the biggest watermelons in five counties—it was impressive, but it didn't really change the course of her life in any way.

But Travis was hot. And he smelled good. And he was pressing closer. And he was here when Joe wasn't.

Fuck.

She'd successfully not thought about Joe for fourteen minutes. Now she was going to have to start over.

"If I'd known that you weren't really in love with Matt," Travis told her. "You were off-limits when he was sure he was going to marry you. Then he found Nadia, but we all thought you still wanted him."

She swallowed. The lighting in the house was nothing more than a dim green glow, and she couldn't see Travis's eyes, or really any other part of him. But she could feel him. Hot and solid and close. He braced his hand on the wall next to her ear.

"If I'd known you were available, I would have taken you up to Klein Hill, festival or not." Travis rested a hand on her hip, angling so they were centimeters from being fly to fly.

Phoebe let her head thunk against the wall behind her and sighed. Dammit. She was finally in the haunted house with a hot guy. Not just any hot guy, but Travis Bennett, ladies' man extraordinaire. He was the perfect choice for a festival rendezvous.

And he wasn't doing a thing for her.

He leaned in. "Phoebe?"

She felt his hot breath against her cheek. She swallowed. "Yeah?"

"I know what you want."

She knew what she *should* want. Maybe if Travis really turned it on. Maybe if he gave her his best moves. Maybe he could convince her...

"You want Joe, right?"

She gasped. Then groaned. And not in the hot-and-sexy way she wanted to be gasping and groaning.

Travis pushed himself back with a light chuckle. "Yes, it's that obvious."

"Well, a lot of frickin' good that's going to do me." She pushed away from the wall and grabbed his hand again.

They had half a haunted house to get through.

"His intentions were good," Travis said, following her past the giant man-eating spider and her web.

"Whatever." She didn't even flinch when the rubber bats came swooping down on them in the next hallway. She swatted one out of the way and continued toward the back door.

"Seriously. He seemed really pissed when he found out no one had taken you out and that Matt was the reason."

"Joe's…" so many descriptors tripped through her head that she had trouble finding one to say out loud, "…a nice guy." He was. He made her feel… Fuck. He made her feel so many things she didn't even know where to start. But he was nice. He seemed to really hate the fact that she didn't have a thousand guys romancing her. "He thinks I've been…neglected."

"You have been neglected."

"Stop it."

A vampire stepped in front of them, fangs dripping blood, his eyes glowing red.

"Not now, Dennis," she told the bank president.

Dennis sighed and went back into his dark corner.

Travis chuckled. "Lots of guys would have asked you out, Phoebe. You have to know that."

"But Matt told them not to."

"Matt was sure you were going to end up together. It's bro code. As soon as he told us, we couldn't do a thing."

Phoebe stopped and Travis plowed into her. She turned. "This is exhausting, Travis. This isn't high school. I don't need anyone, Matt or *Joe*, deciding how things go for me. I don't need them taking care of me, worrying about me, feeling…" She sucked in a quick breath as the tears suddenly welled up, stinging her eyes and tightening her throat. That was the thing, the thing that hurt the most, even more than Matt choosing someone else or Joe pointing that out to everyone in public or Joe not feeling what she was feeling.

He felt sorry for her.

But he liked her. So he was trying to make up for *his* lack of feelings by substituting other guys. Multiple other guys. Even if he had to pay them.

Anger coursed through her, the heat of it evaporating her tears and tightening her jaw. She pulled air in through her nose. Fuck him. She didn't need him. She didn't need any of them.

She abruptly changed directions, plunging through the black curtain to her right and pulling Travis with her. Another right and they were at the side kitchen door. She dropped Travis's hand and shoved the door open, stepped out into the night and took a deep breath.

It would be okay. She was in Sapphire Falls, her home, surrounded by friends. It was festival time, so crazy things happened, but eventually things would go back to normal. Now that Matt was going to Haiti to be with Nadia, Joe wouldn't have a reason to stay and he would not be around every corner. She just had to stay away from him until he left. Then she'd get over him. Probably. Eventually.

"Travis?" She turned to face him.

"Yeah?"

"I don't want to kiss you on the Ferris wheel or make out with you in the haunted house or give you a blowjob on Klein Hill."

"Just twist that knife, babe," he said with a grin.

She shook her head. She was insane to *not* want to do those things with Travis Bennett. "But I can't be alone."

Travis's grin instantly dropped into a concerned frown. "You okay?"

She shook her head. "This is going to sound stupid but...if I'm alone I'm going to want to go find Joe and yell at him."

"Phoebe, I really think he meant well—"

"No." She stopped him. "I want to yell at him. But I'm

afraid I'll also cry or kiss him, and I don't want to do either one."

Travis nodded. "Okay."

"And I really don't want him to come find me."

That was a possibility, she admitted. She was mad at him, hurt by him, but she still knew he was a nice enough guy to come after her to apologize...or something. He'd felt bad that she'd overheard his master plan for the guys to romance her. She'd seen it in his eyes. He hadn't meant for her to hear that. And yeah, okay, maybe he thought he was doing her a favor. But she *had* heard it, especially the part about how he didn't care that the other guys might be indulging in the festival traditions with her. His exact words had been, "Go for it." And she couldn't forget about the part where he was handing out money to make it all happen.

"So you want me to stick close?" Travis asked. He took her hand and gave it a squeeze. "Not a problem, sweetheart. I'd even be willing to start a juicy rumor about us."

She gave him a smile that didn't feel completely forced. "Well, Joe wanted *all* of you guys to spend time with me, right? We wouldn't want him to have thrown all that money away."

Travis gave her a wink. "I don't think anyone will complain."

"Great. I haven't been on a Ferris wheel in a really long time."

Three fucking days. The longest three days of his life.

For three days, Joe had watched Phoebe dance, drink, flirt, laugh and hold hands with the men of Sapphire Falls. And it really did seem like *all* of the men of Sapphire Falls wanted a turn with her. That wasn't true, of course. Mason, for instance, didn't dance with her. Neither did a few other happily married men. But it wasn't just the guys Joe had spoken with the first night of the festival paying attention to her. Oh, they were definitely there, front and center, spending every dime Joe had given them and then some. But there were others as well. Just as he'd predicted.

The minute it became clear that Phoebe was available and that Matt wasn't going to threaten anyone, the guys were lining up.

Literally tonight.

There was a line of guys along the bar at the Come Again who were waiting to dance with her. And they could all do that damned country dancing like they'd been born to it.

Joe took a swig of whiskey. He'd gotten drunk the last two nights and was well on track tonight as well.

"Why are you still here?"

He looked over at Hailey Conner, of all people. He thought that maybe Hailey and Phoebe were friends, but he was never quite sure how to read the mayor of Sapphire Falls. She was gorgeous and confident and walked into any and every room as if she owned it and everyone there was glad she'd shown up. But there was something about her that made him like her. He wondered if Phoebe felt the same way. Like she was fond of Hailey but had no idea why.

He'd love to ask her.

But Phoebe Sherwood was very likely never going to speak to him again.

"This is where the liquor is."

"That's stupid."

It was. There was a liquor store right next door where he could buy a bottle of the meanest alcohol ever made and take it back to his room at Mason's.

The truth was, he was here because this was where Phoebe was. And even though he *hated* watching her with all the other men, he also loved it. She was gorgeous.

Happy. Practically glowing from all the attention. A very cruel, masochistic part of him loved seeing her like that, even if it wasn't because of him.

"Besides, I meant why are you still in Sapphire Falls?" Hailey lifted a glass of red wine to her lips.

"I'm here to…" He trailed off.

Hell, he had no idea why he was still in Sapphire Falls. The woman he'd come to win over was in Haiti while her fiancé prepared to get on an airplane to join her in a little over a week. The woman he'd fallen for instead was currently dancing with Travis Bennett for the fourth time in six songs—not that Joe was counting.

"Fuck if I know," he finally admitted, taking another swallow of whiskey.

"That's what I thought," Hailey said, with a nod.

"I guess I'm…" Yeah, still no idea.

"You're waiting to see if she's going to pick you."

Joe looked at Hailey, just blinking for a moment. He'd only had half a whiskey so far. Shouldn't other people's words still make sense to him at this point? "What?"

"You're hanging out to see if she's going to pick you over all these guys." Hailey turned to face him fully and tucked a long strand of straight blond hair behind her ear with a perfectly manicured red fingernail. "You believe that Phoebe deserves to have a whole bunch of guys gaga over her, but you're also hoping that when that all dies down, she'll still want *you* more. You hope that what she feels for you is about more than the fact that she's never been swept off her feet before."

Joe stared at the woman who could easily be the most beautiful he'd ever talked to. And he'd talked to a lot of beautiful women in his day.

Obviously, her beauty distracted from the fact that she was clearly intelligent and very insightful. It was kind of daunting to think about what she could do with that particular power.

"You can pretty much get any guy you want, huh?" he asked.

Surprise flickered in her eyes, but she nodded. "Pretty much."

"You ever been to Paris?"

"No."

"If a guy offered to whisk you off to Paris in a private plane tonight, would you be impressed?"

"Definitely."

He sighed. "So why don't I want to take you to Paris?"

"Because I'm not Phoebe."

Dammit. He didn't know how to respond to that.

"I never used the word gaga," he finally said.

"You should have," Hailey told him. "It's perfect. It means excessively and foolishly enthusiastic."

It was the perfect word.

"I'm happy she's happy."

Hailey nodded. "I know. I can tell."

"You can?" Why had she been paying attention to him at all?

"Yes. I've been paying attention to you since one of my friends is crazy about you."

So they were friends. Well, that cleared that up.

Hailey glanced toward the dance floor. "I'm not very good at being friends with women. I get along with men better."

Joe wasn't surprised to hear that. At all.

"But I like Phoebe. She's a good person, and I completely agree with you that she deserves guys making asses of themselves over her. Between all the stuffed animals they've been winning for her, the dozens of trips on the Ferris wheel and the fact that they've bought out the flower shop, I'd say they've done a great job."

Joe clenched his jaw. Flowers and stuffed animals were for amateurs. He hadn't resorted to flowers to woo a woman in years. If they wanted to see how to make a girl swoon, he could show them…

He forced himself to stop and breathe. That was exactly the problem. If he wanted to compete with these guys in the awe-her-with-gifts-and-extravagance department, he'd blow them all away. It wouldn't even be a fair contest.

But that wasn't how he wanted to do it with Phoebe. He wanted her to want him as he was. Here in Sapphire Falls in blue jeans while eating burgers. He didn't want all the other stuff coloring her real feelings. He wanted to know that she wanted *him*. Period.

And yeah, okay, that was why he was hanging around.

"Does that make me pathetic or romantic?" he asked Hailey.

She tipped her head as she studied him, seemingly really considering the question. "A little bit of both."

He chuckled in spite of his miserable mood. "Honesty from a politician. I like it."

"Honesty from a friend." She gave him a smile that made Joe sure she could get any man to do anything if she put her mind to it. And there was definitely a sharp mind behind that beautiful face.

His gaze went to the dance floor and found Phoebe. Well, almost any man.

"So, honestly, what do you think I should do?"

"You started this ball rolling, Joe. Now you need to wait and see where it lands."

"Kind of that whole if-you-love-something-set-it-free thing?"

"Exactly that," Hailey told him. "If you really want to see if Phoebe still picks you when she can have every guy to choose from, then you've got to let her *pick* you."

"How do I do that? Just hang out and drink until she gets tired of them?"

"Absolutely not." Hailey reached over and plucked his glass from his fingers. "You need to *not* hang around. You need to go."

"Go?"

"Go. Leave her alone. Don't make this a show. Let her really just be with these guys without it being about you at all. That's the only way she'll actually be able to tell if any of them hit the right spot."

He groaned. "I really hate that terminology."

Hailey shrugged. "Sorry."

He sighed, looked down at the still half-full glass of whiskey on the bar. "But maybe you've got a point."

"Always," she said with another smile. "Remember that."

"Right." He paid for her drink as well and then headed for the door.

At least one thing was clear—Hailey was definitely Phoebe's friend.

জ্যু

He left?

Seriously?

Her feet hurt from dancing, her cheeks ached from smiling, her head hurt from the third night in a row of liquor and loud music and too much sugar, and her heart hurt from not talking to, touching or kissing Joe in three days.

And now he'd just walked out. While she was in another man's arms.

"Thanks, Trav," Phoebe said distractedly and disentangled herself from him.

"You're wearin' me out, sweetheart, just so you know," Travis said with a sigh.

"You're such a baby." She leaned in and gave him a peck on the cheek. Nothing was going to happen with Travis and he knew that, which was why she was spending the most time with him. She liked the other guys who were asking her out and buying her stuff and she didn't want to lead anyone on. Travis was perfect.

Travis headed for the bar and Phoebe bee-lined for the table where Hailey was just joining Lauren and Adrianne.

"I'll take two mojitos," Hailey told the waitress, "on her bill." Hailey pointed to Lauren as she pulled the chair out next to Phoebe and sat.

"Why my bill?" Lauren asked.

"Loser buys."

"Loser?" Lauren lifted an eyebrow.

Phoebe lifted both eyebrows. She sincerely doubted that Dr. Lauren Davis had ever been called a loser.

"Well, I got my part done first," Hailey informed her.

"I didn't realize this was a competition."

Hailey shrugged a shoulder. "I still won."

Lauren leaned in. "Based on what?"

"I accomplished my goal and did it in less than fifteen minutes."

Lauren glanced at Phoebe. Phoebe glanced at Adrianne, who was watching with interest as she sucked on the straw in her diet cola, not saying a word. Phoebe couldn't wait to hear what this was all about.

Lauren looked back to Hailey. "I didn't realize that we had a time limit."

"You want to drag it on even longer?" Hailey picked up the first of her two mojitos and sipped. "I feel like it's been going on *forever*. And you've been getting crabbier and crabbier."

Lauren frowned. "I have not."

"You're bitchier every night," Hailey said, taking another sip. "No one's making you come down here, you know."

"Yeah, well—" Lauren shifted on her chair and crossed her arms. "There's nothing else to do in this damned town after six."

She definitely sounded bitchy now. Phoebe watched the two women with wide eyes.

"Actually, every time she's asked to dance, you get bitchier," Hailey said.

Phoebe looked at Adrianne and then Hailey. Both women were watching Lauren with interest.

"On second thought, you didn't seem pissed when Phoebe was dancing with Tim," Hailey said.

"Or Steve," Adrianne commented.

Phoebe looked at them with wide eyes. "When did she seem pissed?"

"Travis," Adrianne and Hailey said simultaneously.

"Why do you care that I was dancing with Travis?" Phoebe asked Lauren.

"I don't."

Uh huh.

Hailey finished her first mojito and picked up the second.

"What is this all about anyway?" Adrianne asked.

Lauren sighed. "Yes, back to this. I don't believe that you've officially won."

Hailey swallowed. "Did too. He's gone, isn't he?"

"Who?" Adrianne asked.

"Joe."

Phoebe perked up at Hailey's answer. "Yeah, I noticed that you were chatting." And it had bugged the crap out of her. Hailey was totally his type. Or at least the type Phoebe imagined him with—gorgeous, confident, sophisticated. And she'd had something to do with his leaving? Why? How?

"Yeah." Hailey sipped again without elaborating.

"What did you...talk about?" Phoebe asked, trying not to grab and shake the beautiful blond who seemed to not understand that she was at risk for being grabbed and shaken.

"Paris."

Phoebe's throat tightened. "Paris? What about Paris?"

"He asked me if I'd ever been and if I'd be impressed

with a guy taking me in a private plane."

Oh. The tightness in her throat spread to her chest and she had to force herself to breathe deeply. So he'd decided to go back to his old ways, to hit on the girl who could have any guy, to wow her, to become the man above men. Three days was clearly more than enough time for him to get over impressing *her*. Besides, she'd been too easy for him. She got it. For Joe, it was the thrill of the win, of being the best.

What he didn't understand was that he was the best. To her. In the ways that mattered.

She felt the sting at the back of her eyes and blinked rapidly. Fuck. She was *not* going to cry.

"So what was all of this about winning?" Adrianne asked, shooting Phoebe a worried look but effectively distracting the other women from studying Phoebe too closely.

"I got Joe to leave," Hailey said. "That was my job. And, as I believe I pointed out, I did it efficiently too." She toasted Lauren with her half-empty glass.

Lauren shook her head. "You haven't officially won because the competition—which was never set up as a competition in the first place—isn't over. I haven't done my thing yet."

"What's your thing?" Adrianne asked.

"And," Lauren went on, "I can do it faster than fifteen minutes."

Hailey gave her a half smile. "Let's see it."

Lauren sat up straighter, put her hands flat on the table and turned to Phoebe. "Phoebe," she started, "you need to stop fucking around."

Phoebe stared at her. "What?"

"You've been messing with all the guys long enough. Pick one, or two, or three if you want to, and *date* them already."

Phoebe was so surprised she wasn't sure what to say. Which was where her best girlfriend came in.

"What are you talking about?" Adrianne asked. "She's just *dancing*. And you don't want her to date Travis anyway."

Lauren scowled at her. "This isn't about Travis. Besides, Phoebe should *not* date Travis."

"Why not? He's a great guy," Adrianne said.

"Because Travis is an ass. She can do better," Lauren said.

Adrianne smiled. "You're the only woman in Sapphire Falls who thinks Travis Bennett is an ass."

"Well, I'm incredibly intelligent, so you should all listen to me," Lauren said. She turned back to Phoebe. "Do *not* date Travis. But pick any of the other guys and go for it."

She didn't want to go for it with anyone in Sapphire Falls. Phoebe felt her chest squeeze again. Dammit. This wasn't good. Joe was a player. He liked women, lots of women. And he liked them a lot more glamorous than she was. She was no prize. He liked her, sure. They'd had some fun, some great sex. But she wasn't a catch. He needed to go for the gold. She was the bronze, at best.

Phoebe took a deep breath and sat up straighter.

Bronze wasn't bad though. Bronze was good. Bronze was solid. And shiny. It was...better than most. Just like her. She might not be the sexy siren or the exotic beauty, but she was great. Worth the effort. Deserving of romance and adoration.

She looked toward the bar where some of the nicest men on earth were gathered laughing and joking and having a good time. And dammit, every single one of them could dance.

Phoebe looked back at her friends. "They've all been really sweet, haven't they?"

"They have," Hailey agreed. "And they're all exactly the type of guy you've always imagined yourself with."

"So grab one and go for it," Lauren said. "Quit playing

with them, quit using them to make Joe jealous, quit thinking about Joe all together."

Sure, that'd be great. She would love to do that. "How?"

"Well, that was why Hailey got rid of him. He needed to go so you can focus on the guys here, right in front of you, who want the same things and think you're a goddess," Lauren said.

The strange thing was, Joe had made her feel that way. Definitely. Repeatedly.

"But—"

"You need to date, Phoebe," Lauren said firmly. "You've never done much of that. Not with real intentions of seeing if it could go anywhere. You've been too hung up on Matt to really look at other guys as true potential, and Matt had scared them all off so none of them really turned on the charm. You owe it to yourself to find out if you could have something with one of these guys."

Phoebe chewed on her bottom lip. Lauren was right about everything she'd said. None of these guys had ever truly been on her radar. They hadn't flirted or pursued her either, but she'd never lamented the fact really.

But she wanted Joe.

Even though she knew they were a long shot, she wanted him. They wanted different things. They were from different places. They were so different in their approach to relationships. Joe liked things spontaneous and over-the-top, Phoebe wanted down-to-earth with someone she'd known forever.

They wouldn't work out.

But she wanted him just the same.

"Joe and I—"

"Joe walked away," Hailey interrupted. "He walked away without a fight, Phoebe. You heard me say it. It took less than fifteen minutes to talk him into going. And he's been sitting here for three nights watching you with other men. I think that tells us all how he feels."

The tightness that had started in her throat and moved to her chest now dropped to her stomach.

Phoebe looked at Adrianne. Her friend looked...sympathetic.

Dammit.

That meant Adrianne thought there was something to feel sympathetic about.

She took a long shaky breath. "Fine. You're right. So now what?"

"Pick a guy, any guy," Hailey said with a smile.

Ha, Phoebe thought. *So there, Joe. I am the girl who can have any guy after all.* But she didn't feel vindicated. Or anything else except for sad.

Lauren read her face and reached over to take her hand. "Screw him," she said firmly. "He doesn't matter."

Phoebe managed a shaky smile. She really, really, really hoped that would be true for her someday.

CHAPTER TEN

Tim Morton was damned near perfect.

He was good-looking, had lived his entire life in Sapphire Falls, made good money and was well-liked by everyone.

And over the past three weeks, it seemed that he had also scored himself a new girlfriend.

An amazing, sweet, funny, everyone-loves-her, she-fits-right-in redheaded girlfriend.

Who had paw print tattoos on her inner thigh.

Joe shoved his chair back from his computer and paced to the window. He looked out at the lights of Chicago and thought, for the five-hundredth time since coming back to the city, that he really preferred the wide open spaces and deep dark of the country around Sapphire Falls.

"This is what you wanted," the female voice from the computer reminded him.

He turned to face Nadia who was chatting with him from Haiti. "I know." He shoved his fingers through his hair. "It is what I want, if she's happy."

"She is apparently," Nadia said. "That's what she tells Matt anyway."

Matt had joined Nadia in Haiti shortly after Joe had left Sapphire Falls. He'd never seen his friend happier or more content than she was now with the love of her life by her side in the place where she felt most at home. From all reports, Matt was doing very well and had found his calling teaching the kids in the poor villages. Who would have guessed it?

"She'd tell Matt that just so he didn't worry," Joe said. He knew that Phoebe wouldn't want her friend to be concerned when he was so far away for so long. She would tell Matt whatever she thought he needed to hear.

But it was possible that she really was happy.

That seemed strange when Joe was so incredibly *unhappy* being apart from her, but there was no doubt that the guys in Sapphire Falls—like Tim Morton—could offer her things he couldn't. There was no Disney obsession that would make a trip to Cinderella's castle a dream come true, or love of Chinese history that would make a week in Beijing awe-inspiring. No, Phoebe wanted to barbecue and drink beer by a bonfire on a cool fall evening or ride a Ferris wheel on the main street of her hometown. The guys in Sapphire Falls had been doing all of that all their lives. Any one of them could give her that.

It wasn't really Joe's style. Or so he was telling himself.

"She and Tim have a lot in common," Nadia said. "And he's admitted to having a crush on her since senior year."

Well, at least Tim was bright enough to have developed a crush on the most amazing woman in the world. With a low growl, Joe paced back to the computer. "Stop telling me this stuff."

"You asked."

"Next time tell me you don't know."

"If I do that, you'll hop a plane back to Sapphire Falls to check on her."

He opened his mouth and then had to shut it without a word. Nadia was right.

He was uncomfortable asking Lauren or Adrianne about Phoebe, knowing that as her girlfriends they probably knew all the details, including the hot country sex that still wound him up at night *and* the way he'd humiliated her by handing out money to the men of Sapphire Falls.

God, he was an ass.

"Do you think he's good in bed?" Joe heard himself ask Nadia.

She coughed and then asked, "Matt?"

Joe rolled his eyes. "*Not* Matt. Do *not* tell me about Matt. I mean Tim."

"Um." His usually intelligent, articulate friend paused

and then said, "Do you *want* him to be good in bed?"

His first reaction was to say no. He definitely hoped that Tim Morton sucked between the sheets. But then he said, "For her sake, I hope he's good. She deserves to have..." But the idea of Phoebe having *anything* great—whether it was a great steak dinner or great sex—with another man, made him want to put his fist through the wall. "Hell, I don't know. I'm messed up over this woman, Nadia."

She chuckled. "No kidding."

"So what do I do?"

She shook her head. "I don't know. I get where you're coming from. You want her to have the experience of knowing that she can have anything she wants. But you want to be what she wants."

That was it. Exactly. "Yeah."

"I guess you give it more time." Though she didn't sound sure.

"More time for what?"

"For her to hang out with Tim and see how things go, see if he can give her what she wants."

"Or?" Joe asked, hating that.

"You want permission to go storming back to Sapphire Falls to sweep her off her feet?" Nadia asked. "Go for it. I think that's great."

His heart kicked, but he still shook his head. "I think I need to let her come to me."

Nadia sighed. "But you walked away, Joe. I know it was because you thought that was best for her, but from her perspective, you left."

Yeah, and she'd dated four guys in the six weeks he'd been gone. Now she was going out with Tim for the eighth time in those six weeks. More than she'd been out with anyone else. And it had been two weeks since she'd seen anyone but Tim.

Not that he was keeping track.

"Okay, well, since you're not being helpful, I'll let you go," Joe told Nadia.

She chuckled. "Fine. You know where I am if you need me."

They disconnected the Skype connection and Joe sat thinking.

He didn't want Phoebe to forget him. He wanted her to be happy. He wanted her to want him and he wanted her to have the life she wanted.

It was damned confusing.

Finally, he pulled out his cell phone and scrolled to her number.

He couldn't call her. That wouldn't be fair to either of them. What would he say anyway?

Instead, he texted her. Just a short and sweet message to let her know he was thinking of her and wished her the best.

No big deal.

Phoebe felt her phone vibrate against her leg where she'd tucked it under her thigh on the chair during her dinner with Tim.

She really did think that people who checked messages during dinner, especially a social dinner, were jerks. So she ignored it until Tim excused himself to go to the bathroom.

Phoebe was sure it was Adrianne asking if she'd decided to invite Tim back to her house to see if things would progress tonight.

She probably should. None of them were getting any younger, and if the sex sucked she'd know she should end it before it got more serious.

And it turned out that Tim Morton was a really good kisser. How *that* information hadn't circulated amongst the women of Sapphire Falls was a mystery.

Still, the idea of sleeping with the guy she'd done a summer Bible school project with seemed strange. Not to mention that Tim had been the one to intercept a note between her and a friend in social studies when they were freshman that said Phoebe thought Chad Kohls was the hottest guy in school. And he'd, of course, read it out loud to the whole class. Oh, and Tim had actually already kissed her once. In seventh grade. On a dare at Steve's birthday party.

He'd definitely gotten better and he hadn't groped her breast when he'd kissed her in recent weeks, but she couldn't shake the memory.

Yeah, she was finding out that it was possible to know someone *too* well.

The same thing had happened when she'd gone out with Drew. They hadn't even gotten as far as kissing. They'd started reminiscing and laughing about the twenty minutes they'd spent together in the closet in his basement when they were sophomores. He'd hosted a party and his parents had come home early, causing their classmates to scatter to various hiding spots in the house. At the time, they'd talked about how they should spend the time making out. But they hadn't been able to get over the giggles to get anything done. After reliving the memory as adults, every time they'd leaned in to kiss they'd started giggling again. After three tries, they'd decided that they'd still rather laugh together than make out anyway.

It had been similar with Jason Sims. They'd had a nice time, talked baseball and about their grandmothers and then managed to actually kiss when he took her home. But they'd pulled back, neither especially impressed.

Hoping for better tonight with Tim, Phoebe opened her new text message.

It wasn't from Adrianne.

She stared at the message. From Joe.

She felt her heart and stomach flip and even her thumb

was shaking as she pressed the button to open the message.

Tim's a lucky guy.

Four words. That was all.

But she felt immediately lighter.

He was thinking of her.

He knew she was going out with Tim.

And he'd still texted her.

There was no way he would have known about Tim if he hadn't asked someone about her.

That was all she needed to know.

Tim was a great guy. He had and was everything she thought she'd always really wanted.

Before she met what she really wanted.

She typed back only four words and then prepared to tell Tim they could only be friends because she was in love with someone else.

Damned right he is.

ᦌᦎ

Damned right he is.

Joe read the message for the millionth time since Phoebe had sent it back the night before and still felt the urge to grin and groan at the same time.

Phoebe had responded exactly as he'd wanted her to. She needed to know she was amazing.

I really miss you might have been nice though. *I'm madly in love with you* would have been fine too.

It was Saturday night and Joe was pacing his condo's living room, frustrated, bored and missing Phoebe, the coffee at Adrianne's shop, the eggs at the diner, being out in the fields with the dirt and the sun with Mason, joking with the other guys—even the ones who had been dating Phoebe. He missed Sapphire Falls as a whole.

During the week he'd been able to lose himself in work, though no one in the Chicago office had adequately appreciated the joke about the stripper and the call girl he'd brought back from Sapphire Falls. No one had hooted with laughter or toasted him with their jug of iced tea or tried to top him with an even raunchier joke.

His story about the IAS field operations was complete and damned good if he did say so himself, but now he was alone with no work to do and none of his usual activities sounded good to him at all.

So just what the hell was he supposed to do with himself?

Not just today, but for the rest of his life?

Feeling melodramatic about that, he decided to wallow in his morose ponderings. He headed for the kitchen to make a sandwich and thought about his situation. His sad, pathetic, lonely, it'll-never-be-right-again situation.

He didn't want to be here. He didn't want to be in Paris, LA, New York or Rome either. He could travel anywhere in the world, do anything he wanted, with any*one*. And he wanted to be in Sapphire Falls, Nebraska, at the Come Again bar with Phoebe. Or better yet, in her truck bed out by the river. Or even better, in her bed. For at least a week. To start.

He had ham and cheese on bread and decided that even his sandwiches would be boring and sad from here on out when he heard a knock on his door.

Why hadn't he decided to order a pizza? Pizza could be boring but never sad. He crossed to the door and yanked it open.

Phoebe stood on the other side.

"Here's your stuff," she said simply, handing him a big paper sack.

He drank her in. She was dressed in a white skirt with loud pink flowers on it and a light green tank top. Her hair was big and curly, her eyes sparkled and her mouth was curved into a smile.

She was the best thing he'd ever seen.

The second best thing was the suitcase sitting beside her in the hallway.

He looked down at the bag he held. "What's this?"

"The stuff you bought for me."

He opened the top and found a stuffed penguin, several clumps of dried flowers, a couple of teddy bears, a box of gourmet cookies and a bag of cotton candy.

"I bought you this stuff?"

"You paid for this stuff," she said. "They came from other guys, but they did it because you told them to. So really, they bought it for you."

"I'm sure they bought you some things with their own money," he said. She'd been dating for six weeks. Even the cheapest guy would have gone through a hundred bucks in six weeks.

"Oh, I kept the stuff they bought me themselves," she said.

And just like that Joe knew he was madly, irreversibly in love with her.

He dropped the bag beside him and reached out to grab her wrist. He pulled her into his foyer, grabbed her suitcase and tossed it to the side, then slammed the door before starting toward his bedroom.

He didn't care why she was here. Just that she was. With a suitcase.

That meant he could get her rumpled and wrinkled and dirty before worrying about anything else.

Of course, the lack of suitcase wouldn't have kept him from doing any of those things.

"Joe, what are you—"

Her question died as they stepped into his bedroom.

"Oh," was her only response then.

"Yeah, oh." He lifted the hem of her tank top, swept it up and over her head and flung it behind him.

She certainly didn't protest. She reached behind her for the zipper on the skirt while he unhooked her bra. God he loved front clasps. With her hands behind her back, her breasts strained toward him and he cupped them almost reverently.

"I missed you," he said, brushing his thumbs over her already hard nipples.

"Ditto," she managed breathlessly as the skirt parted and then slid over her hips.

"Lose the panties too," he told her. This was it. She was here, she was his, and he wasn't letting her go. Literally. Phoebe Sherwood was going to be tied to his bed for the next several hours and she was going to love every minute. If this was a dream, he was going all out. If it was real...he was definitely going all out.

She wiggled out of the silky white panties and kicked them away. She was completely naked, here in his bedroom in Chicago. She'd come to him.

Now she'd come for him. Over and over.

He cupped her face, bringing her lips to his. He kissed her hot and hard, sweeping his tongue possessively against hers. Then he gentled the kiss, tasting her top lip, then the bottom, nipping at her, then sucking, then pressing closed lip kisses along her mouth, trailing to her jaw, then down her throat.

She arched and moaned as he ran his palm over one breast, her stomach and between her legs. She parted her legs and he immediately moved to claim her there as well, pressing two fingers deep. She was already wet and cried out as he thrust his fingers.

"Joe." Her voice was ragged and she gripped his shoulders, digging in, holding on.

"That's right. You're all mine right now. All." He pressed his thumb against her clit as he moved in her slick heat. "Mine."

"Yes," she whispered.

That's what he'd needed to hear.

He walked her back to the bed, pushing her gently

when the backs of her legs hit the edge of the mattress. His fingers left her body, but the sight of her sprawled back on his bedspread made up for it. For now. Seeing her here, in his territory, no barrier between him and her body, made something very primal and greedy clench in his gut. This was right. This was where she should be. Not necessary *this* bed in *this* city, but in *his* bed, wherever that was. Wherever he was.

"Scoot up toward the headboard," he told her gruffly, turning toward his closet and crossing the distance in four long strides. He'd never tied a woman to this bed—hell, he'd only done it two other times and one had only been the woman's wrists tied above her head—but he was great at improvisation. He wasn't going to let a little thing like lack of experience slow him down.

He grabbed four ties from his hangers and turned, only to pause as surprise, lust and love slammed into him at once.

Phoebe was lying in the center of his bed, her head on his pillow, her red hair fanned out on the pale white cotton. Her arms were above her head, hands grasping the top of his headboard, and she lay with one knee bent and splayed to one side. Everything he needed to see was right there— including the passion and love in her eyes.

"Is this what you meant?" she asked.

He had to swallow before speaking. "Very much like that."

"I don't know where you're going to tie those, but I'll promise not to move if you want," she said, gripping the headboard harder.

He chuckled. How he could get any sound past the tightness in his chest was a mystery, but he found himself amused. Appropriate.

"I don't believe you," he said, approaching the bed, sliding one hand down the length of the four ties he held. "You have this way of wanting to take over partway through, wanting to rush things."

She licked her lips, looking at the ties. "Yeah, okay, maybe you better tie me."

Lust hit him again and he saw her suck in a quick breath at the look on his face. He could only imagine how possessive he looked.

He reached up and grabbed the ankle of the leg that was bent to the side, showing him all her sweet pink heat. He slid her foot along the comforter, making her toes curl. When her leg was fully extended, he looped a tie around her ankle and pulled, stretching her leg out to the side. Then he realized there really wasn't anything to tie it to.

"Dammit."

She giggled.

He looked up. She was stretched out on his bed, completely naked, and was laughing at him.

"I told you it might not work," she said with a grin.

"I'm going to make it work," he promised. "I'll order a four poster bed online and have it delivered today if I have to."

Her eyes and smile widened. "You would do that just so you could tie me up?"

"Oh, honey, you have no idea what all I'd do for you."

Her smile died instantly and her eyes got a shine that looked suspiciously like tears.

"Oh, no, you don't," he said quickly. "There's no crying in naughty, tied-up sex."

Her mouth curved but her eyes still shone. "Who knew that naughty, tied-up sex could be so sweet?"

"I'll show you sweet," he growled. He stomped to the heavy arm chair near the window and dragged it up next to the bed. Then he tried to loop the other end of the tie around the closest wooden leg. It wouldn't quite reach. "*Dammit.*" Why had he bought such a big frickin' bed?

"Honestly, Joe, I can—"

"No. This is going to work. Dammit." He ignored her

soft snort of amusement and grabbed another tie, knotted the two together to make it longer, then managed to get it tied around the chair leg.

Without looking at her—because he'd lose his mind with want or dissolve into laughter—he went to his closet and grabbed all of his ties and dumped them on the floor next to the bed. Then he grabbed his desk chair and put it on the bottom corner of the bed opposite the other chair and tied her right leg to it. He had bedside tables with, thank God, sturdy legs on the bottom to fasten the ties from her wrists. So within minutes, Phoebe was spread out and tied down on his bed.

Then he let himself look.

She looked amazing. Like every erotic fantasy he'd ever had. Yet, the warmth of his love for her was beyond anything he'd imagined. She was watching him with a mixture of affection and desire that was even more potent than pure lust, and he swallowed hard again.

"You are the most beautiful thing I've ever seen," he told her honestly. "I don't even know where to start."

"Just start," she whispered. "It'll be good no matter what."

At that, he gave her slow smile. "Oh, honey, it's gonna be so much better than good."

He crawled up the bed to kiss her, his clothes a barrier between them. The hunger of the kiss made him want to strip immediately, but he held back, kissing her, nipping and sucking on her neck, trailing kisses along her collarbone and down between her breasts.

His lips and tongue tasted the soft mounds of her breasts and then drew on her nipples until she was writhing beneath him. She was tied, but she could get loose if she wanted to. In spite of the way she moved restlessly beneath him, she kept her hands in her bonds and made Joe even more determined to reward her for letting him have her like this. He was playful as he kissed his way over her belly, swirling his tongue in her belly button before continuing lower, but he felt the growing need to claim her, possess her, make sure that she was never this vulnerable or trusting or open with anyone else, ever.

"I want to make you come before I take you," he told her, continuing his kisses over the neat ginger patch covering her mound. "But I fully intend to take you, hard and hot, like you've never had it before."

She moaned and arched closer to his mouth. "Yes, Joe. Do that. Do all of that. A lot."

He smiled in spite of where his lips were. He had other things to do with his mouth than smile, but with Phoebe it was impossible not to smile. "You keep that kind of talk up, and we're gonna be just fine."

He licked along the sweet spot where her leg met her pelvis. She tried to move again, but the ties were keeping her in place.

Perfect.

He moved down to the paw prints that made him crazy even in his memories. He kissed, licked and sucked each of them from the farthest away to the one closest to her center. Her arousal was obvious and he couldn't wait to taste her there. Until she spoke again.

"I wish I could grab your head and make you do what I want," she said through gritted teeth.

Exactly. "I knew you wouldn't hold still," he said, starting over at the bottom print just for that.

"But you've got all the control," she complained, tugging a little on one of her arm ties. It held. If she pulled hard enough, it would come loose, but she didn't test it. "I don't know why I agreed to this."

Exactly. He lifted his head. "Because deep down you want me to have the control."

"No." She shook her head, her curls gliding over his pillowcase and making his heart clench as hard with desire as did the sight of her breasts bouncing softly as she moved, the hard points a telltale sign of her arousal.

"Yes," he said firmly. "Because this is you and *me*. You want to revel, you want to savor every moment, every touch, every kiss…you just don't know how. You've always rushed because you weren't into it. Sex can be fast. Making love takes time."

She lifted her head from the pillow. "What are you talking about?"

Joe hadn't consciously spent time analyzing this, but he knew it was true. "You always rushed through the physical stuff because that's all there was. Lingering, going slow, amps up the connection—or magnifies the lack of connection. Fast and hard—you don't have to really *feel* anything for that. But if you take your time, talk, make eye contact, tune in—you come face to face with your feelings. Or lack of feelings. You thought all those guys in Sapphire Falls didn't have hot, romantic feelings for you. But the truth is, *you* didn't have those feelings for them. So you made it about lust, not love."

"And you connected with and fell in love with all of the women you took your time with?" she asked, dropping her head back on the pillow.

He gently nipped the inside of her thigh. "I'm talking about *your* motivations in bed. Not mine. And who said I took my time? And who says it wasn't for the very same reasons?" he asked. "Maybe that's how I know what you were doing." Then, because he couldn't stop himself, he licked up her inner thigh and into the sweet wetness between the pink folds.

Gasping his name, she arched her back.

When he lifted his head several moments later, she took a deep breath.

"You didn't want to connect with other women? You rushed things?"

He nodded. "I had a short period of time to make an impression on most of them," he said. "And it was never about anything lasting. I just wanted the thrill, the instant gratification of distracting them. I mean, sweeping a girl off her feet only takes a few minutes. It's not like I wanted to carry any of them around for long."

Phoebe chuckled. "Nice metaphor."

"But you," he said. "Whole new ball game, don't you doubt it for one damned minute. I plan to carry you around for…ever. If you'll let me."

She smiled. "Well, okay. But," she added, "if you're going to tie me up and control the pace, then I'm going to keep you from using the wow thing on me. No over-the-top gestures to impress me. Just you. All of you. Real and honest."

"So it's all about emotions, how we're feeling about each other?" he said, lowering his head and kissing the closest paw print.

She gasped softly. "That's right."

"How would you feel about being told that I'm completely in love with you while you're tied up and naked?" he asked, kissing closer to her center.

She wiggled. "It would be a little frustrating, considering I'd really want to hug and kiss you and tell you the same thing in return."

"Oh, well, then we'll have to wait." He lowered his head and licked long and deep along her hot cleft.

Her breath hissed out between her teeth. "Okay, that's probably best. When I tell you I love you, I want my hands free."

"It'll definitely make it easier to put the engagement ring on your finger," he said before sucking her clit into his mouth.

She cried out and gasped his name. When he lifted his head, she said, albeit breathlessly, "And when I say yes to your romantic, heartfelt, emotional proposal, I'll want to hold your face while I look into your eyes and tell you that I've never imagined being this happy and I'll never want anything more than *you*."

Joe swiftly pushed himself back from between her legs and then to his feet.

"Hey—"

She stopped her protest as he stripped his clothes off, rolled on a condom and climbed back up between her knees. "You were saying?" he asked, sliding his hands under her butt and lifting her slightly so he could thrust deep and true.

"I have no idea," she groaned as he stroked in and out again.

"Good. Just *feel*," he told her.

And they did. They felt everything—the physical, the emotional and a bunch of stuff neither of them could describe. And then they felt it all again. And then he untied her and they felt it all over again. Three more times before the sun came up.

శ్రా

Twenty-five hours after her last orgasm, Phoebe approached the door to her hotel room in Paris, France.

After reuniting with Joe—and wow, had they reunited—she'd crept out of bed, headed for the airport, taken the eleven-hour flight and arrived in Paris in time to do some sightseeing, shopping and eating.

Now she was ready to see him. And she expected him any minute.

Smiling she inserted her key card into the door. She could only imagine his thoughts when he awakened alone. All she'd left behind was a note that said, "I love you. See you soon. P."

She expected him any hour.

She knew he'd figure out where she was and come after her. But she really wanted to see Paris on her own first. Because she could. And he needed to think about that.

Maneuvering herself and several shopping bags through the doorway, she mentally planned which of her new outfits she'd be wearing when Joe walked through the door. She'd take a long bubble bath in the biggest bathtub she'd ever seen, spend some extra time on her hair, use her new French perfume and then be waiting on the loveseat with champagne and strawberries—which were already in the suite's refrigerator—for him to arrive.

Mr. Spencer wasn't the only one who could turn up the wow factor when he wanted to.

She was going to sweep *him* off his feet.

"Strawberries and champagne are pretty cliché."

She came up short in the doorway between the foyer and the living area. Joe was sitting on the loveseat, bare feet up on the coffee table, a half bottle of champagne in one hand—no glass—and a huge strawberry with a bite out of it in the other.

She sighed and dropped her bags. "You didn't wait for me?"

"I'll come up with something even better."

She kicked her shoes off. "No. You're missing the point."

Joe just looked at her for a moment. Then dropped his feet to the floor and leaned to set the strawberry and champagne on the table. "What is the point, Phoebe? I woke up without you. I never got to tell you everything I had to say. I didn't get to propose. Then I found out that you'd come to *Paris*, of all places. By yourself. What's going on?"

The word *propose* was still rattling around in her heart and she had to force herself to walk calmly to the couch. She put a foot up and pushed the coffee table out of the way, then moved to stand directly in front of him, her knees almost touching his. "*That* is the point. I wanted to show you that I can come to Paris if I want to, and I can pamper myself and treat myself if I want to. I need you for…more than that."

Joe sat back, watching her with a mix of emotions in his eyes.

Phoebe just waited. He'd get it. Or she'd keep explaining it—and demonstrating it—until he did.

"Okay," he finally said, bringing his hands up and linking them behind his head. "Let's hear this list of things you do need me for. And before you even start, the best orgasms of your life better be on there."

Phoebe breathed deep and smiled. He got it.

"Number one, the best orgasms of my life."

"Damned right."

"Number two, making me feel more beautiful, interesting, funny and sweet than I've ever felt."

He swallowed but just gave her a quick nod.

"Number three, making me laugh and turning me on, at the same time more often than not."

Joe dropped his hands to his lap, clenching and relaxing his hands.

Phoebe moved in closer and he widened his knees so she could stand with her feet between his. "Number four, making me see and love my hometown all over again."

He flattened his palms on his thighs and gritted his teeth.

"Number five, the best orgasms of my life."

Joe raised one eyebrow and clenched his fists into hands again.

"Number six, making me realize that there are no big gestures and small gestures—just gestures that come from the heart and those that don't."

Joe pulled in a deep breath through his nose and let it out through his lips on a long puff of air.

Phoebe inched closer. "Number seven, making me get on a plane and come to Paris. Because this is awesome."

Joe's eyes narrowed.

"Number eight, making me realize that there are more

important things I look for in a guy than being able to country dance."

Joe's eyes narrowed further.

"Number nine, making me really glad, for maybe the first time since doing it, that I got that paw-print tattoo."

Joe breathed deep again and leaned forward. "Are there ten things on this list?"

"Yes."

"Let's hear the last one quick. 'Cause I want to emphasize number one, two, three, five and nine right here and now."

She was now the one to suck in a deep breath. Then she moved forward and climbed up on his lap and cupped his face. "Number ten, making me fall in love. Completely, totally, I-can't-live-without-you love."

Joe looked into her eyes for a long moment. Then suddenly shifted and flipped her to her back on the loveseat and lowered himself over her. "Well, that's perfect. Number ten fits right in with my plans for one, two, three, five and nine."

"That's good since ten fits right in with *all* of my plans," she told him, her heart full.

He leaned in and kissed her long and deep. Her breathing was ragged when he lifted his head.

"I love you, Phoebe."

"I love you too, Joe."

His kiss was hotter, even more possessive than before. When he paused to breathe this time he said, "By the way, just so you know," he said, "you might not *need* me to go to Monaco and Rome and Greece with you, but you do *want* me to."

She did. Of course. She always would. "Why is that?"

"Because of number one—" he kissed her, "—and two—" he kissed her again, "—and three—" he continued counting and kissing all the way to number ten, then added, "—and because I am an *amazing* tour guide."

She laughed as he shifted and started undoing her pants. "Well, when you put that together with…what was that first one again?"

He chuckled and shook his head. "Give me five minutes and I'll remind you. And then some."

He slipped her pants and panties down and off in seconds and then moved to begin unbuttoning her buttons.

"And then some?" she asked, already breathless.

"Yeah, once you're naked, I intend to propose."

There was that word again. "Why do I have to be naked first?"

He freed her last button, lifted his head and grinned. "You don't have to be, but I find everything is more fun when we're naked together."

Yeah, he had a point. So she set about helping them both get that way.

Erin Nicholas

ABOUT THE AUTHOR

Erin Nicholas is the author of sexy contemporary romances. Her stories have been described as toe-curling, enchanting, steamy and fun. She loves to write about reluctant heroes, imperfect heroines and happily ever afters. She lives in the Midwest with her husband, who only wants to read the sex scenes in her books; her kids, who will never read the sex scenes in her books; and family and friends, who say they're shocked by the sex scenes in her books (yeah, right!).

You can find Erin on the Web at www.ErinNicholas.com, on Twitter (http://twitter.com/ErinNicholas) and on Facebook (https://www.facebook.com/ErinNicholasBooks)

Look for these titles by Erin Nicholas

Now Available at all book retailers!

Sapphire Falls
Getting Out of Hand (book 1)
Getting Worked Up (book 2)
Getting Dirty (book 3)

The Bradfords
Just Right (book 1)
Just Like That (book 2)
Just My Type (book 3)
Just the Way I Like It (short story, 3.5)
Just for Fun (book 4)
Just a Kiss (book 5)
Just What I Need: The Epilogue (novella, book 6)

Anything & Everything
Anything You Want
Everything You've Got

Counting On Love
Just Count on Me (prequel)
She's the One
It Takes Two
Best of Three
Going for Four
Up by Five

The Billionaire Bargains
No Matter What
What Matters Most
All That Matters

Single titles
Hotblooded

Promise Harbor Wedding
Hitched
(book 4 in the series)

Enjoy this Excerpt from
Getting Dirty

Sapphire Falls book three!

by Erin Nicholas

Travis Bennett is exactly the kind of guy Lauren Davis has been avoiding for the past nine years. Religiously. Stubbornly. *Successfully*. She knows too well how easy it is to let lust ruin perfectly laid plans. And a small town farmer with no ambitions beyond the borders of his own cornfield is *not* going to change her mind. She's got important stuff to do. Her company is literally working to stop world hunger. Her plans are much bigger than Sapphire Falls. No matter how hot those farmers might be.

The problem is—Lauren is falling in love. With Sapphire Falls. To kick her sudden desire to buy a welcome mat and start baking pies, she asks Travis to help her get over her crush. She wants him to show her what life in the small town is *really* like behind all the sweetness and sunshine and remind her that there's no place for French manicures and Gucci heels on the farm.

Travis has everything he wants or needs—a quiet, simple life in his hometown, a successful farm and his friends and family all around. A hoity-toity city chick who looks down on everything from the local coffee to his favorite music is the last girl he wants sticking around. So he agrees to her crazy plan. He can definitely show her the less-than-glitzy, rough-around-the-edges side of Sapphire Falls. In fact, things just might get downright dirty.

Excerpt

A chicken crossed the road in front of her.

Presumably to get to the other side. There didn't seem to be any other reason.

Not that she thought she really understood why a chicken would do anything.

Lauren Davis stared at the bird as it started to peck the ground on the other side of the path. A chicken. She was in the middle of a place where chickens roamed free.

"*Mmmaaaaaa!*"

She jumped and spun.

And cows. Chickens and cows.

Technically it was a calf. But it was roaming free. And looking up at her with big brown eyes.

"*Mmmaaaaaa!*"

She did not like cows.

"No," she told it. "I don't know what you're asking, but no."

It continued to stare up at her with what she would have described as either affection…or predatory intent.

Lauren gave it a frown and propped her hands on her hips. "No."

The calf moved forward and bumped its head against her leg.

So maybe it was affection. It didn't matter. She did not like cows.

"Listen, where I work, you're food. You might want to keep that in mind." She took a step back. The calf followed her.

She wasn't sure what it was about cows that she didn't like but she didn't. It wasn't a fear or a phobia exactly. But they were big, lumbering things. That didn't smell very good. And that attracted flies. And that turned into steaks.

She was a part of an organization that had a mission to

feed the poor, specifically by teaching them to farm. Her company, Innovative Agricultural Solutions, specialized in crops, but they also partnered with a group that provided livestock. Sometimes that meant chickens and cows for their egg and milk production, but sometimes it was for their meat.

That freaked Lauren out. She worked hard to separate the food that she liked, and that the people she worked with needed, from the animals they supplied. It was silly, but necessary. She wouldn't make it long as a vegetarian.

"Stop it," she admonished the calf. "I can't look at you and think about filet mignon at the same time. That's creepy. And I like filet mignon so don't think you're going to talk me out of that. Just knock it off."

The calf stretched its neck and lapped at the hem of her skirt. Its tongue grazed the skin at the side of her knee and she shuddered.

"I don't think so." She stepped back again.

The calf took a step forward, took a hold of the edge of the skirt and sucked on it.

"No fucking way." She pulled the material from the thing's mouth.

"*Mmmaaaaaa!*"

"Forget it," Lauren said. "You can't suck on my skirt. I draw the line there. And we can't be friends. Go find your mom or something."

It just blinked its big eyes at her.

"Whatever." She was leaving. What the hell she was doing in the midst of chickens and cows, she didn't know, but this was Sapphire Falls and it was the annual town festival—most of both of those things didn't make sense to her.

She turned her back on the calf…and ran directly into a hard chest.

And something cold and wet.

"Ah!" She jumped back, shaking her hands free of the

juicy liquid that cascaded down the front of her, soaking into her shirt and freezing her skin.

It was a warm June afternoon so she was quickly more concerned about the fact that the liquid was purple. On her white shirt. Because of course it was.

She looked up into the grinning face of the man whose grape slush had just soaked her.

Travis Bennett. Because of course it was.

She sighed. Mud, cornstalks, manure...she'd had all of that *on* her at various times in Sapphire Falls and Travis Bennett was always the cause.

"*Why* am I always getting dirty when you're around?" she demanded, grasping the front of her blouse and pulling the wet stickiness away from her stomach.

He chuckled—the bastard. And it was a low rumbling sound that made her realize her nipples weren't perky just because of the cold slush all over them. The bastard.

"Oh, darlin' that ain't *dirty.*"

No apology, no reaching for a napkin, no sheepish look. All she got was "darlin'" and the word "ain't". In a drawl that was like fingernails on a chalkboard. Oh, and a big, fat, cocky grin.

"I'm soaking wet!"

His grin pulled up more on one side. "Now *that* I have some theories about."

Lauren narrowed her eyes and planted a hand on one hip. "Theories about what exactly?" She knew where he was going with this, but she wanted him to say it so she could shoot him down. Like every other time he'd made any kind of sexual innuendo.

"You being soaking wet when I'm around."

She gestured to her clothes. "Clearly, you need carnival food to get me wet, Farmer Boy."

"No kiddin'. I woulda pegged you for a fancy schmancy wine and caviar girl."

Liquor actually. She loved a good martini.

"But hey, a girl who likes meat on a stick and funnel cakes is my kinda lady."

Meat on a stick. Yeah, right. Though funnel cakes weren't *horrible*. They involved powdered sugar after all.

She blew out an exasperated breath. Travis talked like a hick. *Why* did she want to put her hand down the front of the blue jeans that had been covered in who-knew-what in the course of the *years* he'd owned them?

Travis was a farmer. A small town farmer. A small town farmer who had never traveled outside of the county in which he'd been born—and his father had been born and his grandfather had been born. She knew the type. Too well. She'd been surrounded by the type, involved with the type, in *love* with the type, until she escaped to the *city*. Where she'd found real life. Real culture. Real *coffee*.

And it didn't matter what city. She loved them all. Traffic, people, action…*life*. And not a cornfield or haystack for miles.

She was a city snob, a small-town-phobic. She knew it. She owned it.

And no good-looking, suntanned, slow talking, cheap beer guzzling small town *farmer* was going to change her opinion.

"Clearly the slushie needs to be applied externally for it to get me wet," she told the cheap beer guzzling small town farmer she wanted to lick from head to toe. In a cornfield.

She hated him.

"You city chicks are into some weird stuff," Travis said. "But darlin', I'll apply anything you want any*where* you want."

Stupid tingles all over her body.

She put on an unaffected expression. "And I suppose it would be some sexy set-up like the bed of your truck with mosquitos buzzing around and maybe some straw poking me in the ass while we're at it?"

He gave her a slow grin. "You, me, the bed of my truck... I'll put twenty bucks on soaking wet in five minutes."

The bed of his truck. Of course.

But it wouldn't take five minutes and he knew it. Somehow.

Damn him.

She was hard to read. She worked at being hard to read. She'd practiced it for years. And yet this guy...

Either he was really insightful—she almost snorted out loud at that—or he was really, *really* full of himself.

Lauren looked him up and down, from his well-worn seed corn cap to the brilliant blue eyes, past the day's growth of scruff on his chin, the red wrinkled t-shirt and the worn-and-washed-over-and-over blue jeans all the way to the scuffed work boots.

He was really, really full of himself.

She reached into her purse, pulled out a fifty and handed it to him. "It's pretty clear you need this way more than I do. I'd feel so bad taking that twenty off of you."

Travis grinned, took the fifty and tucked it into his jeans. "I don't care what they say, Dr. D. You're not all bad."

She wanted to smack him.

She hated when he acted like he didn't care a bit what she thought of him. She had yet—in the almost two years of running into him on and off in Sapphire Falls—to really feel like she'd gotten the best of him.

And she also hated when he called her Dr. D.

And said stuff like "I don't care what they say". They who? What did they say?

Dammit.

"Well, you can tone down the country-boy-charm because I don't do farmers."

His grin hadn't faded a bit. He leaned in. "Is it the

penises?"

She narrowed her eyes and leaned in as well. "Actually, it's the smell. Eau de Barnyard, doesn't really do it for me."

But that wasn't the problem with Travis. At all. He smelled like man and laundry that had been hung outside to dry. And sunshine. He smelled like sunshine. For god's sake.

Travis wasn't bothered by her comment. He chuckled. "Well, glad to know I don't smell like all those pretty girls you usually go for."

No, he sure didn't. He smelled better. And that was saying something since she really liked how those girls smelled.

She wasn't a lesbian. But she'd had relationships with women. She had embraced her bisexuality during her sophomore year of college. But on the spectrum of sexuality, she still went for men more often than women. She hadn't been with a woman in over a year. She hadn't been with *anyone* in almost seven months.

But Travis Bennett did not need to know that. He didn't need to know anything about her sex life. Like that he was totally her type. Totally.

She loved men like Travis. Men's men. Guys who used their hands to get things done and had muscles sculpted by hard work rather than by a gym. Men who were comfortable in their own skin without any hair products or a daily moisturizing regimen.

Country boys.

But country boys made her stupid.

And she was *not* going to live in the country. Never again.

So she steered clear. Really clear. She dated men who knew wine and theater and spa treatments. And there was nothing wrong with any of those things. She was attracted to them, she enjoyed spending time with them and they were okay in bed. Some had been better than okay. A couple had been damned good.

It still took more than a smile and a "darlin'" from them to get her going though.

Which was good. She didn't want to be falling for anyone. She had important stuff to do.

"So you could move back a few feet," she said, giving him a little push. "Or across the sidewalk. Or across the square completely." He always stood so damned close.

Of course, she noticed how hot and hard his chest was when she pushed him.

He chuckled again and the sound washed over her, making all the body parts she didn't want to think about when Travis was around say *well, helloooo, Travis.*

"Aw, I'm not goin' anywhere, darlin'," he said in that irritatingly sexy slow way he had. "This is my town, remember? You'll never get away from me entirely."

It seemed to be true. She ran into him every day. All. The. Time. Of course, Sapphire Falls was a small town with only twelve hundred and six other people besides Travis. The odds were against her. Especially when she figured in the facts that there were only two places in town with coffee and she and Travis were both devoted morning coffee drinkers, that there was only one bank, one post office and one gas station—and they both used all of those places regularly—and that Travis was one of the farmers working with Lauren's company, Innovative Agricultural Solutions, also known as IAS. They were bound to run into each other. Like it or not.

"You could at least try to keep your stuff off of me."

He grinned at that. "You mean my stuff that's making you wet and sticky?"

She *really* didn't like him. Or the way he got to her.

"Well, I'm nothin' if not a gentleman," he said.

And he stripped off his T-shirt.

He handed it to her. "You can use this to dry off."

She was vaguely aware of a scattering of gasps and a

wolf whistle from the people wandering through the square, but there was no way she was going to glance at any of them. Not when she had *this* view. Her mouth never went dry when seeing a man's chest for the first time. Then again, it had been a long time since she'd seen a chest like Travis'. Toned, tanned and completely lickable.

16824535R00158

Printed in Great Britain
by Amazon